EDGAR GRAHAM

Nancy Veldman

ISBN: 1452854017
ISBN-13: 9781452854014

No matter how long we have lived, no matter how much we have done, there is always one more thing we can achieve that just might push mankind over the creaky edge of mediocrity. The dreaded acceptance of an unfulfilled life because we were afraid to step out and try. Everyone has words that need to be written so that those who read them are changed forever. How many manuscripts never make it to print, but remain unfound in a dusty drawer. Well, this one manuscript survived.

CHAPTER 1

It had snowed in Portersville, Illinois every winter for the last 20 years. The temperature was down below thirty degrees as soon as the frost was on the pumpkins, and the leaves had fallen to the ground in feathery piles with a fragrance of fall. It was almost magical to be up at night and see the transformation of the town, whose streets were lined with huge oak trees that had stood proud and colorful in the early fall. Suddenly they would become a white fairy land with piles of white snow that would turn into snowmen by early morning. Most of the town was halted for a while by the covered streets and icy patches on all of the roads and bridges. It was unusually quiet as Edgar plodded from house to house, opening mailboxes and inserting catalogs that boasted of winter sales for holidays coming soon. His gray boots, bought years ago from a discount store, left bigger than life footprints as he trod through piled snow. He wore a gray coat, a gray hat, and gray gloves, almost invisible in the blowing snow, but he was more important to the people in the houses than their morning coffee.

Edgar had been delivering mail in Portersville for so long that people couldn't remember their last mailman. He still walked his route, even though other mailmen in the town used their vehicles and got through the route quicker than he did. He decided long ago that he liked walking and knowing his customers. He loved seeing the children playing in the streets, catching an occasional ball for them, and reminding them to watch out for cars. He had seen many children grow up to be young adults and it made him proud to be a small part of their lives. He knew all the parents, what they did for a living, and many of their sorrows. He listened long and hard to the stories of mothers left to raise their children because their no-good husband had left them behind. Oddly, if you asked anyone on his route, none of the people would say they knew anything about Edgar Graham. He was an enigma to the whole town, yet a vital part of their lives.

There was a young family at the end of Maple Street that Edgar was just beginning to know. He had seen the wife out several times but as soon as she saw him coming, she ran back into the house. The husband was usually out washing his truck or working in the yard; he was friendly enough, but something about him made the hair stand on the back of Edgar's neck. This was quite unusual, because Edgar Graham liked almost everyone in Portersville. Today, as he approached the house, Edgar saw both the husband and wife outside with a small child. As he delivered to the few houses on the curve of the road, he watched the young family, trying to figure out the mechanics of that household. He loved doing this, and it was a great pastime while he was walking on his long route. He had learned to read people pretty well, and something about this man just did not feel right. He came up to their driveway and yelled hello. The wife looked up and he thought he saw a black eye. She ran inside quickly, without a word. The man walked up to Edgar and took the mail out of his hand.

"Good morning, sir. Thanks for the mail. Pretty cold day for you to have to walk your route." He smiled and Edgar noticed some teeth missing. "Name is Peterson. Doug Peterson."

Edgar shook his hand and looked straight into his green eyes. "Morning Doug. My name's Edgar Graham. Been a mailman here for years."

"We been noticin' you for a while, but glad to meet ya. Stay warm." Doug turned and walked back to the house.

Edgar finished the street, and cut across to Eastland Avenue. He was enjoying the crispness of the air, even though it was very cold outside. He had done this so long that his body was accustomed to the cold. He saw people out scraping their car windshields as the sun was beginning to blare down on the cars parked in the driveways. They were lined up like a used car lot in front of many houses, but taking on different shapes covered in snow. Everything took on different shapes in the snow. A lot of things were hidden from sight until the spring thaw. Edgar's footprints were covered up suddenly by a little snow flurry that was a mixture of large and small flakes coming down like confetti from the gray sky. As he walked his route, many thoughts went through Edgar's mind; he learned to use this time to work through problems or situations that were bothering him. He made many decisions while walking his route; important decisions. His head was clear and his mind ready to think. So he was enjoying his solitude when James Edsom drove up and rolled down his window.

"Hey Edgar! How's it goin?" James smiled and raised a furry eyebrow.

"Things are good, James. You stayin' out of trouble?" Edgar was worried about James, who was always getting in trouble with the law. When he stopped to speak to anyone, he either needed money, or was going to tell about his latest girlfriend. Edgar kept walking, hoping to escape the smell of alcohol on his breath, and the swirl of cigarette smoke that was curling out of the truck window.

"Oh yeah, Edgar. I'm doin' fine, just fine. Wonderin' if you were nervous or anything? The police keep comin' around my house lately, and it's makin' me nervous as a cat." Black smoke poured out of the muffler as James idled at the curb. Edgar shook his head and smiled. *One day James would end up in the State Prison if he didn't clean his act up. I've done all I can do for that boy,* thought Edgar.

I've told him not to speak to me on the street anymore and now the police are drivin' by his house. What has triggered that? *What is he talkin' about around town that would raise suspicion?* He leaned on the door of the truck and looked James square in the face.

"James, now I have told you not to talk about anything in town to anyone. What have you been sayin' to people?"

"Nothin, Edgar. I swear. But for some reason this one cop keeps showin' up at my house at night, shining the light into my yard. Why is he doin' that, Edgar?"

"I don't know, James. But for the time being, you need to stay out of trouble and not draw attention to yourself. Go about your business as normal and just stay clean. Can't you get a job at Joe's Hardware store in town? That would give you somethin' to do with your time, James, and bring in some money."

"I'll try, Edgar. I just get nervous, is all."

"I'll talk to you later, James. Need to finish my route. Don't worry about anything and get on with your life, like I am. No need to worry, you hear?"

James looked at Edgar and smiled. His teeth were yellow and several were missing in the front. "Ok, Edgar. I'll try to get busy living my life. I don't want any trouble. Sure don't want any trouble."

—   —   —

The mail route ended on Black Forest Road, where the Morgans lived. All five children were out playing in the yard. Edgar walked up to the mailbox and put the catalogs and letters into the box and closed the door. He called out to the kids and grabbed up some snow to throw at the oldest boy, Dan. The kids screamed with delight and picked up snow and threw small snowballs back at Edgar. He knew this family was struggling to make ends meet because the father had cancer. He worked some, but money was tight and the children needed clothes for school. New winter coats. Edgar headed home with a slight tug on his heart. He walked up to his house with ideas dancing in his head. *This was going to be a fun Christmas this year*. He had a lot of things he needed to do, and one of them was for this family. He had been to the bank yesterday and cashed his paycheck, so he pulled the money out of his wallet and laid it on his desk. There were about ten envelopes lined up on the desk, and he took the money and split it up between all of the envelopes, making sure they all got the same amount. He had been saving all year and the envelopes were getting fat. He did this every year. He picked ten people or families to give to, and this year it was going to be tough to pick them.

The phone rang and it was Jane, his one and only daughter. No one in the neighborhood had ever seen her, but Edgar loved her with all of his heart. She was an attorney and one of the best in the firm; she grew up being a perfection-ist and it came in handy in her job. He was so proud of her, and missed seeing her around the house. She was dating a young man and it sounded like they were getting very close to getting married. When Edgar hung up he sat down at his desk to think. He hadn't planned on what James told him about the police coming to his house. It made a sweat come up on his brow just thinking about it. Nothing would ever happen. He just needed to go on with his life and relax. He took a deep breath and checked all the envelopes that were on the desk. All the money was there, each one the same. He put them back into the slots on the back of the desk and went into the kitchen to make supper. It had been a long cold day, and he was more than ready for a good meal and rest.

CHAPTER 2

Mary Williams had been a widow for twenty years and was a retired school-teacher who was loved by all. She had a soft face with feathery wrinkles and a twinkle in her eye. She was always baking cookies and taking them to the Wilton Nursing Home on the outside of town. It was a dreary place filled with people who were forgotten by their families, and they loved seeing Mary coming in the door. Mary had three children who lived down south and hardly ever got home to Portersville. She was lonely, but no one ever knew it. She was first to volunteer for any job and used her skills as a teacher to pull it off without a flaw. She still dressed in suits and a low heel, even though the bones in her back were as thin as paper. Her doorbell rang and Mary hurried to answer it, wondering who in the world it could be. When she opened up the front door, there was no one there. She walked out on the porch and looked both ways down the street, but saw no one. As she closed the door and turned around, an arm went around her throat and she screamed out.

"Don't move lady! I'm not goin' to kill you!" The voice was deep and scratchy. Mary could not see his face, but was trying to recognize the voice. "I want you to keep quiet and git' me all the money you have in your house."

Mary was shaking but was too old to be scared. She shocked the burglar by being so calm. "Of course, I'll get my purse right away. I don't keep money loose in the house, but you can have the money in my purse." She moved very slowly, leaning on her cane for support. She was determined not to act afraid.

The man stayed with her the whole way, and when she picked up her purse, he grabbed it and dumped it out on the kitchen table. He had a black hood over his face and his clothes were black. She couldn't tell anything about him, except that he was tall and strong. He shuffled through her things and found a wallet that was full of ones and a couple of tens and a twenty. He searched all the pockets in the wallet and found a hundred dollar bill folded up. He put all the money into his pocket, threw down the wallet, and turned to Mary. She avoided looking directly at him, hoping he would leave now that he had her money. But instead of walking out, the man knocked Mary to the floor and ran. When she fell, she hit her head and blacked out. There was a pool of blood forming next to the wall, near her head.

Hours passed and no one had found Mary. It was snowing again and all the footprints that might have been found were being erased by the white feathers that were falling from the sky. It was bitter cold as Edgar walked up to the porch to put Mary's mail in her mailbox. She was one of the few who still had a mailbox near her front door. And perhaps because of her age and good standing in the community, this was overlooked by the post office. Edgar really enjoyed his conversations with Mary and always looked forward to her peeping out of her door to see if her mail had arrived. He had decided that she watched through the sheer curtains of her living room window for a glimpse of him coming up her walkway every day. As he stepped up on the porch, Edgar noticed the front door was slightly ajar. This was not all that unusual; she almost always at the door by the time he put her mail in the box. Today, however, there was no sign of Mary at the door. Edgar called out her name as he put the mail in the box, but there was no response. He called louder and still no response, so he decided to open the screen against his better judgment and look inside. He kept saying her name loudly, hoping she was in the kitchen or somewhere in the house where she could hear him. The house was dead quiet, with only the sound of a clock ticking in the hallway. Edgar knew he should not be in the house alone, and just as he was about to turn and walk out the door, something caught his eye through the doorway of the kitchen. He froze for a moment, not sure whether to go into the kitchen or call for help. He decided to walk to the edge of the living room where he could see clearly, and it was then that he saw the lower part of Mary's foot on the floor near the kitchen table.

Edgar could feel his heart pounding as he reached for the telephone. He called for an ambulance and gave the address. He ran to Mary and knelt down to see if she was still breathing. He thought he felt a weak pulse in her neck and then saw the blood on the floor next to the wall. Nearly tripping on her feet, he ran to the kitchen sink and ran cold water over his face. He could hear the ambulance coming and went back to Mary. He was afraid to move her at all, so he touched her shoulders and talked to her softly, trying to reassure her that she was going to be okay. He wasn't even sure if she could hear him, but he still wanted her to know he was there. His hands were shaking with rage as he stroked her back. Mary was an old woman and did not deserve this at all. Anger welled up in Edgar as he sat there waiting for the EMTs to arrive. His hands went into a fist and he was sweating, thinking about someone hurting an old lady like this. Quickly he stood up and looked for anything that might have been left behind that might tell him who the intruder was. Nothing. He saw nothing out of place except her purse on the table, lying on its side with the contents dumped out. Obviously the intruder wanted money, and he knew burglars often preyed on the elderly, but this woman was so loved by everyone in the town, that it was hard to believe someone would want to hurt her.

The EMTs were finally coming through the door, and behind them were the police. Edgar spent the next thirty minutes talking to Fred Perkins, the sheriff, explaining how he found Mary laying on the floor in the kitchen. He scolded Edgar for entering the house, but at the same time was glad that he did, as Mary would not have been found for days if he had not. A report was written and the police drove away, leaving Edgar there to lock the house up and finish his route. He was going to visit Mary later in the evening after he was done with his work. He was also going to be thinking hard about who could have done this horrible thing. Right now he was angry enough to shoot someone. But he knew better. The law might need to handle this one on their own.

CHAPTER 3

The Peterson house was in an uproar because Chloe and Anna were asking their father for a new puppy, and Doug didn't have the money for anything right now, except the basic needs of the family. He was already behind on the house note and this brought out a temper in him that was always right underneath his collar. It didn't take much to make him angry, but money did it every time. After Anna was born, he had wanted Shelley to get a job to help out, but then she came up pregnant with Chloe and it ruined his plans.

"Shelley, I told you over and over that we ain't gettin' no puppy right now." Sweat was forming on his brow as he stood at the doorway of the kitchen.

Shelley felt a knot form in her stomach and tried to make light of the conversation. "Oh Doug, just relax. You know how kids are. They all want puppies."

"Well, we ain't gettin' one, so I don't want to hear no more about it." He stomped out of the room and went back to the bedroom to clean up for supper. He reached into his pocket and pulled out the money he had hidden all day. He had a hundred dollar bill, a twenty, and a few ones. He tucked the money into a drawer and closed it, his heart beating just thinking about what he'd done. Nothing seemed to go as planned for him and it didn't look like things were going to change. He would use this money to help pay his house payment, and hope that things would pick up in his work. He painted houses for a living and things were slow. He was doing some small repair work for the Jeffersons down the street, but there was nothing more on the horizon. He was worried sick about losing the house, but tried to keep his chin up.

The phone rang and Shelley picked it up. She was quiet for a moment and then shouted out loud. "Who in the world would break into Mary Williams' house and steal from her? Is she going to be ok?"

Doug listened and cringed. *Who was callin' Shelley and what did they find out?* He ducked out of the house and headed for the garage, hoping to miss the conversation that would follow when she hung up the phone.

"Oh my goodness! I can't believe it. Well, let me know if she's okay, will you? She is such a sweet person and so giving. I'm sick about this, and it's kind of scary to think we have someone breaking into houses on our street, and robbing people." Shelley hung up the phone and shook her head. She headed to the living room to settle the children down and break the news that there wasn't going to be a new puppy anytime soon. She passed the kitchen window and looked out to see Doug talking on his cell phone. Hopefully he was getting another job.

She shrugged and tried not to feel hopeless. Their relationship was not what she had hoped for in a marriage, but she was determined to stick with it and make it work for the kids. She did want to get Doug to learn another way of dealing with things instead of losing his temper so quickly. And if he hit her again, she was gone.

— — —

Doug put his cell back in his pocket. He was relieved to know Mary was doing okay. He didn't mean to knock her down like that and hurt her. He got scared and pushed her, that was all. It was an accident and he was nervous about what this would bring. It was one thing to take her money, and another thing to face murder charges. The hospital believed he was a nephew when he called, and told him that Mary was recovering nicely. He cleaned up his brushes and closed up the garage. No one would ever know he took the money, and he needed it badly. Somehow he had to find some work, or some way to make some money, and fast. When he walked back into the house, Shelley wanted to talk to him about the break in, but he acted like he was not that interested and she finally shut up about it. He hoped the nervousness would leave his stomach soon. He hadn't done this in a very long time, and the *fear of being caught* was gigantic. He knew he had to get a grip, just in case anyone decided to ask questions. His father had spent some time in jail when he was growing up, and he didn't want to be like his dad. But times were tough. What was he supposed to do?

Doug put his head in his hands and closed his eyes. One thought was bothering him about this whole thing. *What if Mary had recognized his voice? If she did, he was a dead rat.* He hoped she did not, but there was nothing he could do but wait. And waiting was not something he was good at.

— — —

Mary was laying in her hospital bed with a tremendous headache and determination to find out who broke into her home. She felt like the voice was familiar but at the moment drew a blank. She was shaky from the fall, and not quite over the scare of having a stranger in her home, rummaging through her purse. If she were still teaching, this would have made a great story to share with the class! But she hadn't taught in years and there was really no one to tell, except her three children. And they weren't going to hear about this from her lips. She didn't need them rushing up to Portersville to check on her, demanding that she move south to live near them. She was happy in Portersville, and that was where she was going to stay. Lying there in her own little world, she looked over and to her surprise, Edgar was standing in the doorway of her room, smiling at her.

"Hello dear Mary. How in the world are you?" Edgar walked towards her bed and sat down in the chair next to her.

Mary smiled. She absolutely loved Edgar. He was so sweet to her; so caring. "Hello, Edgar. What a sweet surprise to find you in my doorway. Can you believe we have a burglar in Portersville?"

Edgar shook his head. He was tired from his long walk in the snow, but he just wanted to be sure she was okay. "I don't believe it, Mary. I'm sick about it. But I'm so glad I walked into your house today and found you. What would have happened if I had not come by? I shudder to think."

Mary smiled again and shook her head. She took Edgar's hand and thanked him for saving her life. "I will not forget you, Edgar. This kind thing that you have done deserves a reward, and I'll make sure you are taken care of." Mary had an idea, and decided to keep it to herself. She would call her lawyer as soon as she made it home.

"Edgar, I have some repair work that needs to be done on my porch. I noticed that the paint is peeling off and I may need some boards replaced. Do you know a good painter?"

Edgar thought a moment and then remembered Doug Peterson. He hated to give her that name as a source, but thought it would be nice to give him the work. He was sure they could use the money. "I think Doug Peterson is a painter, Mary. You want me to call him and see if he can do the job?" Edgar took out a pen and wrote down a note to himself to call Doug tomorrow about this work.

"That would be so nice of you, Edgar. I would feel better if you would do it. I'm not sure when I'll be home, but I do need that work done. Be sure to tell him I'll pay him well for a good job." Mary yawned and this did not go unnoticed by Edgar. He stood up and stretched and said good night to his favorite neighbor in all the world.

"I'll check on this tomorrow, and also come by and see how you are. Take it easy, Mary. Rest well, and come home soon."

Edgar walked out of the hospital thinking about Doug Peterson. And he also thought about the black eye he had seen on his wife. A knot formed in his stomach again and acid came up in his throat. He could smell a rat a long way away, and he was hoping he was wrong about his neighbor. When Edgar pulled up into his driveway, he noticed a small package on his steps near the front door.

He got out of the car and picked up the package and walked inside. It was fresh banana bread from the Jeffersons next door. What a great gift for him! He rarely had homemade food, and it was a delight when one of his postal customers gave him food they'd made for him. He savored a slice even though he had already eaten his supper. Later, when he was taking out the garbage, his other next door neighbor, Jim Rutherford, was about to walk his dog. Edgar decided to have a short chat with him.

"Hey Jim! How are things goin' at the bank?" Edgar shook his hand and patted the dog.

"Well, things are slow for all of us, especially in this kind of weather. Not much building going on in the winter, and not many sales either. But it's this way every year, Edgar. So we just have to hunker down and wait it out." Jim always like chatting with Edgar, but knew nothing about his family or personal life. He was an interesting sort; he seemed to know a good bit about a lot of different subjects, so the conversation never had a lull.

"Jim, did you hear about Mary bein' robbed? I just got back from the hospital and a short visit with her."

"Really? I did hear something about it at work. What in the world happened? She is such a sweetheart and has been here for so long. Was she hurt badly?" Jim was interested in finding out who did it, as there hadn't been a robbery in Portersville in years, that he could remember.

"She's doin' great. You know she's a trooper, Jim. We don't know yet who did it, but she's recovering from the fall and will probably come home in a day or two. I'm hopin' she will remember somethin' about the man that will help the police find him. All she could say at the moment was that he was dressed in black with a black mask."

"Well, we need to re-activate our neighborhood watch, don't you think, Edgar?"

"I sure do, Jim. That's a great idea. I'll pass the word. Maybe we need to have a meeting of sorts to get everyone on the same page with this."

Edgar told Jim good night and walked back into the house. He was tired and ready for bed. He always thought that when he got older things would slow down and get easier, but it seemed like the world was getting worse and nothing was getting easier. He yawned, pulled back the covers, and lay back on the pillow. The room was cool and he tucked the covers around his neck to warm himself up. By the end of the night, Edgar had wrestled those covers off the bed, and was almost as tired when he got up as when he went to bed. He could not get Mary off his mind.

CHAPTER 4

Before seven o'clock in the morning Doug's phone was ringing. He bolted out of bed hoping to catch it before it woke the girls up. *Who would be calling this early in the morning?* He was shivering because the heat had been turned down to save money while the family slept under tons of covers to keep warm. He answered the phone and was surprised to hear Edgar on the other end.

"Sorry Doug! Edgar here. I was up talkin' to Mary Williams, our neighbor who is in the hospital recovering from a fall, and she mentioned she had some paint work to be done on her porch, and some small repair. You up for that?" Edgar felt the pause on the other end of the line and waited. *Surely Doug needed this work,* Edgar thought.

"Yeah, sure," Doug said with a shaky voice. He cleared his throat to sound calmer, giving him time to pull himself together. This really caught him off guard. "I'll do whatever she needs done, Edgar. Just let me know when she wants me to start, and uh, I will need to check out the porch to see what supplies I'm goin' to need."

"Ok, Doug. I'll let Mary know today when I go up to visit her. She'll be relieved. Oh yeah, she said to tell you that she'll pay you well for a job done right. I figured you could use the work with things so slow 'round here." Edgar could sense something, but could not put his finger on it yet.

"Just let me know, Edgar, and thanks for callin' me. I'll do my best, you can tell Mary that."

Edgar hung up the phone and smiled. Mary would be pleased about this, and a family would get some money. He needed to work on his feelings about Doug. All he really knew was that his wife had a black eye, and that wasn't enough to build a case against this guy. He had never been wrong in his estimation of people, but he decided to give Doug some slack for now.

He walked into his kitchen to make some fresh coffee and a big breakfast. It was so cold that his body needed a lot of food to keep him warm. He also packed a thermos of coffee to take along the route with him. He opened up the morning paper and glanced at some of the headlines, noticing a small article about Mary being robbed, but it didn't give out much information. He tossed the paper into the trash, grabbed his thermos and lunch, and headed out the door. Whoever broke into Mary's house probably would make another move soon, and hopefully the law would be watching.

As Edgar worked his own street, he noticed Greg Morgan out scraping snow off his windshield again. The weather had lightened up a little and there was talk of a melt soon.

"Hey Greg! How you doin' this mornin'?" Edgar stuck out his hand to Greg.

"I'm makin' it, Edgar. Kind of a rough time for me right now." Greg looked tired and there was sweat on his brow even in the below freezing temperature. "Doc says I may not make it through this cancer, man, and I just don't want to accept it."

Edgar shook his head. "I can't imagine what you're goin' through, Greg. But I want you to know I'm here for you, man. Are you able to work at all right now?"

"Some. But there are days I can't even get out of bed. So I try to work when I can, but I don't know how long they'll keep me on at Masons. I've worked there for 15 years, and have made a lot of money for the company, but I know they have their limit on how long they'll allow this to continue. My insurance is good, but if I lose my job, I'm not sure how I'll pay all these medical bills. Hopin' to hold out long enough to complete this treatment, and then I just don't know what will happen."

Edgar looked at Greg and his eyes watered. He looked away and swallowed the lump in his throat. "Hey, Greg. I'm here for you no matter what. Just let me know if you need anything and I'll be there, okay?" Edgar walked away knowing that this family needed some financial help and he was going to let them be the first family he helped this year. He kept on walking his route, but his mind was not on his work. Today his mind was on James Edsom and whether or not he had found a job or not. He was worried about this guy getting into trouble again with the law. Edgar wondered if this would ever stop; this worrying about who might find out. James had sworn on his life he would never tell anyone, but Edgar had his doubts. Somehow he needed to get James a job and keep him busy.

Just as he rounded the bend in the road he spotted James' truck pulled over to the side of the road. The truck was empty so Edgar was wondering where he'd gone, when suddenly James appeared, coming out of the backyard of a house in the cul-de-sac. *What was he doing in this neighborhood?* Edgar shook his head. *This could not be good.* He called out to James, but James acted like he didn't hear Edgar. He jumped into his truck and sped away. Edgar shook his head and stood in his tracks, thinking of what he should do. He had to finish his mail route, but he decided to call James as soon as he got home. *Hopefully he isn't doing drugs again. That is all we need,* Edgar thought. He finished his route, tiring out on the last street.

The cold took a lot more energy than when he did his route in the spring and summer. Edgar walked into his house and noticed that someone had been in his house. *What in the world was going on in this neighborhood?* He hurriedly ran through the house, looking for things that might have been taken. The kitchen was fine, but the desk had been destroyed. Papers were everywhere, the check- book was on the floor, and all the envelopes with money in them were gone. Edgar was shocked. He stood there in disbelief. *Who would have come into my house to steal from me? Was it the same person that robbed Mary?* Edgar picked up the phone to call the Sheriff and then decided against it. He really didn't want the law to get involved in his life, so he made a quick decision to wait and see if he could solve this on his own. And the first person he was going to check out was Doug. He picked up the phone and dialed Doug's number, but it rang and rang and no one answered. He was surprised that the whole family was gone, but shrugged it off. No point in jumping to conclusions. It could be anyone at this point.

—   —   —

James raced out of town as fast as his beat- up 1980 Chevy pickup would go. The bumpers were holding on with rope he had found in his garage. There were numerous dents in the truck, and the hood would not completely close. The truck was rattling something fierce, but he was determined to leave town. He had a brother in Jamestown, miles away, and that was where he was headed. No one even knew he had a brother, so he would be safe for awhile. Guilt was setting in, but James tried hard not to give in to it. Edgar was going to be very upset when he found out that his money was gone, and James hated taking it. But he had somebody he had to pay off, and it was either steal it from Edgar or lose his life. These men didn't want to wait for their money, and James had nothing to give them in lieu of the debt. He was stuck and didn't know what else to do. Edgar was his best friend, the one man who would go to bat for him, and he had stolen all the money Edgar had saved to help other people. *I must be a no- good bum, a piece of slime. A bottom dweller.* James broke out in a sweat thinking of how Edgar would feel when he got home. *Edgar will never see me again, that's for sure. I can never come back to Portersville.* It made James sad in one way, but hopefully he would start a new life in Jamestown and get a regular job. He would love to buy a better truck and maybe even get him a wife. "Somehow I will pay Edgar back." He said it aloud in the car. The words hung in the air while James lit up a cigarette and turned on the cheap radio. Just as he was about to go over the state line, a patrol car pulled out of a stand of trees and cut on his lights and siren.

James looked down and realized he was going over 90 mph and crossed the state line not knowing whether the cop would chase him or not. He should have been more careful, especially after what he had just done.

He looked back in his mirror and the cop car was gone. He kept watching as he drove into Jamestown, but no sign of the cop. James swallowed his fear and drove to his brother's house. *That was too close a call. How stupid can I be?* He didn't need any attention from the police right now, and he was determined to start a new life with no problems attached to it. He was going to forget his past and move on. He only hoped Edgar wouldn't find out that it was him. That would be harder to live with than never going back to Portersville. James pulled up to his brother's house with a sigh of relief. When he knocked on the door, his brother greeted him with a bear hug and a sheet of paper with a message on it. A phone call from Portersville. From Edgar.

CHAPTER 5

Edgar was sick inside. He had saved all year long and put money back and now it was all gone. He sat down at his desk, after picking up the mess on the floor and took inventory to see exactly what was missing. As far as he could tell, the only things gone were the envelopes of money. He sat there thinking. *This must have been what Mary felt when the burglar took her money out of her purse. It's a pretty sick feeling. Intrusion of privacy to say the least.* He knew there was no getting the money back, so he didn't waste any time worrying about it. But he did want to know who did it, and that was going to be a priority in his life for a while. He picked up the phone and called Doug again, but still no answer. *Maybe they went out of town to see family. Who knows?* Edgar looked out the window in the living room for a while with a blank look on his face. He was tired. Not a good time to solve any problems. He got up, put on his hat and coat and drove to the hospital to see Mary. She could use the company, and tonight so could he.

The hospital was buzzing as there were new arrivals, and the nurses were getting all the patients settled into their rooms. Edgar knew right where Mary's room was, so he just walked in like he owned the place and went directly into her room. She looked like she was asleep so he just stood at the door surveying the room. It was small and light green. Reminded him of the color of his elementary school. Ugly green. *Why don't they paint hospitals a bright color? Wouldn't it be more cheery?* Edgar laughed at himself. He walked over to the bedside and sat down in a chair near Mary. She was peaceful and he didn't want to disturb her. He leaned his head back and dozed off waiting for her to wake up. A nurse came and went, not wanting to wake Edgar while she was changing a bag at the head of Mary's bed. She closed the door and Mary stirred. She turned her head to see Edgar snoring in his chair and she laughed out loud. That laugh woke Edgar up and he jerked awake. He had forgotten for a moment where he was, and when he got focused again he smiled at Mary.

"Hey lady! How in the world are you doing? I must have dozed off waitin' for you to wake up." Edgar laughed.

"I'm doing pretty darn well, Mr. Edgar. It's good to see you again. You must've had a tough day dozing off in my room and all." Mary looked pink in her cheeks and was feeling pretty good tonight. "The doctor is going to let me go home tomorrow morning and I'm thrilled to be able to get in my own bed. I'm feeling much stronger and am more than ready to get out of the hospital and get back to my routine."

"Well, I had somethin' interesting happen today, Ms. Mary." Edgar paused and raised an eyebrow. "I came home from my mail route to find out that someone had broken into my house and stolen some money I'd put back." He didn't mention that the money was to help other people, even Greg around the corner. That was something he didn't want anyone to know about.

Mary looked amazed and frowned. "Who in the world is doing this, Edgar, in our quiet town of Portersville?"

"I wish I knew the answer to that, Mary. But I can promise you that I'll find out. I plan to get to the bottom of this. I didn't call the law. I hate havin' them come around and they never seem to get the robber anyway, so I'm goin' to solve this on my own. I wanted to ask you tonight if you could remember anything about your robber. Do you remember a voice or any mannerisms that stood out? Anything at all."

Mary thought and thought. "I've been laying here for hours thinking about that day. I can't think of anything that would make the man stand out. I might be able to recognize his voice but I can't promise that. I'm getting old, Edgar. I doubt we'll find the burglar by my description of him. He was in solid black from head to toe. That's all I can say about him."

"Well, if you think of anything in the future, write it down. It might help us to solve this problem before they do it to someone else. I had plans for that money but now that has gone awry."

Edgar looked so sad that Mary laughed. "Edgar, you and I'll figure this out. Don't worry. Just get me home tomorrow and we'll work on finding out the truth. Can you pick me up tomorrow around eleven thirty? Will you be through with your route?"

"I won't, but I can stop and get you and come back and finish the route. It won't take me long to pick you up."

Edgar got up and leaned over and kissed Mary's forehead. "You rest while you can, and I'll see you tomorrow. Let's not say anything to anyone about my robbery. It will just upset the whole neighborhood for nothin'."

Mary nodded and off Edgar went. He wasn't looking forward to going home because that would remind him that his money was gone. He tried Doug on his way home on his cell phone and Shelley answered. "Hey Shelley. This is Edgar. Just wonderin' how your family was doin'. Is Doug in?"

"No, Edgar. Doug went to see his father in Shelby. He's not doing too well and Doug thought he better go see him while he was still alive."

Edgar frowned. He guessed it couldn't have been Doug after hearing this bit of news. "I'm so sorry, Shelley. Please give him my regards and I'll stop by and see you guys when I deliver mail tomorrow."

Edgar hung up the phone and sat down. He just knew it'd been Doug, and now he was frozen. He didn't know where to turn. Something would show its ugly head. The truth would come out. He'd saved for so long and it was gone. He went into the kitchen to make some dinner and something caught his eye on the floor. He leaned over to pick it up and stood there in the light of the kitchen sink holding a glove in his hand. A black glove. *So they didn't want to leave any fingerprints,* he thought to himself. The glove looked slightly familiar but he could not for the life of him think of where he'd seen it. He laid it on the table and finished making his supper. He walked into the living room and turned on the television and sat down in his favorite leather chair to eat in peace. His back was hurting, and his chair felt so good after the kind of day he'd had. The news was inconsequential so he turned on a game show and turned down the sound. His mind was on the glove. Somewhere in the back of his mind he was remembering something and if he sat there long enough it would come to him. *The back seat of a car.* He could almost see it in his mind. He was straining to think when the phone rang. It was Greg Morgan.

"Hello Greg. Anything wrong? Have you had a good day?" Edgar was surprised by the phone call.

"Okay, I guess. Say, Edgar. You told me to call you if I had a need. Well today we found out that my job is only going to last another two weeks. I knew it was coming, but was hoping it would wait until after Christmas. It looks like I am going to be without a job during the toughest time of the year. I was wondering if I could borrow some money until I pick up another job. Just to help out on the mortgage. I hate calling you, Edgar."

Edgar was sitting straight up in his chair, listening to Greg with a heavy heart. His money was gone that he had saved up. And he had planned to give it to Greg. "Greg, how much were you wanting?"

"Oh, maybe two thousand would hold us until I find something. Susan may have to go back teaching until something breaks here. I didn't want that to happen, but things are getting tougher as I get sicker."

"I understand, Greg. I'll bring you the money tomorrow. I'll have to make a quick trip to the bank, but I'll bring it on my mail route, if that's okay." Edgar put his head in his hands and sank deeper into his chair. *What else is goin' to happen? And where in the world was James?* His mind came back to the glove but the image was gone. He would have to think of it again. He picked up his half-eaten supper and took it to the kitchen. He was so worn out from the excitement of the day that he decided to turn in early. Tomorrow was going to be another long day and he just was not up to any more excitement.

— — —

James had locked his house up tight and left only one light on in the back bedroom before he pulled out of town. A patrol car was parked in his driveway and two deputies were walking around the house. They had gotten wind of a drug deal and wanted to check James out. He had a bad background and it would be just like him to be involved in another drug deal. They searched the outside of the house and then knocked on the door. There was no answer and the house was pretty dark inside. The deputies broke into the house and called out for James. Of course he didn't answer; the house was empty of all his clothes and anything important. This raised some suspicion for it looked like he just packed and ran. After an hour of shuffling through what was left of James' personal items, the men walked into the kitchen, pulled the door to, and locked it. One of the deputies walked into the backyard and just stood there looking around with his flashlight. He was about to turn around when he saw something sticking up in the ground where the snow had melted away a little. It looked like a shoe, but he wasn't sure. He bent over to pick it up and sure enough it was an old shoe with a torn sole. It was a large shoe and the deputy knew James wasn't a large man. He wondered whose shoe it could be, so he took it with him to the car where the other deputy was waiting.

"Hey Joe, look at this. We know James has a small foot, so what's this shoe doing in his yard? I know it could be anyone's shoe…but I just wonder. Let's take it in and see what Sarge says."

"Okay, Al. It may be a dead lead, but I guess it doesn't hurt. It looks like it has been outside for a long time. So I doubt it has anything to do with the drug deal that just went down."

They headed to the precinct and walked into their sergeant's office with the shoe. "Hey Sarge! We just checked out James Edsom's house and no one was there. Thought you might want to see what we found in the backyard. It may be nothing important, but just thought I would bring it in, all the same."

Jesse Stryker picked up the shoe and studied it. Suddenly, he turned pale and sat down in his chair. There was a dog tag tied to the laces of the shoe. He recognized it immediately and knew it belonged to his son. The two deputies noticed it and came over to him. "You okay, Sergeant?"

Jesse recovered quickly and looked at the men. "First of all, men, you have just taken something from the scene of a possible crime. What in the world were you thinking? If the shoe was important at all, you have destroyed the crime scene. This cannot be used as evidence now in a court of law. I'm not going to write you up on this one, because you are wet behind the ears, but don't ever do this again, or your badge will be pulled. Can you imagine the ramifications of this had this been a real crime scene? Don't tell anyone you found this shoe, do you hear me?"

"No sir. We won't say a word to anyone. I guess we did the wrong thing here." Joseph scratched his head. He wasn't thinking right when he picked up the shoe. He got too excited about the possibility of finding something important. He was so embarrassed he could hardly talk.

"You boys get out of my office and get back on the street. And try not to do anything else stupid today will you?"

They left the sergeant's office and went back out on the street. All night they were discussing what that shoe would be doing in the backyard of James Edsom. It looked like Sarge recognized the shoe, but they couldn't be sure. He was too upset with them about their stupid mistake.

When Jesse Stryker was alone again he turned to look out the window of his office. It was a sunny day but cold outside. His stomach was in a knot. *I can't believe that this shoe would turn up now, after all this time. What were the odds of it showing up now? Sarah would know immediately.* I have not covered my tracks very well. I should have never allowed James to be around when I shot Mason, or asked him to bury the body. I was afraid Mason's involvement with drugs would lead the law right to my door and blow my whole operation to pieces. Jesse put his head down on the desk. *This was not the time for anything to come up that would ruin my chances of being promoted to detective. That boy was nothing but trouble growing up. Always rebelling. How ironic that he might even in death ruin my career.* This would have to be kept quiet if he wanted to move up in the department. He decided not to show his wife the shoe and do some checking around on his own. It might take longer, but this didn't need to leak out. He picked up the two-way and radioed the deputies who had just left his office, and reiterated that they not to speak a word of this to anyone. He stood up and looked out the window at what looked like a lazy beautiful town. You just never knew what was going to pop up in your life at the most inopportune time. Drugs were in every city on the map. *Why would I be a suspect in the death of my own son?* He looked at his watch and took a deep breath. *I need to keep my mouth shut. No one knows anything at all.* He decided to grab a bite of lunch. Something had to settle his stomach down and maybe Susie's Diner would be just the ticket. In the car he thought about Mason. *He had been dead for a couple of years now, and here this shows up. When we leave this world we should have a legacy that follows us. Not a friggin' nightmare.*

—   —   —

James was sitting in his brother's house where he was supposed to feel safe, but his blood pressure was up and he was nervous as a cat. *How did Edgar know this number? Had he slipped and told Edgar about his brother? And why did he call?* James decided not to return the call because there was nothing good that could come from a conversation with Edgar. It was difficult enough to steal the money, but it would be near impossible for James to keep the truth from Edgar. Edgar had a way of looking right through what you say and seeing the truth at the end of the tunnel. No matter what you put in front of the tunnel, old Edgar could still see it. So James didn't want to even begin that conversation for he knew how it would end. He took a deep breath and walked outside to check his truck and lock it up before he went to bed. He looked up in the sky and saw a white round moon. He breathed in the fresh cold air and said a quick prayer to a God he didn't know. He was grateful for a new start in life, even though it bothered him badly that he hurt his good friend Edgar. James went inside and walked into his small bedroom that his brother turned over to him. He lay down on the pillow but his eyes would not shut. For every time he closed his eyes, a man's face would pop up. That face just happened to be Edgar Graham.

CHAPTER 6

E dgar awoke before the rooster could crow. He had so much to do today and knew he better hit the road running. After breakfast, he went directly to the bank to withdraw two thousand dollars for Greg. He put this in an envelope with Greg's name on it and tucked it into his jacket's inside pocket. Then he started his mail route and moved along without talking much to anyone so he could be on time to pick up Mary at the hospital. He stopped at Greg's house and knocked on the door. Greg answered and did not look good at all. He was very white and pasty looking, but smiled when he saw Edgar.

"I'm so sorry, Edgar, to have to borrow this money. But I promise that I'll pay it back somehow."

"No problem, Greg. Just let me know how things are going, okay? I really care about your family and hope that things work out for you." Edgar smiled to himself as he turned and walked away. It felt good to give the money to Greg, for Edgar knew how badly he needed it, but he was saddened that he could not give more. He was running a little behind but made it home to get his car and arrived at the hospital at eleven forty five. Mary was sitting on her bed waiting patiently, with a smile on her face. She was so glad to be coming home and it was especially nice to have Edgar pick her up. She trusted Edgar explicitly and would not have had anyone pick her up but him. She would rather have taken a cab than have another man take her home.

When Edgar walked in the door Mary stood up and took his arm. He put her in a wheelchair and rolled her to the elevator and down they went to the car. Mary was talking about nothing in particular until they got inside the car where she felt more private.

"Edgar, first of all, I want to thank you for picking me up. It was so kind of you to take time off your mail route. I was embarrassed to ask you to do it, but as usual, you did it with such grace. Secondly, I have a proposal to make and I want you to think about it very carefully before you answer me. I have thought it out for quite some time now, and this hospital stay has given me long hours to work out the kinks. I know you had some money stolen, and I also know that you have given money out to people over the years at Christmas time. Anonymously. However, I was smart enough to figure it out and that is why I want to make this proposal."

Edgar tried to interrupt but she held up her hand to stop him. "I am not through, Edgar. Please hear me out. I know this upsets you that I have figured you out, when you are the one who is good at figuring everyone else out. But this time I think you'll be pleased. I have decided to allot a certain amount of money for giving, as I am aging at the speed of light and don't know how much longer I'll be around. I don't know how you feel about it, but I gather that we feel much the same about giving. I don't want anyone to know where the money comes from, but I want you to pick out who gets it. I don't get out much anymore, except for my work at the Wilton Nursing Home, and that may be ending soon enough. Now what do you think about that, Edgar?"

Edgar was speechless. He had no idea she paid any attention to what he did, and this floored him that she had figured out his giving at Christmas. "I am flabbergasted, Mary. I don't know quite what to say to you, but I'd be honored to choose the families who receive money. I already have one family for sure that needs it. Greg Morgan is one of the people I wanted to give to this year. But my money was stolen. I'm still sick about it and angry because I haven't discovered who did it yet."

"Oh Edgar, don't worry about that money right now. I'm sure you will figure out who took it sooner or later. Right now we need to take care of the people that you have been thinking about all year, and I want to be a part of it. You have to agree with me that no one will know who gave them the money. You and I will remain anonymous forever; is that agreeable to you?"

"I agree totally, Mary. Again, I'm surprised but not if I really think it through. You've been so giving in your life, Mary. I think we make a great team. When do we start this venture?"

"Immediately! As soon as I get home and settled in my house, I'm going to withdraw some money for you to give away for me. I will have to speak with my accountant so he doesn't have a heart attack when he sees the withdrawal in my account." Mary laughed at herself and looked at Edgar. He was laughing too. It was like they were involved in a secret caper and this time it was actually a good thing for Edgar. He felt a little better about the theft on both their parts, but wanted to find out who did it. He didn't want to say too much to Mary, so as not to upset her. She was happy about her new idea, and Edgar would not do anything to upset her now.

Once Mary was home safe and sound, Edgar hit the route again so that he could finish it before it got to dark. He was getting cold as he approached the last street, as he usually delivered the mail long before it got this late. He saw Bill Jefferson walking out to get his mail and walked over to him. "Thanks for the banana bread, Bill."

"Hey Edgar! How is our Mary was doing?"

"She came home today. She has recovered nicely and is glad to be back in her own home and bed."

"My wife was going to take Mary some food and I wonder if this is a good time, Edgar?"

"It would be the perfect time to do it. She hasn't been to the grocery store since she got back, and I know she would love some home cooking. That would be great, Bill." He caught himself before he let on that he had had a burglary, because he didn't want to scare his neighbors. Although they might need to be more careful and lock up their houses, for some reason Edgar didn't feel like the person who robbed him was going to hit anyone else. If he could just figure out the glove issue. While he was finishing up his route he kept thinking about the black glove, and all he could see was the back seat of a vehicle. *There were black gloves lying on the seat, but I can't remember where yet. It will come to me at some point. Until then I have enough to keep me busy. I still need to talk to Doug, and I am worried about Greg. And come to think of it, why did James not call me back? Could life get any more complicated?*

---   ---   ---

Edgar ate alone again for the millionth time. He sat in his living room with the television on, not listening to anything, but thinking about everything. He didn't enjoy his life all of a sudden. It had gotten way too complicated and this was not what he wanted at all. He never minded being alone, but for some reason he was feeling lonely. That was not like him at all. He had no one he was interested in, and really had enjoyed his life as a hermit. He talked to enough people each day on his route to satisfy any social needs that he had. When he came home it always felt good to just relax and think about his day. He loved being unnoticed for the most part, and didn't need much from others. Maybe he was just tired. There was so much going on and no answers for most of it. That would wear anyone out; even a young man. And he was anything but young. He did hope one day he might meet a woman who wanted the same thing as he did in life. He was getting too old to start over. He wanted peace most of all; peace and quiet. He was a strong man who had strong legs. He could outrun a rabbit when he was young. He had always been a loner, but now, since this thing had happened with James, he really enjoyed his anonymity. His mother would turn over in her grave if she knew what he'd done. He had covered for a friend. It was a bad situation that got worse and the only solution was what he had done. He prayed it would never surface for it would ruin his life forever. The town was too small and too tight. There was a possibility that no one would understand the circumstances and that was critical in the decision he made. The sheriff's department was a joke; right out of Mayberry. If all of this had happened years ago, he would have handled it in five minutes. But here in this sleepy little town, no one knew who he was. He took a deep breath and headed for bed, only wanting a deep sleep to keep his mind from thinking too much. He needed to see his daughter sometime soon. She always brought light back into his life. He would call her in a day or two and set up a time to see her. His eyes were heavy when he lay down to sleep. He dreamed about Greg and his illness; he dreamed about Mary being so fragile, and he dreamed about the black glove he found on the floor near his desk.

Edgar Graham did not have a bad bone in his body. But he was not perfect. No one is.

CHAPTER 7

The sun was shining brightly over the horizon, and there were clouds lining up like a crowd at a football game, threatening a storm at some point during the day. Edgar opened his eyes and the phone rang. It was Mary on Saturday morning, bright and chipper, talking so fast he could hardly keep up with her.

"Edgar. I have already been to the bank this morning, and you have no idea how good it feels to be able to drive again and get out in the fresh air. I withdrew a sum of money and I want you to come over for a moment when you get up. Why don't you have your coffee with me, before you start your route? Then we can talk." She hardly took a breath she was so excited about this venture.

"I sure will, Miss Mary. Let me get going here and I will walk over and have a cup of coffee and we can make plans." Edgar jumped out of bed and hurried into the shower. *This woman is amazing*, he thought. *No grass under her feet. She just got home from the hospital and she is already back driving and ready to go. I hope I hold up as well as she has*, he thought, as soap ran down his back. He stood in the hot water for a moment and closed his eyes. This might be the only moment of peace this day holds, and he wanted to savor it as long as he could.

Edgar walked up the steps to Mary's house and knocked on the door. She had to have been watching for she answered before his arm went back down to his side.

"Good morning Edgar! Come right in. I have a small breakfast for us and so much to talk about."

Edgar grinned and wiped his brow. This woman never failed to surprise him. As he walked down the short hallway to the kitchen, he noticed the framed photos on the wall, and there was a certain smell in her house that he could not put his finger on. It brought back memories of his childhood; perhaps an aunt's house or his grandmother's. She always had something baking and the aroma was enough to make you hungry even if you had just eaten a huge meal. They sat down at the table and Mary poured him a fresh cup of coffee, and served up a perfect breakfast of eggs, homemade biscuits, bacon and two pancakes that were perfectly round.

"Edgar, I am so excited. When you are as old as I am, there is not much in life that excites you; but this is doing it for me. Just the thought of being able to help others like you have done is something that could get me out of bed in the morning."

"Well, Mary, you are making too big a deal out of what I've done. I'm sure lots of people save money during the year to give to people during Christmas. It's something I started years ago and it just wouldn't seem like Christmas if I wasn't able to give to people like this." Edgar took a huge bite out of the biscuit, and the butter ran out on his fingers. He licked them without thinking and then looked up at Mary. She was grinning from ear to ear.

"Edgar, I love to see a man enjoy his meal. Now, let's get down to business." She pulled out a stack of money and laid it on the table. "This is the money I want you to give out. It is exactly ten thousand dollars. You could choose ten families and give them a thousand each, or whatever you want to do. I'm totally trusting you to do what is right, and I just want to know how it all turns out."

Edgar nearly choked on his food. *Ten thousand dollars? How much money did this little woman have?* "Oh my heavens, Mary! Are you sure you want to give that much away? I mean, we can start with a lesser amount and see how this thing goes, don't you think?"

"No, Edgar. We want to start big. I want to make an impact on a family, so you just be sure when you give the money that it takes care of the source of the need. I trust you completely. I realize it seems like a lot of money, Edgar. I have made some good investments in my life, and I cannot take this money with me, you know. I would rather die knowing it helped people, than just give it all to a charity and not know what is done with it, you see."

"I can relate to that. I have saved up enough for my retirement, and the rest I enjoy giving away. I will do my best in this venture we are doing together, and report back to you about what I do with the money. I appreciate your trust and will do nothing to alter it." Edgar took the money and put it in the large envelope and set it near his plate. He pushed away from the table and smiled.

"I am so full that I don't know if I can walk my route!" They both laughed and Edgar stood up.

"I better get going. I'll keep a journal on what I do so you can read all about it. Everything will be down in the journal and that way you have record of where your money went, Mary. If you think of something you want to do, let me know. Otherwise, I'll be watching for people who are hurting and see how we can help them out. Is that okay with you?"

Mary walked over and hugged Edgar. "I have never been so sure of anything in my entire life, Edgar. You have a good day, now. And if you need anything at all, please call me. This might be the most exciting thing I've ever been a part of in my entire life. And to think it is coming when I'm in my eighties. I guess better now than not at all!'

Edgar left the house with a big grin on his face. His stomach would never be the same. However, it was a cold winter day, and he was going to need that energy to finish his route today. He walked over to his house and looked for a safe place to keep the money. For now he decided to put it in his closet in a box that he stuck way back under some other blankets he had stored there. He made a mental note to purchase a safe of some type that would deter a burglar. Sticking money in envelopes and putting it in his desk slots was pretty stupid. He just never thought about being robbed before. Now it was the first thought each morning, when his feet hit the ground. *No more leaving my doors unlocked,* he thought. *I might even invest in a security system.*

He pulled on his heavy gray boots and his heavy coat and hat and walked out the door. He decided to stop in and see Doug and mention the work he needed to do for Mary. He also would check on Greg to see how things were going with him. As he walked his route, his mind wandered back to James. *Where in the world was he? And why did he take off so quickly?* That spelled nothing but trouble and this made Edgar worried. He would try the brother's house again in Jamestown to see if he could get an answer to some of these questions. Maybe it would be best if James lived out of town. He couldn't seem to get a job around here anyway.

—   —   —

Saturday night was Edgar's night to go grocery shopping so he made a short list of things and drove to the center of town to Marvel's Grocery Store. He had been shopping there for years and knew where everything was. Some new manager had come in and had the bright idea of moving everything around, so now Edgar had to look harder for what he came for. He ended up buying more than was on his list, and this made him frustrated. But the manager just sat back and smiled.

When Edgar got out of the car, he noticed a young woman leaning against one of the stores that was closed. She had a small child with her and she was on a cell phone. It was so cold outside he could not believe she was just standing there with her child. He entered the grocery store and started down the aisle. He kept running into people he knew that were on his route, or went to the town meetings with him, so it took him longer to shop than he had planned. When he got to the checkout, a man and wife walked up behind him with two carts of food. He overheard them saying that it was getting harder and harder for them to feed their five children. He turned just a little to see what they looked like, and the woman had dark circles around her eyes. The man had on a torn jacket and his shoes were worn out. He thought about his talk with Mary, and decided to pay for their groceries even though he had not brought any of the money with him. He told the checker not to let the people know his name or anything, and he paid for their groceries by leaving four hundred dollars with the checker. He walked his cart out to his car in a hurry and unloaded his groceries. He wanted to be gone before the family came out of the grocery store.

He was about to get into his car and noticed that the girl was still standing outside the closed store. He got out of his car and walked over to her.

"Hello, young lady. Is there anything wrong? It is so cold out here, and you have a young child. Can I do anything to help you?"

"Oh no, we're fine," she said with her head down. Edgar could see her shivering. The little girl began to cry and tug on her mother's coat.

"I'm Edgar Graham, and I live in Portersville and work for the Postal Service. I know these are tough times and it's so cold. Tell me what's going on and let me see if I can help you out any." Edgar was wondering where her car was, and if she had a husband.

"My husband left me. I have no money and no place to go. I called my parents and they said I have to fix this mess that I've made. They didn't want me to get married anyway. So here I am standing here in this cold weather with my daughter, and I don't know where to go." She began to cry and Edgar walked over to her and hugged her.

"Hey, don't cry. Let's get you to a hotel and get you both warm. We can work something else out in the morning, but you need a warm place to sleep. How does that sound?"

The girl was embarrassed and didn't want to take the help at first. But she saw how cold her little girl was and shook her head yes. Edgar picked up the little girl, tossed their small bag into the trunk, and got into his car. He drove straight to the closest motel and got a room for them on the first floor. He paid for two nights and got them settled in for the night. There was a concession area near their room where they could get drinks and light snacks until morning. The motel served a light breakfast, and then he would have to think of something else for them. She wrote their names down on a piece of paper, and Edgar put it in his pocket.

"Now, you guys stay here for the next two nights and we'll figure something out. Don't worry. I know you're upset, but something will work out. Just take a hot bath, turn on the television and get your mind off it. You don't want to scare your child, Linda. She's so young and I know she is wondering where her father is. I'll call you in the morning, ok?"

Linda had been so nervous to give her name out to this stranger and allow him to get them a room. *Who was he anyway?* Maybe she was nuts to allow him to help, but he seemed to be genuine and she was so cold. "Thank you, Edgar, for what you've done. I will pay you back somehow."

"Don't worry about that right now. Just have a good night and we'll talk in the morning." Edgar had an idea running around in his head, but he would have to talk to Mary about it tomorrow. It just might be a great idea if she went for it.

Edgar got back into his car and drove home feeling pretty good about the night, and his first venture of giving with Mary. He took out the money in Mary's envelope and repaid himself. He started a ledger so that Mary could see where this money had been spent, and put it up in the closet with the money. The only problem with helping Linda was that he had given her his name, and he had wanted to remain anonymous. He didn't see how he could have handled it any different but he would work that out with Mary in the morning.

— — —

Jesse Stryker was not having a good night. He avoided telling his wife, Sarah, about the shoe, which he decided to leave at work, and went to bed early. Tossing and turning, he was wondering what he would do if everything broke loose. They had raised the boy right and it just never paid off. Even now, after he had been dead for a few years, something was still happening that could ruin his career. The embarrassment was what Jesse could not handle. He didn't want anyone to even remotely guess that he was involved in any way with the drug situation in Portersville. His marriage was shaky and had been most of their married life. This would put his wife over the edge. She blamed Jesse for their son's lack of discipline, as Jesse was so busy building his career and working night shifts that he did not spend enough time with the boy.

Maybe he should tell the guys not to look into this at all. Play it down a little. That way he had a good chance to get the promotion that he had worked so hard for, and no one would be the wiser. He made a mental note to call the dogs off on this one, and laid back and fell sound asleep. He woke up in the middle of the night sweating and felt his cell phone buzz. There was a text from Linda. *What in the world was she doing here? Why would she text me at home? I have told her never to contact me at home.* Jesse got up and went into the living room and texted her back. He told her not to contact him at home but that he would get in touch with her tomorrow. Now he really couldn't sleep. He walked to the door, grabbed a coat, and got into the squad car and drove around for a few hours. His mind was racing between finding the shoe and now Linda popping up. He knew he should never have slept with her, and then to find out she was pregnant with his baby was just too much. He would regret this for the rest of his life. If this came out, his marriage would be over and possibly his career. They wouldn't respect him at all at the precinct and the gossip would be endless.

Jesse parked the car in his driveway and hung his head. *When you make a choice to do something that you know is wrong, you better be prepared to handle the consequences,* he thought. *For even though you stand in the dark to do the thing you know is wrong, it has a way of finding the light at the most inopportune time.* He opened up the door and got out of the car. He did not see Sarah standing in the window of the doorway watching him. Her heart was heavy and she knew something was eating at him. It could be his job, but somehow she sensed that it was not.

Sarah shook her head and went back to the bedroom and climbed in bed before he had time to open the back door. *The truth has a way of coming to the surface,* she thought. And if it is what she feared the most, Jesse would pay for the rest of his life for putting her through it. She had sacrificed a lot so that he could do what he wanted in life. He slept, drank and ate being a Sergeant, and now he wanted to be a detective. That was fine, but she had worked hard all these years adding to their income so he could play cop. The pay was ridiculous and no deputy could raise a family on what he made. So the women had to go out and leave their kids at smelly day care centers so that their husband could play cops and robbers. She should have run for Commissioner and fought to change this flaw in the system. She turned over and closed her eyes just as Jesse climbed back into bed. She could feel the tension coming off of his body, but she didn't speak. This would have to be one thing that Jesse worked out on his own. She didn't have one ounce of energy left to hold this marriage together. If one more thing happened, she was gone.

CHAPTER 8

Edgar awoke with a start and realized it was Sunday and he didn't have to deliver mail today. He laid his head back down on his pillow and thought about last night. He needed a plan and had worked something out that he needed to run by Mary. He hoped it would work, but you just couldn't tell how someone might react to something like this. Linda was in a mess and needed a place to stay, and the only solution would be to find her an apartment or ask Mary if she could rent a room from her. That way Mary wouldn't be alone in that huge house and Linda would have a safe place to live. Mary might even watch the child and allow Linda to get a job. There were all sorts of options, but Edgar made himself get up and shower. There was no point going over all of that without talking to Mary first.

He waited as long as he could to call her, and then dialed her number. She answered on the third ring, but was wide awake.

"Good morning Mary! Hope you slept well last night?"

"Of course Edgar. I'm in my own bed. All you have to do is spend one night in a hospital to really appreciate your own bed." Mary chuckled to herself.

"I have something I need to talk to you about. Do you have a minute? I would like to walk over and discuss several things with you and also share about last night at the grocery store."

"It all sounds intriguing. Come on over and I'll start our breakfast."

This could become a habit, thought Edgar, as he shaved and dressed. *One could get used to having a breakfast like Mary fixed to start his day*. He took his journal down and headed next door. *Boy, this would be a heck of a conversation. I just hope that Mary sees this situation like I do, and allows Linda to room with her. That would solve this problem and help her out too*. Edgar still was amazed at what was happening between him and Mary, and how quickly people were being put in his path that needed help.

He didn't even get in the doorway of Mary's house before he smelled that heavenly aroma of hot coffee, biscuits baking, and the smell of maple syrup. He was going to weigh five hundred pounds if he kept this up. Good thing he walked every day. He headed back to the kitchen and there Mary was, with her red apron on and her hair all pretty and red lipstick on. I bet she was quite a woman in her day, thought Edgar.

"Boy does it smell good in here, Mary. Hope you are feeling good today. I have a lot to share with you and also have a few questions for you." Edgar sat down and was served the meal of his dreams all over again. This time with fresh squeezed orange juice.

"I'm all ears, Edgar. Don't tell me our little venture has started already! Now, you eat and talk at the same time, for I don't think I can stand waiting to hear what all you have done."

"I was doing my regular Saturday run at the grocery store and headed for the checkout counter. In back of me were a man and wife who looked pretty rough. I couldn't help but overhear what they were saying about how much food it took to feed the five children, and how tight things were. So I told the checker that I wanted to leave some money for them, but not to mention my name. He happened to be a checker who checks me out regularly and he nodded that it would be fine. I left four hundred dollars for the groceries, hoping there would be some left over for them to use for something else. I had forgotten to put any of your money in my pocket just in case I ran into someone who needed help, so I just paid out of my account and took the money out of yours when I got home. Is that alright with you, Mary?"

"Perfect, Edgar. I am so excited about this. I had no idea it would start so soon, but I know there are a lot of people hurting out there." Mary's eyes were twinkling.

"Well, there's more. Before I went into the grocery store, I noticed a young woman standing outside of one of the stores that was closed, and she had a small child with her. They had to be very cold, and she was on her cell phone. When I came out she was still standing there and the child was whining, so I walked up to her and asked if I could help and she told me her story." Edgar took a sip of coffee and thought a moment before he continued.

"Mary, they are obviously in trouble. She said her husband left her and she had no place to go. Her parents didn't want to help her and she was standing there trying to figure out what to do, so I offered to take her to a motel for a couple of nights so that we would buy some time to figure out what to do about her situation. I got them both settled into the motel and they have a free breakfast this morning when they get up. I left her a few dollars and told her I would call her cell today."

Mary thought a moment and then looked at Edgar. "We can't leave them there, Edgar. What do you think we need to do? This is a complicated situation. You can't just give her money, can you? I mean, do we need a plan?"

"Well, I've been thinking, Mary. You live alone here in this huge house and you have a lot of bedrooms. You are getting older and it might not be a bad idea if someone lived here with you. I don't mean you are old, Mary! But what do you think of the idea of her moving in here with you for a while, and renting a room. she needs to get a job and I didn't know if you would watch the little girl, or if there was a nice day care center we could get her into. This is just an idea, Mary."

Edgar could see that she was thinking. She stood up and walked to her window over her sink and looked out. It upset her to think Edgar saw her as fragile. But she knew she was getting older and it was very lonely at times in this big house. *Could she tolerate someone living in her house? This would be a total stranger. What if she did not like her?*

"Edgar, this is a big thing we are talking about. I don't know this girl and she doesn't know me. We would have to get along pretty well to live in the same house. Can I meet her today? Can we meet first before I make this decision?"

'I think it would be a great idea for you both to meet. I haven't said anything to her about this, and she may not even want to do it. But I was trying to come up with a solution to her problem and this popped into my mind." Edgar scratched his head and looked at Mary. She seemed a little nervous about it. Maybe it wasn't such a good idea.

"Let's go see her now and you two can meet. We won't mention it at first, until we see how you both get along. The child is very quiet but maybe she will take to you. You just never know with kids."

"Okay, Edgar. You go get your car, and I'll get my coat and hat. I guess this is part of the adventure we are doing together. I just didn't think for a moment that I would have to share my home with someone. Giving comes in different clothes, right? Sometimes it is a simple dress and sometimes it is a whole wardrobe."

Edgar laughed. Mary was a piece of work, for sure. "That's right, Mary! Sometimes it requires a commitment on our part when we step out and help someone. I'm finding that out myself with Greg. I'll pull my car into your driveway. Be careful. I don't need you falling, Mary."

—   —   —

The Motel wasn't too shabby, but also wasn't one of the better ones in town. It certainly looked more run down in the daylight. Edgar went straight to the room and knocked on the door. He could hear little feet running around, and the television on. Linda came to the door with her hair up in a pony tail. She was smiling a little and glad to see Edgar.

"Good morning Linda. Hope you slept well. I wanted to check on you this morning and brought someone else with me for you to meet." He walked Mary into the room and they sat down in the two chairs by the bed.

"Hello Linda. I'm Mary Williams, Edgar's neighbor. How are you this morning?"

"We slept very well, thank you. I don't know what we would have done without Edgar Graham and his generosity."

"Well, don't worry about a thing. We just want to talk to you about your plans, if you have any, Linda. Are you planning to live here, or did you come to see someone?"

Linda was caught off guard by the question and took a minute before she answered. "I did come here to see someone but they're not too happy about my being here. It sort of surprised them, I think. Anyway, I don't know what to do now." She looked down and tears streamed down her face. Mary was taken back by the girl's sorrow and reached out for her hand. Her little girl, Lacy, came running to her mother, crying and saying she wanted to go home. Mary reached over and took the little girl and held her close. Lacy took one look at Mary and fell into her arms, crying.

"I think we need to take you two to my house," Mary said with a smile. "I know I'm old, but I have a lovely big home and we will figure this all out together. How does that sound, Linda?"

"Well, until I can do something on my own, I guess that's the best option. I really appreciate it, Mary. I don't want to cause you any problems or be any trouble to anyone. Edgar has been so nice already, and you really don't owe me anything at all."

—   —   —

Edgar walked over and took Linda's hand and looked her in the eye. "Hey girl. We want to help you if we can. I know this feels strange and a little awkward, however, for whatever reason you are here, perhaps we were meant to meet. So let's give this a try and if it doesn't work, we'll work something else out. I know you're lonely and Mary will be good company for the both of you. And wait until you taste her cooking!"

They all laughed and Linda walked over to pick up her purse and their coats. This all seemed like a dream and she hoped and prayed it ended up a good dream and not a nightmare. Jesse had let her down in a big way. She knew she shouldn't call him but what was she supposed to do? She needed money to raise this child of his, and she planned to get it one way or the other. If she had to go face his wife, she wasn't too proud to do it. Hopefully it wouldn't come to that. She headed out the door with Edgar and Mary, not knowing where this journey would take her.

It didn't take long to get to Mary's house, and as they pulled up in the driveway, Linda gasped in disbelief. The house was lovely and larger than the others on the block. "So this is where I'll be staying, huh?"

"Oh yes, Linda. It's a beautiful place for you to find your way. Now let's go in and let Mary take you upstairs to your room so you can get settled."

Edgar led them all inside and after Linda was upstairs with Lacy, he sat down at the kitchen table with Mary to make out a plan of action. "We need to probably take her shopping for clothes, Mary. She didn't bring much with her for herself or her child. I can get some money for the clothes and any personal items she may need. Can you handle that Mary, or do I need to take her?"

"I can do it, Edgar. You have done more than enough. I'm going to enjoy their company and this will give us time alone to get to know each other. You go rest or do whatever you need to do. We both have had a pretty exciting day so far, and it's not over yet."

Edgar made it home and collapsed on the bed. He wondered who it was that Linda came to see in town. *Maybe she will share more about her life as time goes on*, he thought, as he pulled some money out of the closet for Mary. He walked it back over to her and reminded her to call him when she got back. He sure didn't want to tire her out too much, but he wanted her to feel a part of this new venture.

Dialing James' brother's number, Edgar sat down in the recliner waiting for someone to answer. The phone rang and rang. There was no other way for him to get in touch with James except through his brother. He didn't know anyone else to call. He closed his eyes to think about the black gloves, hoping to figure out where he had seen them. He fell asleep, weary from trying to figure everything out.

— — —

Mary called to Linda to come downstairs so they could talk. "Let's go shopping, Linda, for things that you will need for a few days or so. If you decide to stay longer, then we will buy more clothes. I know you and Lacy both need pajamas and a couple changes of clothing. So let's go find a store that suits you and pick up a few things. Are you up for that?"

"Oh Mary! I'm overwhelmed by your kindness. Yes, that would be nice. Lacy will need a nap this afternoon sometime, though. I'm still in shock about meeting Edgar, and now you. It's almost too much. But I would love to go shopping with you, and really, it won't take much for us to get by."

They left to go to the mall and were gone about two hours. Mary was sizing up Linda, and also trying to get as much information out of her as possible. Twice while she was out with her, Linda's cell buzzed. Someone was leaving her a message. Mary wondered if it was the father of the child, or the person she came to see here in Portersville, but she held her questions for another time. *There may be more to this story than we know,* she thought as she walked them all to the car.

— — —

Jesse Stryker was frantic inside knowing Linda was in town. Everything was going so well until those two over- eager cops found that shoe, and then Linda showed up. He had texted her twice, telling her not to call his house, that he would contact her. But he was scared to death that she would show up at his door unannounced. He had been weak and lonely and done something stupid. He thought he had taken care of it, but now it had raised its ugly head right on his doorstep.

He would have to find a way to take care of the girl and get her out of town before his wife found out about her. That one task may be more difficult than the career move he was attempting. In fact, it may be one of the hardest things he would have to face in his whole life. His knees were weak but his determination was strong. He would get this taken care of one way or the other.

CHAPTER 9

Doug decided to make a phone call to Mary to check on what she needed done on the house. He was very nervous, but decided to suck it up and make the call. He needed the money, and in a sick way, it would make him feel less guilty about robbing her if he did some honest work for pay.

"Hello, Mrs. Williams? This is Doug. I heard you need some paintin' done and small repair, is that right?"

"Oh yes! Hello Doug. Edgar said you might be interested in doing a little work for me. I am so glad you called! Can you come over tomorrow and look at my porch? It may be too cold for you to paint, but perhaps you could start the repair work on some of the boards in the floor now. You may have to wait for spring to paint, don't you think?"

"That's probably right, Mrs. Williams. But I'll be glad to come by tomorrow and see what all needs doin'. Thanks for the work. I'll see you tomorrow mornin' at around ten oclock."

Doug hung up the phone and breathed a sigh of relief. Now *I'll have a little work to do, and maybe Mary will come up with more things to do in that old house. I could offer to paint her rooms or somethin'. Anything to keep me from stealin' again. I hated to do it, but what does a guy do when he has a mortgage and no work?* He walked into the living room and Shelley was there with the girls.

"I know the girls need winter coats, Shelley. I just got some work from a Mrs. Williams who lives round the corner. It's not much, but it'll hold us until I pick up a bigger job. You may need to go back to work, Shelley, just to help make ends meet. Or what about keepin' kids at our house?"

"Doug, I'll gladly get a job. But we need to also work on your temper around here. I am sick and tired of your yelling and flying off the handle. It's not good for the girls to hear, and frankly, it is ruining our relationship."

"Okay, babe, I hear ya'. I'll try to keep it under control. I'm stressed out 'cause I have no work and I don't want to lose the house, Shelley. We're in trouble, do ya' get that?"

"I get it alright. Let's put our heads together and figure out a way to make it work, instead of destroying each other and this marriage. Okay?"

Doug walked out of the room and sighed. He went to his shop to think, and to have a smoke. He had picked up this nasty habit after things got so bad. *Wonder if Edgar has any ideas? He talks to people all the time on his mail route. It would be worth a shot. I think I'll call Edgar tonight and see what he thinks. He got me a job workin' for*

Mary. Maybe he would come up with somethin' else. He walked back towards the house and noticed a basket on the front porch with a towel over it. He picked it up and pulled the towel off, and there in the basket was a pair of black and white cocker spaniel puppies. each had a red collar on and a note tied to it that read: *To Chloe from a friend. Hope you enjoy this puppy. Take good care of her and give her lots of hugs and kisses.* The other note said: *To Anna: Enjoy your new puppy. Love her and take good care of her.*

—   —   —

Doug was shocked. He looked up and down the street but saw no one. He took the puppies inside and called for Shelley. "Look what I found on the front porch! Can ya believe this?"

"Oh my gosh! Who in the world would leave puppies outside our door? Did you see anyone at all outside? They are adorable!" She called the girls in and they squealed at the sight of the puppies. The whole household was turned upside down and so was the mood of the family. Doug laughed and got his camera out to take some photos of the girls with their puppies.

"I just don't know who'd do this, Shelley. We have told no one about the girls wantin' puppies, have we?"

"I don't think so, Doug. But whoever it was, I'm happy it happened. This is just what we needed around here. I know it will cost money to feed them and take care of them, but this will do wonders for the girls. And you."

—   —   —

Edgar had hidden two houses down to watch Doug when he found the dogs. He had talked with the girls one day last week when he had delivered their mail. They told him they wanted a puppy but their father had said they didn't have the money. He didn't totally trust Doug, but he knew the family was really struggling. Sometimes if you help someone out, they turn a corner in their lives. He was watching to see if they needed more help. Like winter coats and shoes.

He drove back home with a smile on his face. Life was getting better. As long as James didn't come back home.

CHAPTER 10

The drug traffic was increasing in Portersville. Fred Perkins had no idea where it was coming from, but as he sat in his office looking out on the city, he was worried. There were a lot of rookies in the department now, and he felt like he did not know most of them very well. He had been sheriff for many years, and had always worked with a team of men who covered each other's back. Things were different now. He was getting people in from all over the state and it was more and more difficult to track their backgrounds to be sure he was getting qualified people he could trust. It made his job much more difficult. He was noticing a loosening in the department and too many unanswered questions. He needed to bring in an outside person to find out what was going on, but he didn't know who at the moment; someone familiar with the structure of the sheriff's department and also the drug situation. He decided to talk to Internal Affairs and get someone who could really figure this department out. Something was not right and he could feel it in his gut.

Two rookie cops were in his office the other day and shared that they had found something in the backyard of James Edsom's house. These boys had disturbed a possible crime scene. They should have never taken the shoe and it raised his blood pressure to even think about anyone being so stupid. It was not like Jesse to brush something this important off, and Fred might have to call him on it. Cases were not being solved. Too many things did not add up; Jesse's own son's death was never solved. He wondered if there were drugs involved in that death. *Did Jesse know something? Was he trying to protect his son?* He decided to have a talk with Jesse in a couple of days and get a feel for what was eating at him. He liked to run a tight ship and right now it felt like a cruise ship out to sea. He was going to get to the bottom of things or his job might be on the line. It was close to re-election time and he didn't need to be looking for another job at his age. He really wanted to retire as sheriff.

— — —

Jesse was waiting in Fred's office early Thursday morning. It was his normal day off, but he had received a phone call from Fred on Tuesday to schedule this meeting. He had no idea what was up, but tried to calm himself down for whatever was going to come up at this meeting. Fred came through the door with a strong stride, closed the door with a slam and sat down at his desk looking at Jesse with a stern eye.

"What in the world is going on Jesse? I need to know how your pulse is, buddy. Those two young punks came in here saying they found something in James Edsom's backyard, and that you told them to shove it under a rug. Let it go. What is that about? Was it nothing? They shouldn't have picked up anything in that backyard. I don't have to tell you that, for heaven's sake. What were they thinking? They had no business around that house in the first place."

"Oh Fred, relax. I assure you it was nothing to be excited about. It was an old shoe, for heavens sake! A shoe. I know they should have never taken the shoe, but I didn't see any connection in a shoe that obviously had been outside for a long time and the drug ring we are dealing with. I saw no reason to check it out, but if you prefer, I will go over there myself today and check out James' backyard. Would that make you feel better?"

"Hey Jesse! Your slack attitude really surprises me. With all the drug trafficking we have had lately and knowing James' background with drugs, why would you not check it out? And you want to be moved up to detective? Give me a break, Jesse. It ain't happening with that kind of attitude. We need to get our department back, Jesse. This is serious business if you and I want to retire in our positions here. I don't like the feel of the department right now; it feels very unstable and immature. Are you preoccupied with something? Anything going on in your life that you need to tell me about? How is your wife?"

"I assure you my life is in order, Sheriff. There are no skeletons in my closet. I have been under a little stress and that has nothing to do with my job or my marriage. I agree that the new guys are weak and do not seem to know what they're doing. I'll crack down on them."

"Your son was not involved in drugs, was he, Jesse?"

"No way, Fred! He was a good boy. Sure he got into trouble now and then, but no drugs. Not to my knowledge, anyway. We went all through this when he got killed, Fred. Remember? We turned over every stone, but came up with nothing. I don't know if we will ever find out how Mason died. It used to keep me up at night, but I finally let it go. Hard to bury your own son, you know?"

Jesse stood up and excused himself. Fred rolled back his chair and propped his feet on his desk. He was worried about Jesse and he didn't know why. If he was a bettin' man, he would say that Jesse was hiding something. It showed in his posture, his face, and this lack of zest for his job. He could not put his finger on it, but something was going on that Jesse was not happy about.

Edgar got in from his route worn out and hungry. He sat down heavily and took off his boots, wishing spring would come early this year. He was already sick of the snow and Christmas was only two weeks away. He walked over to the refrigerator and opened it, bent over to look inside, and pulled out leftovers from last night's roast dinner. He loved cooking but didn't take the time most nights. Eating alone ruined the desire to cook. He had talked to his daughter long into the night, and they had hit on every single topic that either one of them could pull out of their brain. He loved talking to her and missed having her near him. She had a life of her own, and he knew marriage was around the corner. In a way it would be nice, because one day he would have grandchildren. But her aging meant he was aging and he was not ready to be old.

Lost in his thoughts, Edgar sat with his meal on his lap and rested his head back against the recliner. The television was on low but he had no interest in watching it. He was thinking of his dead wife, of their life before Jane was born, and the work that he did. No one in the town knew what he used to do and he intended to leave it that way. They would never find out that he had once worked for the FBI and had solved many cases that otherwise would have remained a mystery. His life had been on the line way too many times so he finally reached a point where he hung up his hat and came back into civilian life in Portersville. It was a quiet town, and he made a home here, making few friends but meeting a lot of people. He chose the mail route because he would be able to be alone in his work, yet still talk to a lot of different people on the mail route. It was a great job for it gave you all the time in the world to think. He had risked his life for years and now he wanted to sit back and take it easy. He was finding that much easier to do with James gone. His venture with Mary was interesting, and it filled a lot of his time. But he wanted to find out who stole the money out of his house, and he aimed to do it. He kept dreaming about the gloves and he was pretty sure now that it was in the back of James' truck that he saw them. He had tried to call him again at his brother's but was getting nowhere. He had mixed emotions about finding James, because he had a sick feeling there was always more to the story than it appeared at first glance. James invited trouble. He made wrong choices time and time again, even though he would give you the shirt off his back. The only thing was that the shirt might be stolen.

He put his dishes up in the kitchen, turned out the light and picked up the phone to call Mary.

"Hello Edgar! What a nice surprise. How are you? We are having a wonderful time here together. I am so glad you called!"

"I was dyin' to know how things were goin' with Linda and little Lacy. Are you gettin' along okay? And is Linda more settled, or is she still trying to work things out in her head?"

"I think she has settled into my house for the time being, but she has a lot on her mind. She won't share it with me yet, but she is warm, eating well, and has her child with her. That is the main thing right now. You and I need to speak with her about work, perhaps. I really don't know what direction to take this, Edgar."

"We'll talk to her together, Mary, and see what she says. I'm hopin' she will tell us why she came to Portersville, and who it was she was comin' to see."

"That would be an interesting point, alright. I will let you know if I hear anything pertinent and you let me know when you want to have this talk. How are you coming along with giving the money away?"

Edgar smiled and shook his head. "I'm tryin' hard, Mary. It takes time, and I always like to make sure I'm doin' the right thing by meetin' the real need, you know? I gave Greg two thousand dollars of my own, but I know the children need coats and probably shoes. He's in real trouble with his health. I'm not sure he's goin' to make it."

"You use your own judgment, Edgar. I trust you. Let me know how that all turns out. I am sure we will talk soon. Good night, Edgar."

— — —

Edgar hung up the phone and got in his car. He was thinking about driving over to James' house and just looking around. It was dark enough now that no one would be able to see him. If he could get into the house he might find out some information that would help him know if James stole his money. He drove around the block first to see if anyone was around, then he parked the car down the street and walked on the other side of the street to the house. He was crossing the street when he thought he saw someone go into the backyard. It was dark but for a second he saw a flash of light. He decided to go around the backside of the small house and look around the corner. There was a large tree that he stood behind that was away from the house and gave him a great view of the entire backyard. There was someone there, looking at a place in the yard with a flashlight. He could not really tell who it was it was so dark but he crouched down and waited to see if the man got any closer to him. The flashlight cut on again and for a nanosecond the face of the man came into clear view. Edgar stood up and rubbed his face. It sort of *looked like Jesse Stryker.* He was not dead sure, but it sure looked like him. *What in the world would he be doin' here this time of night?* He kept his position, hidden from view, and watched for a few minutes. The man bent down and dug around in the dirt in a few places, got up and walked around the yard. It was like he was looking for something in particular. Then he suddenly looked at his watch and walked around the other side of the house. Edgar followed closely as the man walked down the driveway and off into the night.

Edgar stayed still for a while to make sure he was gone. Then he walked into the backyard and pulled out his own flashlight. He didn't see anything in the yard. He walked the entire border of the yard and there was nothing, so he tried the back door and it was locked. Edgar pulled out the tool he had used for years with the FBI and unlocked the door and went in quickly. The house was dark except for one light in the bedroom. He put on some thin surgical gloves and rummaged through some drawers and ran upon James' old address book. There were not too many names that Edgar recognized, but he did find the address of his brother. He tore out the page and put it in his pocket and walked through the other rooms. The house was full of old pieces of furniture and was pretty bare. In the bedroom there was a bed and nightstand with a lamp, and nothing else. The closets were empty and the bathroom had some medicine in the cabinet. He did find some needles under James' bed. *Stupid of you to leave these here, James,* Edgar thought, as he picked them up and put them into a plastic bag he found on the floor. There was nothing else here that could incriminate James or connect him with the drug dealers. Edgar had a thought and went back to the address book. He decided on a whim to put the small book into his pocket. No one else would know the book even existed except James. He walked out of the house, locked it, and walked the outer edge of the yard, crossed the street, and got into his car.

On the way home, Edgar was thinking about Jesse Stryker. *What was Jesse doing at James' house this late at night? What was he looking for?* Edgar found it hard, with his background in the FBI, to let this just drop. But he had to be careful because he didn't want to draw any attention to himself or allow anyone to think he had much of a connection at all with James Edsom. He planned to take their secret to his grave, and he was pretty sure that James would agree to that. He drove home wishing he had never met James, and he could not help but wonder why Linda came to Portersville. He learned in his line of work that events seemed to line up in the universe to a given point and then it all would fall into place. If he waited and listened, all the answers would show up right in front of his face. All he had to do was see them.

CHAPTER 11

Linda sat in her room with tears streaming down her face. Jesse obviously was going to leave her hanging and anger rose up in her like bile. Lacy was asleep on the bed beside her and she glanced over at her precious daughter. She had some of Jesse's features, so he could not deny she was his. How could he sleep at night knowing a child was in this world that belonged to him? They should have never slept together; she knew he was married and that he was going to leave her and come back to Portersville after his seminar. She had lived in St. Johns, Illinois for all her life, and that is where she thought she would marry and raise a family. She never dreamed that she would have a child out of wedlock with a man who could care less about her.

The moon was shining through her curtains and she walked over to the window and looked out. Thoughts were running through her head like deer running through the forest. Inside she felt like a wild animal, but instead of running she felt caged. Trapped. She was too young to be in this situation and it made her angry at herself for allowing it. She had to think of a plan that would work, so that she did not have to stay with Mary much longer. It was nice of Mary to take her in, but this was not going to be a permanent arrangement and Linda did not want to wait for them to come up with something. She wanted to be in control of her life. She smiled. How was she going to do that with no money and no place to go?

She sat down on the huge bed and opened a nightstand drawer and pulled out a pad of paper and a pen. She began to make a list of her options, and one of those options was to tell Sarah about what Jesse had done. *I hate to do this, for it would ruin Sarah's life forever. At the same time, Jesse didn't want to respond to me and help in any way. He hasn't texted me again so what am I supposed to think? He wasn't even concerned about where I am sleeping or getting any food. His own daughter out in the cold.* It made no sense, yet she had heard all her life that this was how men were. They wanted to sleep with you and then you were trash. The more she thought about Jesse the angrier she got. *Should I make a phone call to his house? Should I wait until morning and do it when Jesse was gone to work?*

Mary was downstairs fixing hot chocolate and set it on a tray with a few homemade cookies, and walked up the long flight of stairs to Linda's room. She saw a light under the door so she knew Linda was still awake. It was early yet, and Mary wanted to have a quiet chat with her before she went to sleep.

Mary tapped on the door softly. "Linda, may I come in? I have brought up some hot chocolate and cookies for you and Lacy."

Linda hurriedly put the list inside the nightstand drawer and shut it quietly. She broke out in a sweat for what she was thinking about doing, and walked to the door to greet Mary.

"Of course Mary. How sweet of you to bring this all the way up to me. I'm not used to being waited on, you know."

"Well, all of us need pampering from time to time in our lives, Linda. I thought we might have a quick chat before you go to sleep. Does that sound good?"

Linda looked over at Lacy sleeping. "I guess we could sit in these two chairs across the room so we don't wake her up," she said smiling.

The two women walked over to the old antique chairs and sat down to have their hot chocolate. As Linda sipped hers, Mary began to talk.

"I've been thinking about things, Linda. I know we don't really know each other yet, and it's none of my business what you do with your life. I don't even know if you want to remain in Portersville for long. I thought I would see what you are willing to share with me, so that I could possibly help you make a short term plan until you are more settled."

Linda was uneasy and wasn't really ready to talk to Mary about Jesse. She really did not want to tell anyone about him, but it might come to that if he didn't respond to her. "I'm not sure yet what I need to do, Mary. I know I can't stay here with you forever, and I was hoping to get in touch with the person I came to see here in Portersville. Perhaps I will pursue that tomorrow, and if it doesn't pan out, then you and I can work something out. How does that sound?" She paused and ate one of the cookies. Mary was watching her closely to see if she could read what the girl was thinking.

"Linda, we all make poor decisions in our lives. The key is to turn it around as quickly as possible so that it does not ruin our lives. You think about it, and let me know after tomorrow if things don't work out. I don't want you to think I'm nosy. I just want to help you. My intentions are pure and I wouldn't want you to ever think I'm prying or trying to run your life. Just keep in mind that if you are in any kind of trouble, it might be good to have someone on your side, since you are a stranger in this town."

At that, Mary got up and walked to the door. "I hope you sleep well, Linda. Breakfast will be served around eight o'clock, if you are hungry. If you need to go out tomorrow, I will be more than happy to watch Lacy for you, okay?"

"You're so kind, Mary. That would be wonderful! I'll let you know if I plan to leave the house. I don't think Lacy would be any trouble for you; she seems to have taken to you so quickly."

Mary left the room and closed the door quietly. Linda sat in her chair, sipping the hot chocolate, developing a plan for tomorrow. Her head was spinning and her heart was racing; she wasn't sure whether to try to text him or to call his wife. She decided to text him one more time and see if he responded. Then her conscience would be clear on the fact that she had tried every angle she could before she went to Sarah. Her stomach was sick just thinking about how a visit with his wife would turn out. However, there was a little girl's life at stake and she wanted the best for her. She didn't want Jesse. She wanted him to support his daughter. That is all. And she deserved it, even though they really didn't know each other.

Linda lay back on her pillow and thought about her life, her parents and where she was now. Two years ago she would never have dreamed that she would be lying here in a stranger's house with a daughter who was two years old, whose father was also a stranger. Her parents had raised her in a strict home, going to church, monitoring every single thing she did. They had just about disowned her over this, and it really hurt her that they wouldn't help at all. In the situation she found herself in, she had to face the fact that she had to grow up quickly, and that no one was going to come in and bail her out of this mess. She waited about two hours for Jesse to respond but there was not a word from him at all. He had to be home, as it was getting pretty late. Of course, Sarah may be sitting right next to him and he wouldn't have a chance to answer her. So she decided to go to sleep and wait until morning to see if he found a way to text her back. If he didn't, then she was going to plan B. She said her prayers, thanking God for a warm bed and roof over her head, and curled up next to Lacy and fell fast asleep. She dreamed again of a night in shining armor who would sweep her off her feet and marry her. Mary walked upstairs to check on the two children, as she did consider Linda a child. She opened the door and smiled, seeing Linda curled up beside Lacy. It was kind of nice having someone on the upper floor of her house. She had a reason to get up in the morning and fix a good breakfast. It had been a long time since anyone had spent the night in her house, and she found herself loving it. She went downstairs and set the table for breakfast and turned out the lights. She walked back to her bedroom, changed into her robe and got into bed. She looked around her room at all of the familiar things she had collected all the years of her marriage. Sidney had been such a good husband and made a lot of money in the banking business, and because he had died so suddenly at such a young age, she was left with a lot of money to manage. She hoped she has done a fair job at taking care of things, and she felt very good about putting Edgar in charge of giving to people. She had plans of leaving some money to Edgar because he had taken such good care of her. Even more so than her own children. They called her a lot and sent her things. But he was right next door where he could come and sit with her, and now they were actually doing something wonderful together. It made her feel useful and caused her to look forward to getting up in the morning.

She closed her eyes and was asleep in seconds. That used to drive Sidney crazy, for it took him an hour to turn off his mind.

— — —

Upstairs Linda's phone buzzed and a message came in. She was sound asleep dreaming of a life that might never come to pass.

Jesse was sitting on the front porch shaking inside, not knowing what to do. He had been a jerk to Linda and he felt like a dog for not responding to her. He wasn't responsible for her whole life; but he knew that her husband left her because she got pregnant with another man's child. He wished he could buy her a train ticket home so that the problem was gone. But he had a sick feeling that this woman was not going to go away easily. How was he going to get the money out of the savings without Sarah knowing it? He needed to pay her off, but he didn't have that kind of money lying around. He got up and went to bed.

Sarah was upstairs waiting when he got there. He closed his eyes and fell asleep but it was a restless sleep. Sarah watched her husband with a tear coming down her face. There was something in the air that did not feel right, and she dreaded finding out what it was.

CHAPTER 12

It was a cloudy morning, cold and windy, with branches of the large oak trees blowing up against the house. Linda woke up with a start, thinking she had heard something outside. She walked over to the window and looked out but didn't see anything. It was cold in the room so she climbed back in bed and snuggled against the warm body of her daughter and fell back asleep. She awoke the second time to Mary knocking gently on the door saying that breakfast was ready. She sat up in bed and stretched, feeling foggy and disconcerted being in a strange house. Lacy started moving around and Linda kissed her forehead. It was then that she remembered her cell phone and reached over and took it off the charger to check it for any messages. There was one text. The number on the text she recognized as Jesse's. Her stomach was churning as she opened the text. The message was cold and to the point...

Listen girl. I know you need money for your daughter, but I don't want you calling my house or trying to find me. I will take care of it. Just give me time to get some money together and then I want you out of here and on your way home. If you think you came here to get rich off me, you got another thing coming, you here? Now stay put and let me have a few days to get some money to give to you. If you contact my wife or ring my phone at home, you will not get a dime from me. And you won't like what happens next.
Jesse

Linda sat back and leaned on the headboard. His words stung as she read them, but she knew he was trying to bluff her. Her father had been a policeman, so she knew all about the law. His words made her even more determined to get what was coming to her, so she got up and rinsed her face and woke the sleeping princess.

"Come on, little angel. Aunt Mary has made a wonderful breakfast for us, and we don't want to disappoint her."

She bent down and picked up the little girl and down they went to the kitchen. Lacy was talking up a storm and touching everything in sight. Mary didn't seem the least bit concerned about having a two year old running around her kitchen, which tickled Linda. It was also a relief because it would have taken both of them to keep that child sitting in one chair for five minutes at a time.

"The food smells fabulous, Mary. What in the world are you fixing? We don't really eat that much in the morning."

"Oh, sit yourself down, child. You need to eat. I was thinking the other day when we met that you were way too thin. You need your strength raising your daughter. I hope you find something here for her to enjoy too." Mary had made fresh scrambled eggs, biscuits, jelly, bacon, pancakes, and pastries. Linda had a large glass of fresh squeezed orange juice by her plate and somehow Mary had dug up a child's mug for Lacy, full of cold milk. There was even a small bowl of oatmeal for Lacy if she wanted it.

"Oh my gosh! I don't believe all the food, Mary. We should have asked Edgar over for breakfast. This is way too much food for us." They all laughed and ate until they were stuffed, without much conversation until they were through. Mary cleaned up the dishes while Linda helped to put things back into the large refrigerator. Her mind began to wander back to the text that Jesse sent, but not for long, because Mary began to talk to her about what she wanted to do today.

"Linda, have you decided about what you want to do? Are you going out? I am available to take you anywhere you want to go, or to stay here with Lacy. You can take my car if you want to go shopping, or look for your friend. You just let me know, okay?"

"I'm so grateful to you, Mary. You've been such a good friend to me to take us in like this. I know it is hard to have strangers in your house. I want you to know I appreciate it so very much. I'm trying to decide what I want to do. My head is spinning right now. Maybe I'll take Lacy back upstairs and we'll take a long hot bath together, and I'll get my head clear."

"That's fine, angel. Just take your time. We have all day ahead of us. I'll be down here paying my bills, so anytime is fine with me."

—   —   —

Linda went back upstairs and reread her text. She decided to be bold and call his cell phone. He had to be at work by now so it wouldn't cause any problems. The phone rang about five times and then he picked up, but there was silence. He didn't say anything.

"Jesse, I need to talk to you. Just meet me somewhere today so that we can talk this out. What do you expect me to…."

Jesse hung up the phone and shook his head. This broad wasn't going to quit. His heart was racing and he had to think clearly about what to do. His wife was home alone and he was worried that Linda would call. Maybe he should have talked to her. He sat for a moment and called her back. Her phone rang and rang. He waited. Finally she picked up.

"Jesse, don't hang up on me! I'm sick of this. You were a part of this child too."

"I'll meet you in the park in the middle of downtown at ten thirty. Be there alone."

"I'll be there. But don't be so cocky. You don't hold all the strings to this puppet. Isn't it odd that you were so sweet to me when you wanted to sleep with me? Now you act like I'm a piece of lint on your brand new suit. I want some respect here, Jesse. Simple respect."

Jesse sat there feeling like crap. He knew he was messing up, but just couldn't give in to her. He was afraid it would never stop. "I will meet you there. Just don't be late, Linda. I have a job, you know."

Linda hung up and nearly screamed. Then she caught herself and hurried into the bathroom to take a quick shower. She pulled Lacy in the shower with her and laughed and sang, worried she had frightened her. She went downstairs hurriedly, looking at her watch. It was nearly ten o'clock now.

"Mary, I do have a plan today. I need to run in town for a couple of hours. Can you sit with Lacy while I am gone? I really do appreciate your offer."

"Of course, Linda. My keys are on the seat of the car. Please be careful, and here is my phone number if you need anything." She handed Linda a card with her phone number on it and also a fifty dollar bill. "I thought you might need some cash on you. You never know what is going to happen."

Linda thanked her, gave Lacy a quick hug, and walked out the door. She couldn't get to the park fast enough. She wasn't sure where it was, but she was pretty sure she could find it. Her heart was up in her throat, for she hadn't seen Jesse since the night they were together. She had really liked him then. Of course he was wining and dining her to get what he wanted. *I feel sorry for his wife*, she thought. *I was stupid to give in. Most men love waitresses and he was one of them. What a flirt he was. I should never have fallen for his lines, but I was upset over Josh and I got weak. Stupid, stupid, stupid! Well, he is not going to get away with this one. A child has been born that needs to be taken care of and it was not up to Josh to be her father.*

Linda pulled in and parked the car. She could hardly breathe and was shaking badly. She tried to calm herself down as she didn't want Jesse to know how nervous she was. Suddenly she saw him sitting on a park bench way back underneath some trees. She walked his way but looked around to make sure he was alone. There were other people in the park so she felt pretty well protected. She wouldn't be alone with him for anything in the world. There was no telling what he would do.

"Well, I see you finally showed up," Jesse said with a smirk.

"I had no trouble finding the park. Look, Jesse, I don't like this anymore than you do. But you are not going to abandon me with this child. I had no idea I would get pregnant and you sure did nothing to protect yourself either. So we need to be mature about this and take care of Lacy like two adults. All I am asking is that you pay me some money to help raise her. That's all, Jesse."

"Let's get this straight on the front end, Linda. I have no plans on getting involved in your life or the child's. This was all a big mistake and I don't want you around here trying to interfere with my life. We made a mistake, don't you get it?"

"Oh, I get it alright. But I'm the one who has to take the brunt of this mistake. My marriage is gone because of this baby. My whole life is going to change because of that one time with you. You need to step up to the plate and help me with this, Jesse."

"Hey girl. I'll find a way to give you some money. But I want you to promise you'll leave town and not come back. Is that a deal?"

"I don't plan on living here Jesse. I just came here because I didn't know what else to do. Give me a break, will you?"

Jesse got up and walked around for a moment and came back. "Okay, here's the plan. You give me a couple of days to get some money together and I will text you to meet me here again. I give you the money and call you a cab, and you disappear in the sunset. Is that understood?"

Linda looked at him with disgust in her eyes. She couldn't believe he was being such a jerk to her. "I'll tell you how it is going to be, Jesse. You're going to give me some money and I'll leave town and not talk to your wife. But if you don't give me enough to make it, or arrange to continue giving me money so that I can take care of her, then I'll go to your wife. You are not going to threaten me, do you hear?"

Jesse had a lump in his throat and got up again and walked around. He didn't like what he was hearing at all. He knew his wife would be gone before he could blink if she found out about Linda and a child that was his. "I said I would give you some money, Linda. But I don't have a lot of cash to give to you. I'm going to have to figure out how to go into our savings without Sarah knowing it. You have to give me some time. After all, I didn't know you were coming into town. I had no idea you were coming."

Linda looked down and then back at Jesse. He was pathetic. She had no time either. She had to walk around pregnant knowing it was not Jeff's child, and when she confessed about Jesse, Jeff lost it and left. They were so new with each other when they got married, and he left her alone too much, going out with the guys and drinking. He got into a lot of trouble with those friends and she put up with it. He had no mercy for her when she made a mistake. Only this mistake changed her life forever. His went unpunished and hidden. It didn't seem fair, but life wasn't fair. She was seeing that real fast.

"I'll give you until tomorrow afternoon. If I haven't heard from you by three o'clock, then your wife will get a visit from me. And don't try to send her off somewhere because I will only be waiting for her when she comes back. I have a wonderful place to stay and someone who really cares about my welfare. I could settle down here with no problem, Jesse. It will be difficult enough for me to go back home after this. But you don't have to handle any of the shame."

Jesse didn't allow his emotions to come to the surface. He remained cold as steel when he spoke to her. "You go back to wherever you are staying, and I'll meet you here tomorrow at three o'clock. After tomorrow, I hope I never see or hear from you again."

—   —   —

Linda got in her car shaking like a leaf. She could not remember being so mad at anyone in her entire life. If she had had a gun, she would have used it. Thank God she didn't. She headed back to Mary's not really wanting to talk to anyone yet. Her heart was sick and so was her stomach. It was hard to stand there and take that from a man she had slept with. For two cents she would call his wife right this second. He deserved it. She picked up her cell and dialed his home number. It rang once and she hung up. Better wait until tomorrow to see if he comes up with a decent sum of money. She smiled. *Surely this will work out and I can get out of this town. I'm not too happy about heading back to St. Johns, Illinois, but where else can I go? At least I do have some girl friends there that will help me get settled and find a good job.*

She walked back into Mary's house and down the hall. The house was unusually quiet so she wandered back to Mary's room and sure enough, piled up on the big bed she found Mary and Lacy, sound asleep. Linda smiled and tiptoed out of the room. Lacy could get spoiled living here with Mary.

—   —   —

Jesse sat at his desk fuming and worried about how he was going to come up with the money. He was sick of Linda and her little attitude. He better think of something quick or his world would come tumbling down.

CHAPTER 13

Christmas was a week away and Doug could feel it in the air. The snow had come and gone, and now it was just plain cold. The kids were expecting a big Christmas and his pockets were empty. What in the world was he going to do? Mary was ready for him to do some work, but he didn't think it was good to do it right before the holidays. So he told her he would start right after Christmas if that was okay with her. She seemed agreeable and it wasn't as hard to talk to her as he had feared. He really felt good about fixing her porch; almost like he was making amends for what he'd done. Of course he still was going to take the money she was offering. He needed it desperately. He just needed to hold out until spring when his work would pick up.

He was sitting in his truck making a list of things he needed at the hardware store when he glanced up at his rear view mirror. Edgar was delivering the mail. He stuck his head out the window and hollered at Edgar.

"Hey Edgar! How's it goin'?"

"Hey Doug. Cold. Really cold today. How are things?"

"Pretty darn slow, if you want to know the truth. Hey, I did call Mary and talked to her about the work she needs done. But I'm not goin' to start it until after Christmas. Just doesn't seem like the time right here at the holidays, ya' know?"

"I can see that, I guess. I'm glad you called her. How are the kids? You ready for Christmas around your house?"

"Well, it's goin' to be a light Christmas around here. The girls love their puppies; we never did find out who left 'em at our door. But they want new bikes and they need shoes and coats for this winter weather that doesn't seem to be lettin up any."

Edgar shook his head. "I know, Doug. It's tough when you have young children."

"Well, we'll get by. We always do, Edgar. Thanks for askin'." Doug stuck his head back in the truck and went back to his list. Edgar watched for a moment and then walked on down the street. He was going to leave some money for Doug soon so that he and Shelley could buy the things they needed for the girls. He would wait until it was dark and leave an envelope in the door. He could put it in Doug's truck if the window was down. He would decide later.

— — —

Three streets over there was a large family that Edgar had gotten to know. The husband was gone and the wife had to work late in the evenings to make enough to provide for all the kids. He knew she was struggling; he could see it in her face. He had put money in an envelope and tucked it into her mail bundle. She wouldn't think it came from him as he addressed it and stamped it. It was coming at a perfect time for her, with Christmas so close. On his own, he ordered Christmas dinner from the local diner, and it would be delivered the day before Christmas. This was the most fun he'd ever had in his life, and he was relishing it.

Greg was someone he wanted to give more to. He really liked that guy and it hurt him to think that one day soon Greg might not be around anymore. That family was really going to miss him, and nothing would replace what he could have brought into their lives. Edgar waited until he had finished his route; it was almost dark and all the lights were on outside the homes as he walked up the driveway. It got dark so early that it really ate into his day. He went inside to warm himself up and made a fresh pot of coffee. He turned on the news to see if anything interesting was happening in town. He sat down at his desk and pulled out some of Mary's money and put it in an envelope for Greg. He wrote his name on the front and wrote "Merry Christmas to a wonderful family!" on the outside. He had put a thousand dollars in the envelope but he opened it back up and added another thousand. This family needed it for sure, and he might even have to do more for them when the time came for Greg to die. It was hard even saying it, but Edgar knew it was coming. He could see it on Greg's face.

He got into his car and drove over to Greg's house and parked down the street a ways. He walked quietly to the edge of the yard and cut through to the porch where he rang the doorbell and wedged the envelope between the two doors. He ran as fast as he could to the outer edge of the yard and hid behind a tree. He could see Greg open the door and the envelope fell. Greg bent over and picked it up and opened it. He yelled out and looked around the yard. He saw no one and shut the door. Edgar grinned from ear to ear and left, heading to his car. It was more fun because he remained anonymous. Mary would be delighted. He should carry her with him the next time he did this. She would get a real kick out of it.

He drove over to Doug's house and stuck the envelope in the doorway and rang the bell. He ran again to the outer edge of the yard and hid so he could make sure they got the envelope. Doug opened the door and saw the envelope at his feet and leaned over to pick it up. He opened it and looked around. *Who was this leaving money at my door? This is unreal! Who would know we need this money so badly?* He rubbed his head and walked back inside. Edgar could tell he was really puzzled. He almost laughed out loud, but caught himself. That would ruin everything. Heading back to the house Edgar thought about who else he would help. Mary had about four thousand dollars left in the envelope on his desk. He wanted to give some to Linda and Lacy, but he would talk to Mary about it tonight. When he walked back into this house he went straight to the desk and wrote down who he had given the money to. He was putting up the pad in a slot when something fell off the desk. He leaned over to pick it up and saw it was a lighter. *What in the world is a lighter doing on my desk? I don't smoke and don't even own a lighter. Has someone been in my house again?* He checked the envelope again and counted the money. All of it was still there. *So where did this lighter come from?* He looked at it in the light and suddenly anger rose up in him. He sat down in his chair by the desk and put his head in his hands. It was James's lighter. He was sure of it.

Edgar checked the whole desk again but there was nothing else there. No other hint of James that he could find. *Was James the thief? Would he have taken my money and headed out of town?* Edgar had asked that question out loud and something about the words ringing in the air made it very clear to Edgar. It was James who had stolen his money. *So he was into drugs again. That rat. What in the world had he done that he would steal money from his friend?* And Edgar was probably the best friend James had, even though they really didn't know each other that well. But they did hold a secret together that neither could ever share with anyone. *That would make one pretty close,* thought Edgar.

He was going to call Mary tonight, but now he wasn't in the mood to talk to anyone. He was thinking of how he was going to find James and what he would do with him if he found him. Or would it be better to leave it alone? The guy sure didn't need to come back to town. It was better now that he was gone. He was just too fragile and would get into trouble if he was here. Edgar went straight to bed. Too much for one night. A small lighter had taken the joy he had of giving right out of his heart. His sleep was restless, but vindictive. For in his sleep, Edgar had made James pay for all the times he had let him down. *Be careful what you dream, he had been told when he was young. It just might come true.*

— — —

James was lying in bed looking up at the ceiling. For some reason he was thinking about Edgar tonight and feeling pretty lousy. He had really liked Edgar and didn't want to lose him as a friend. But he'd blown that for sure. He could never set foot in Portersville again. His house was just sitting there empty, and he was pretty darn sure that the cops had been by there to check for drugs. He had cleaned it out pretty good but he couldn't be sure he got everything. He was so tempted to call Edgar back, but it would open up a can of worms as sure as he was lying there. So he left it alone.

He had gotten a job and would receive his first paycheck on Friday. He wanted to save up and get a new used truck and rent a house. He loved his brother but they both needed their privacy. He wanted a new life and this was the only way he knew to get it. Edgar would be proud of him if he knew he had a job. He turned over faced the wall and closed his eyes. Tomorrow was coming fast and he wanted to be fresh for work. For the first time in more years than he cared to admit, he was drug free, alcohol free and working.

He fell asleep quickly but in spite of his start on a new life, he was haunted over and over about Jesse Stryker's son, and the money he stole from Edgar. He woke up in a sweat, breathing hard. He suddenly felt a cold chill come over him, and he sat up in bed. *What if they found something in my back yard that would lead them to me? How can I be dead sure that nothing would come back to haunt me?* All he could do tonight was roll up in a ball and pull the covers up around him. This was when he needed his friend Edgar. And he had cut that tie when he left town.

James was lonelier than he had ever felt in his entire life.

Chapter 14

Mary was expecting Edgar for breakfast, so she spent the early hours getting wonderful things ready for him. Too bad she wasn't a younger woman, because she would have loved to date Edgar. He was the perfect gentleman and always entertained her well. Just as she put the biscuits in the oven, he knocked on the back door. She let him in, smiling, and they both sat down at the kitchen table.

"Good morning Mary. How are things going over here? Is Linda settling down a little?

"I think she is, Edgar. But I do sense that she's really upset about something and she hasn't felt free to share it with me yet. The fact that she hasn't opened up to me makes it really difficult for me to help her like I want to. Do you think we need to give her some money to help her get on her own? We could find her an apartment and maybe a used car. I know that's expensive, but I would be willing to do that if it would change her situation."

Edgar was stunned by Mary's huge offer, and he thought a moment before he answered her. "I think we can give her some money, but I'm not sure she wants to settle down here, Mary. I was really hopin' that she would open up to you, so that we'd know exactly what her needs are. Now we are sittin' here guessing. Maybe we need to really have a heart to heart with her and see what she says."

Mary served their plates and they both dove in, eating while the eggs were still hot. She had outdone herself with fresh strawberries and powdered sugar, bacon, eggs, black eyed peas, biscuits and gravy and fresh banana nut bread.

"I think that is a wise idea, Edgar. I'll have dinner ready when you get off work. Just come on over unless you hear from me."

——— ——— ———

Linda was upstairs standing on the balcony. She could hear bits and pieces of what they were saying in the kitchen. So they were wondering what she was upset about. Interesting. She couldn't tell them right now. She had to wait to see what happened at the park. Jesse would either come through or he would let her down big time. She was hoping it was going to go smoothly because she wasn't looking forward to calling his wife. It could get very ugly and all she wanted was a way to raise her daughter. She had nothing against Sarah but that was who would suffer if the truth got out.

She dressed Lacy and walked downstairs to breakfast, smiling, but with a nervous stomach. Mary pulled out a chair for Lacy with a large book for her to sit on. Lacy loved sitting in a big chair and ate her breakfast without a word. Linda filled her plate with a few things and picked at her food. Edgar talked about his mail route and engaged them all in laughter. But he was also eyeing Linda and trying to figure out what was on her mind. He noticed that she didn't have much to say. He offered to take her where she needed to go, but she turned him down.

"I really need to be alone for a little while, Edgar. Thanks so much for your offer. Mary, this food is delicious but for some reason my stomach is upset this morning. Please forgive me if I don't finish my breakfast." She got up and went out to the sun porch and sat down. It was lovely out there because you could look out at the trees and sky but not feel the bitter cold. It was one of Linda's favorite rooms in the house, and she loved being alone with her thoughts. She dreaded this meeting with Jesse. She wished things had turned out another way; she would have loved to have stayed married, but it just was not in the cards. She tried to gather her thoughts and make a plan if Jesse fell through with the money. It might be difficult, nearly impossible, for him to withdraw a large sum of money without his wife finding out. She knew that was going to be a big problem. However, he should've thought of this when he charmed her and took her back to his hotel room. All he wanted was a good time. Now he was facing one of the worst times in his life, all because of one fun night. She suddenly felt sad, used up, and tired. She was way too young to feel this way about herself or life. *I hope I have learned a lesson from this*, she thought sadly.

Edgar came up behind her quietly and stood watching her at the window. He cleared his throat so that he wouldn't scare her, and she turned around. Her face said it all. But he didn't speak about what he saw in her. "I was wondering, Linda, if you're homesick? This is a pretty big deal, you comin' to Portersville alone with no place to go. Have you connected with that person you came to see?" Edgar watched her pupils and her body language.

"I haven't. But I hope to today, Edgar. Thanks for asking. I'm a little home-sick, but not as much as you would think. Mary has been such a good host that I'm very content being here in her house. She has a wonderful gift of making people feel very welcome. I can't thank you enough for bringing me here, Edgar. I hope to be able to leave soon, but I'll never forget what you have done for me."

Edgar knew she was lying about something. But he didn't push the point. "So what's on the agenda today, if I may ask? Are you meetin' someone today?"

Linda turned and looked out of the window. *What am I supposed to say?*

"I am, Edgar. But I won't be gone very long. Mary has said she'll gladly sit with Lacy." She looked at her watch and excused herself. "I need to run upstairs and make a few phone calls, Edgar. It's so good to see you again, and I'll let you know how my day turns out."

She walked out of the sun room and ran up the stairs. Edgar made a silent decision that he would keep from Mary at this time. He went back into the kitchen and hugged Mary. "What a wonderful breakfast, my dear. I've gained a lot of weight visiting you in the mornings!" He paused and took a slow deep breath. "I'll get back to you on Linda. Have a wonderful day, and let me know if anything comes up."

—   —   —

Edgar started his mail route but kept his eye on the time. About two o'clock he headed home to take care of some things. Mary's car was pulled out of the garage but Linda hadn't left yet. He decided to pack some food and water in his car and pulled out of the driveway. He parked at the end of the street back off the road on a lot that had a lot of trees. He could see the road from where he was and turned off his car. It was cold, but he had layered his clothing so that he wouldn't get cold on his mail route. It would come in handy no matter where he ended up today.

Thirty minutes went by and no Linda. He waited patiently; that was one thing he learned in the FBI. He had tucked his gun in his belt; he wasn't even sure why he did it. It never really hurt to have a gun no matter what the situation. But today he just felt like it might be a smart move on his part. He was dozing when a car went by and woke him up. It was Linda. He waited a few seconds to let her get ahead of him and he pulled out and followed her. There were several cars separating them so she wouldn't see his car. It was a gray day and a little hazy outside, which helped his cover. She was headed into the center of town, and he guessed that she would probably stop at the park, or a restaurant. Sure enough she headed for the park and pulled in. He waited as long as traffic would allow and pulled in. He parked on the other side of the parking lot and got out of his car. He skirted the edge of the park so that she wouldn't see him. He found a group of trees and stood behind them, keeping her in sight. She looked around to see who was in the park, and then sat on a bench to wait. Edgar kept looking at his watch and at Linda. It was nearly three fifteen and so far no one had shown up. Edgar decided to sit on the ground by the tree, still out of sight. He was watching a woman with a child and got engrossed in what they were doing. Suddenly he looked back at Linda and someone was standing there talking to her. It was a heated conversation and Edgar stood up and slowly moved closer. He didn't want them to see him, so he had to be very careful. There were plenty of trees for him to have good cover, and he found that it felt pretty good to step into his old routine again, after so many years. He suddenly realized it was Jesse Stryker and his jaw dropped. *What in the world had Jesse done? He was married. Highly thought of in the community. Was he nuts?*

— — —

Jesse was so angry he could hardly speak. She was demanding so much from him and he had no way of meeting those demands. "Linda, for gosh sakes will you settle down? I can't come up with the amount of money you are wanting! Do you get that? I'm sick of you thinking you can show up here in my town demanding things from me. Who do you think you are?"

"I'm growing to hate you, Jesse Stryker! You have a part in this child and you need to step up to the plate. I'm well aware of your marriage and your big career. But what about me? What in the world do you expect me to do?"

Jesse was getting madder by the moment. "Do you really think your life is up to me? That I'm totally responsible for making sure you're okay? You are nuts! I'm not going to stand here and allow you to talk like this. You're either going to take this money I'm offering you now, or I'm going to walk away and you'll get nothing. And don't you dare threaten me with calling my wife! You won't live to raise that child if you do that, Linda."

Linda was shaking inside. She had never been so mad in her entire life. She hated this man who was standing in front of her with his fist in the air. "You can threaten me all you want, Jesse. I'm not afraid of you. I know you won't hurt me; you know what will happen if you do. So stop with your threats and let's get real. I have a child to raise and I need help, and I want you to get serious about it."

Jesse had had enough of her talk. He saw no way out of this mess. His chest was tight and he felt sick. He didn't want to hurt her, but he only had so much money to give to her and she was refusing to take it. He got in her face and yelled, losing control of his temper. "Linda, I am at the end of my rope with you. Either you take this money or I'm going to leave and you'll get nothing out of me." He grabbed her shoulders and shook her, and she hit him in the face. Edgar was watching and nearly came out of the trees, but decided he better not show his face just yet.

Jesse pushed her away from him and she fell and hit her head on the park bench. She was still for a moment and then sat up, rubbing her head. Jesse squatted down and grabbed her arm and pulled her to her feet. "Listen to me, young lady. This isn't a game here! You could get hurt real bad if you keep this up. Is that what you want? Now stand up and take this money I have for you, and let's call it a day."

She was bleeding somewhere on her head, and the blood was dripping down her forehead. But her anger took over and she didn't feel a thing. "Jesse, I was hoping that this meeting would turn out differently. I see you are going to be stubborn about this, but I can be stubborn too. What are you going to do, Jesse? Kill me? I hardly think so. That would be pretty stupid out here in the open where people can see you. It's getting late, and I'm freezing! Now be a man and do what you are supposed to do."

Jesse looked down and Linda didn't see it coming. She heard a noise in the woods and turned to look, and right at that moment, Jesse pulled his fist back and hit her hard in the stomach. It knocked the wind out of her and she fell to her knees, gasping. It took everything Edgar had to keep from going to her, but he refrained. He had to wait and see what Jesse would do. It would do no one any good for him to come out of hiding now. Jesse walked away and got into his car and drove off, squealing his tires on the wet pavement. Linda sat for a moment and got her breath and stood up. She sat down on the park bench for a few minutes to sort things out, and walked slowly back to the car. Edgar waited to see what she was going to do; it looked like she was dialing her cell phone. *Who in the world would she be calling?*

Edgar had a sick feeling it was Sarah Stryker. This wasn't going to end well. He had figured it out the minute he saw Jesse. *The child was his. What a jerk he was. Got her pregnant and then wanted to dump her.* He stayed on the outskirts of the park and made it back to his car. There was nothing he could do right now, so he headed back to the house to finish up the last street on his mail route. He was glad he had gone to check things out, and to be there in case their argument had brought out a gun on Jesse's part. Thank God it didn't. He would have shot Jesse for sure if he'd tried to really hurt Linda. *What a mess that would have been. I thought I was just helping a young girl out when I saw her at the grocery store. I had no idea what I was getting myself into.* He rubbed his eyes and shook his head. *Nothing was simple anymore. What a complicated mess!*

He had a strong feeling that this wasn't the end of this conversation. *If Sarah was called, all hell would break loose. But maybe that is what it'll take to get Jesse to pay attention. He could've handled this in a more mature way and then things would've gone back to normal. Instead, this was going to turn into World War III. And somehow I'm going to end up in the middle of it,* he thought, shaking his head again.

— — —

Mary was in the kitchen when Linda drove up the driveway. Watching her get out of the car, Mary could tell that Linda had been crying. *Things must not have turned out well,* she thought. *The poor girl needed a break.*

Linda came in the door and ran upstairs. She rinsed her face off and checked her phone. She had put in a call to Sarah but no one answered the phone. She decided to wait and try tomorrow when Jesse would be busy at work. She wasn't going to stop until her last breath; he was going to pay. She headed back downstairs and faked a smile. "Hello Mary! Thank so much for keeping Lacy for me. I sure hope she wasn't any trouble."

"Oh my heavens! She's an angel, Linda. You've been such a good mom to her and she minds so well. She's a joy to be around."

"Well, it meant a lot to me to be able to go out today and I don't know what I would've done if you hadn't kept her for me. Is she still sleeping?"

"Yes, she's taking a longer nap today for some reason. I may have worn her out playing hide and seek, but she was having a wonderful time and I lost track of the time."

"That's okay, Mary. Is it alright with you if I fix some coffee? I need something to perk me up and some hot coffee might do the trick."

"Sure Linda. I made some fresh coffee cake, so help yourself to it. I'm going to see if Lacy is awake and bring her in here." Mary walked back to her bedroom and called Edgar.

"Hello Mary. Are you okay? I just got back from delivering the mail. Had to run some errands today."

"I was wondering if you knew what Linda was up to today. She came in crying and her face was so red. I'm worried, Edgar. Something isn't right and I don't know how to find out what it is.'

"Let me take care of this one, Mary. Trust me, will you? I promise I'll let you in on whatever I find out. I have a way of getting to the bottom of things. Have you noticed that?"

"One would think you used to be a policeman yourself, Mr. Mailman. Please do let me know if you find out anything. I'm going to go to bed early tonight, as that baby wore me slap out. But I'll be up bright and early in the morning if you need me."

— — —

Lacy was awake and grinning on the bed. Mary grabbed her up and took her into the kitchen where Linda was sitting at the table. The little girl ran to her mother, giggling.

"Hey little baby. Have you been good for Aunt Mary?" Linda pulled her up on her lap and kissed and hugged her. She almost started crying again, but caught herself. She really needed to get control of her emotions. Things could get out of hand real quick.

"She was a perfect child, Linda. I think she might be a little hungry, and I made us a light supper. You game for a vegetable dinner with blueberry muffins? I thought that would hit the spot this cold winter night. Christmas is in a couple of days and I wanted to put up a tree for Lacy. Will you help me if I get it down from the attic?"

"I'll get the tree for you, Mary, and Lacy and I'll help you decorate it if you like. It wouldn't be Christmas without a tree." Linda took a deep breath and let go of some of the tension. Putting up a Christmas tree was the last thing she felt like doing. But maybe it would take her mind off her confrontation with Jesse. *I will remember this Christmas the rest of my life*, she thought, shaking her head.

CHAPTER 15

Linda sat on the sun porch with her hands in her lap, dead still. She was worn out with the stress of this trip. It hadn't turned out at all like she thought it would. Jesse was scared, she could see that. He overreacted about her being in town, and the fear of what she might do was propelling him forward into a frantic rage to keep her away from his wife. *The smartest thing he could've done was be nice about it and set up some kind of arrangement with me for taking care of Lacy. No one would ever have to know. We could have opened up a separate account for him to deposit the money. But no, he was going to be a real jerk about it and threaten me.* She smiled for a moment but it faded into a worried look. She had to think about what to do next. This was too important a decision and she knew that if she went to Sarah, it would impact her life as well as theirs. She would play up the fact that she didn't want to disrupt their lives, but wanted her daughter to have a good life. *Sarah was a mother. And Sarah had lost a son. She would be sensitive to my fears about my child's future; but the wrath she would feel towards Jesse might overshadow any compassion she had for me.* She sipped on some coffee and let her head fall back on the chair. Her body was sore from the punches he had given her. She wanted to break down and cry but she had no one to really lean on at this point. Edgar had been so wonderful and she would never be able to repay Mary for the kindness she had shown. *My options are slim; tell Sarah or go home with nothing. What would most people do in this situation?*

Just as she was about to tear up she turned and Edgar was standing in the doorway again. *Why did he keep doing that? It was unnerving.* "Hello Edgar. Please come in and sit down with me. I was just enjoying a little peace and quiet here on the porch. This has come to be my favorite place in the house to just sit and think."

"I can see how you would like this place, Linda." Edgar looked around the room at the chintz fabrics and open windows. All the furniture was comfortable and the colors were relaxing. "Hey. I thought we might go look at Christmas lights tonight with Lacy. How does that sound?"

"Why that sounds wonderful Edgar! I haven't been in the best of moods lately and I apologize for that. But I do have a lot on my mind. What time did you want to go?"

Edgar noticed the tiredness in her face and the worry. He wanted to tell her he knew what was going on, but withheld it for now. "I was thinking around seven thirty. Not too late because I know Lacy goes to bed early. I really think she'll enjoy seeing all the lit up houses. Some people really go all out to decorate for the holidays."

"Great! I'll make sure we are ready at seven thirty. Is Mary going?"

"Yes, I think she will. It has been years since she enjoyed the Christmas lights, so she is excited."

— — —

Doug was sitting in his garage on an old keg thinking about his money situation. He had an idea that might drum up some work. He had decided that maybe he would go door to door in a mile area from his house and ask people if they had any repair work that needed to be done. It wouldn't hurt, even though he knew how people felt about someone coming to their door. He wasn't that well known in the community so that was a strike against him. But if he dressed nice and smiled, maybe people would feel at ease with him. He had to do something or he wouldn't be able to pay his house note. He didn't move to Portersville to fail. He wanted to start a new life with Shelley and the girls, and he knew he better get his act together or go under. He looked at a calendar and decided to wait a week after New Years, so that everyone would be over the holidays and back into their normal routines. Spring would be on everyone's mind because people get sick of the cold, wet weather of winter. He would get Shelley to print up what he could offer people, with his name and phone number on the paper. It would give him something to hand people so they wouldn't forget him when they were ready for some work to be done.

He walked inside and shared it with Shelley. She was busy folding laundry but sat down to hear what he had come up with. She smiled and agreed it would be a great idea. Then she shared with him her surprise. "I've been doing my homework too, after our conversation the other night. I checked at the school and they do need substitute teachers for the next semester at the girls' school. So they have put me on a list to call when a teacher is out. I knew you would be happy to hear this news!"

"Hey! That's great! Maybe we'll make it after all, Shelley. We love this house and the girls love bein' in this neighborhood. We are goin' to have to buckle down and make it through this tough time. If you get this job, you'll be home when the girls get home, so we don't have to deal with babysitters or daycare. I know that makes you feel better about workin'."

"You have no idea. I was worried about finding someone for them to stay with and now that isn't even an issue. I'll look forward to getting out of the house and feeling productive again, too." Shelley paused and looked at Doug. "After Christmas, give me the things you want me to say in the handout, and I'll type it up and print a lot of copies for you. We can make it look as professional as possible."

Doug walked back outside to work in his shop. He felt better all the way around about Christmas and how he was going to pay his bills. He just hoped things worked out like he planned. *It would be the first time in his life that it did*, he thought, and laughed out loud.

— — —

Down the street, Greg was laying in bed taking a short nap. He could tell he was going down and it really was tearing at his ability to stay up for the family. He didn't want to die and could hardly think about not being with his wife to watch the kids grow up. *How was she going to make it? I have a life insurance policy, but will that be enough for her?* Tears fell down his face as he lay there with his eyes wide open. He never allowed anyone to see him cry. It was a rule he gave himself when he found out that he was terminal. Instead, he helped them with their feelings about it, always smiling and saying it would all work out fine. Inside his heart was ripping out of his chest. Talk about sadness. This was the deepest sadness he had ever felt in his entire life. Way more than when his own father had died of a sudden heart attack. That was bad enough; this was entirely overwhelming every single part of his body, mind and soul. It made it difficult to get up in the morning or have a desire to do anything. For what was the point?

Constantly working on his attitude, he pushed himself beyond what the doctors said he could do, or should do, so that his wife and children had what they needed. He didn't want them to feel like they were watching him slowly die. He really wanted to go off somewhere, near the end of his time, and die alone or with a nurse. He didn't want his family to see it. *But how do you share that with your wife?* He now understood why people who were terminal killed themselves to spare the family. It made perfect sense. On top of that, the person who was ill didn't have to sit around and wade through the deterioration of the illness for the long awaited for peace of death. He had seen people last forever in a stage that was pure torture for them and the family. He didn't want that for his own life or for his wife. He would make the decision about what to do as the time approached. He couldn't promise himself that he would be able to kill himself. But he would have that option available if he chose to do it.

— — —

Mary was meeting with her accountant this afternoon to see how much money she had and talk to him about what she wanted to do with it. She had some ideas, but wanted to talk with Edgar about them before she made any decisions. She almost trusted Edgar more than she did her sleazy accountant. He actually gave her the creeps. Tall, thin, and stern, he was formidable even to Mary. The odd thing was that it was her money, not his. But after talking to him, she always walked away feeling like she had just spoken with her father. This man was just the opposite of her father, who had been gracious, giving and very intelligent. Mr. Poppinwolf was a stiff necked, mediocre CPA who thought he knew more than he did. He had been the family accountant for years and Mary hadn't even considered finding a new one. But today, after this meeting, she was going to look into it. He made her life miserable at times, and she didn't know why. It wasn't like she was going to leave him all the money. Funny man. He was very odd, and she couldn't put her finger on why. Maybe she should bring Edgar with her to this meeting, so he could size up this penny-pincher.

She picked up her phone and dialed his cell phone. It rang and rang. Finally he picked up, out of breath. "Hello? Mary? Are you okay?"

"I'm doing fine. Just wanted to know if you would ride with me to see my accountant today? I'm thinking about changing and I wanted your ruthless opinion of him!" She laughed at her own humor.

"You are feelin' pretty frisky this morning, Mary! Of course I'll go with you. What time?"

"My appointment is at two o'clock. I know that's pushing you on your route. What do you think?"

"I'll be there with bells on. It might be good for you to have a man by your side when you are with this guy. He sounds like a real bundle of joy."

Mary smiled and hung up. She could always count on Edgar to be there for her. She trusted his opinion now over anyone else in her realm of vision. She surmised that he came from a very intelligent background and chose the postal route as a way of escape from stress. But he had failed to share much about himself with her. *I will get it out of him one day,* she thought. She was very concerned about Linda and needed to talk to Edgar again about her. They never did make a decision about giving her any money. Christmas would be the perfect opportunity to do it. She also wanted to know about Greg who lived around the corner. So much to talk about. But Mary loved every minute of it. Her life would be empty without Edgar Graham, to say the least.

— — —

Edgar had been making his own plans for the New Year. He was going to give Sheriff Perkins a call first thing after the New Year came into play. He sat in his car looking out across the rows of houses he new so well on his mail route. Inside a few of those homes lurked drug dealers that he knew were part of the corruption of Portersville. They were sneaking into the schools, engaging the children to get involved with delivering drugs, getting them hooked on the easy drugs first, and then the hard stuff. It made Edgar sick to think about it. He knew exactly how they worked and could almost peg them after having one conversation with them. What was once a clean, beautiful, safe place to live, was fast becoming a drug Mecca. Odd that it would happen in a small town. There had been some influx of industry that had carried with it outsiders coming in from larger cities. With that came some corruption and opportunities for the drug lords to move in. No place was safe from drugs. He also felt like something was going on inside the sheriff's department, for he had observed a few things himself that were obviously against the law. He let it slide because he didn't want to get involved. But after seeing Jesse behave like he did with Linda, and finding him in James's backyard with a flashlight late at night, he suspected there was more behind that badge than met the eye.

What he decided to do was talk with Fred and watch and wait. The right time would come for him to make his move. He learned a long time ago, to make a move too soon would be worse than not making it at all. He felt an old excitement come up in him that he thought was dead. *Nice to feel it again.* It gave him something to look forward to besides the mail route and the venture with Mary. A nice balance.

He picked up his cell and phoned his daughter. He would run this past her and see what she said. They had a great way of communicating and he loved the sparring that resulted in a clash of opinions. She had his temperament, but also a little fire from her mother. *Too bad we couldn't be a team, somehow, but she needed to have her own life,* he thought.

Edgar looked at his watch. It was one thirty. He'd better finish his route and head home. Mary was waiting, and he couldn't wait to meet this accountant. He sounded like a real bird.

CHAPTER 16

Looking around the office of Mr. Poppinwolf was like seeing the destruction of the worst tornado Edgar had ever witnessed in his entire life. There were files and papers everywhere, with no order at all. Everything was random. *How could he find anything in this office? The walls are a drab green like a hospital, and there is a musty smell that was not surprising with all of the paper stacked everywhere. He probably never threw anything out. What happened to having a secretary who filed things?* Edgar was having a chuckle to himself when in walked the CPA himself. Mary looked at Edgar and they both had to hold back a laugh. Edgar stood up and reached out his hand, trying his best to be polite during his first meeting with this man who managed Mary's money.

"Good afternoon, Mr. Poppinwolf. Name's Edgar. Edgar Graham. I'm here with Mary to listen in and help her make some decisions."

It was obvious that Mr. Poppinwolf wasn't happy to see Edgar. He sat down without shaking his hand, and growled. "I don't shake hands, Mr. Graham. Too many diseases going around in the winter. Have a seat."

Edgar looked at Mary and raised his eyebrows. *This should be a fun visit.* Mary spoke up right away. "Gregory, be nice, please! Edgar is my best friend in all the world and I trust him explicitly. Now let's get down to business. I want to know how much money I have and where it all is, and I want Edgar to hear it in case I have trouble remembering in the future."

Gregory winced at this request. He preferred to withhold information from his clients unless it was absolutely necessary for them to know it. He had operated this way for years and he didn't plan to change for Mary. "Well, you are perfectly aware of how much money you have, Mary. We have discussed this numerous times in the past. I don't see the need in going over it again today. Why do you need to know?"

"Well, for one thing, Mr. Gregory. It is my money and I have a right to know. And secondly, I have a plan and I need to know how much money I have to work with."

This alarmed Gregory and he stood up without thinking. "And what plan would that be, Mary Williams? You have never mentioned any plan to me before. I need to be the first person you tell about any plans to spend your money. After all, I do manage it for you, is that correct?"

"Yes, you do, Gregory. But if you don't change your attitude towards me and how you talk to me, I'm going to find someone else to manage my estate. How do you like that, Mr. Poppinwolf?"

"Now, Mary. Calm down. Don't get all emotional on me this afternoon. We can take a look at things, of course. I just don't advise you to go out and spend without thinking about your future."

"My future, Gregory? Hell, how old do I have to get before I'm allowed to spend like I please, may I ask? You aren't the keeper of my money, you know. You keep my books. And you give me financial advice. That is all, Gregory. I can spend it all if I like and die poor, which is sounding better and better to me as the years go by. Who else is going to get it, might I add? You? I hardly think so! And why can't you keep a neater office, Gregory? This is a pig pen in here! I'm embarrassed for Edgar to see it this way."

Mary paused and cleared her throat. She was on a roll, and Edgar was afraid he was going to have to excuse himself before he burst out laughing at the whole situation.

"Are you so tight you cannot hire a secretary, Gregory?"

"I have never had a secretary, Mary. I'm perfectly capable of running this office the way I see fit, and I don't like having to deal with emotional females who have to take off every other day for one thing or the other. Now, let's get down to business."

He pulled out the files and brought up figures on the computer. He had done books for years without a computer but he finally broke down when his clients demanded reports that could be printed out for tax purposes and other issues. He hated it though. He hated change.

"Here are your profit and loss statements for the last three years. You can see how you have earned a lot of interest on the money in your accounts. At the bottom of the page it shows your total net worth. The figure is ten million dollars. That is what you are worth at this time, Mary. Ten million dollars."

— — —

Edgar almost fell out of his chair. Was he hearing this guy right? *Ten million dollars?* He looked over at Mary and noticed she was in shock too. "Mary, are you okay? Did you not realize you had that much money?" Edgar put his hand on her arm and tried to soothe her.

"Oh Edgar. This has surprised me to say the least. I had no idea it was that much. Think of what all I can do with it. Since you came into my life, I realize more and more how much we can do for people. I'm very excited, Edgar. This is huge. We are talking about a lot of money here."

For a moment Mary forgot about Gregory Poppinwolf sitting there. She looked up and his face was ashen. He looked like had lost his favorite dog. She smiled and looked him in the eye. "Thank you. You have been very helpful. Is there something wrong, Gregory?"

"No, Mary. I am fine. If we are finished, I will show you out." Gregory stood up and came around his desk to usher them out the door.

"Gregory, please, hire yourself a secretary and get some order in this office. This is ridiculous! And could you smile once, do you think? The whole time I have known you I have yet to see a smile. I'll call you when I start drawing money out of the bank. This is going to be the best time in my life."

Gregory was speechless and turned white as a ghost. He just stood there shaking his head in disbelief. Or was it fear?

— — —

Edgar walked Mary to her car and they laughed all the way home. *Poor Gregory. What a mess he was.* Mary was so excited about what she could do for the rest of her life, that she could hardly contain herself. "Edgar, just think of what we can do. There is no limit. Talk to me, Edgar. Talk to me about Greg and Doug. About anybody else you have met. We need to discuss Linda, too. I could set her up in a nice place and give her enough money to get started. We need to make a plan, Edgar."

"Hold on, Mary. Let's get home and see what we have here. Tonight I promised Linda that I would take her, Lacy and you to see the Christmas lights. Let's get through Christmas and see what comes up, okay? There will be a lot going on for the next couple of weeks, through the holidays. Let's get through that, Mary, and then decide what to do."

"You're right, Edgar. I guess I got overwhelmed. I'm so glad you came with me. Now you know what I deal with when I go talk to Gregory. Is he a mess, or what? It's hard to believe he is successful at what he does. You couldn't even find a pencil on that desk. What a mess!"

They laughed as they walked into the house. Mary fixed some fresh coffee and they sat down at the table. She pulled out some home made cookies and called for Linda. Lacy came running in the kitchen and jumped on Mary's lap. She was really taking to Mary; it was quite obvious.

"Linda, where are you? Come on in here! We had a great visit with my accountant. Are you hungry? Would you like some cookies I baked yesterday?"

Linda came through the door smiling at the two of them. "Listen to you two. What in the world are you so giddy about, Mary? You must have had a great meeting!"

"Well, when you get my age, sweetheart, you like to know where you stand with your money so you can plan how you are going to live out the rest of your life. I took Edgar so he could understand everything. I don't know what I would do without him."

She winked at Edgar. She knew better than to tell Linda what she had discovered this afternoon. No one would know. She was going to call her attorney after Christmas and set up a meeting. She wanted to leave Edgar some money for taking such good care of her. He would be surprised, but she would not be around to see it.

CHAPTER 17

Christmas Eve came like a thief in the night; quietly, and with more snow than Portersville had ever seen. There was not one single footprint in all of Portersville, for everyone was asleep and unaware that the town was being transformed again into a winter wonderland. Mary had given specific instructions to Edgar along with two envelopes. She wanted those envelopes placed before Christmas morning, so poor Edgar might be the lone soul out in the middle of the night, along with Santa Claus of course, to leave an anonymous card at the door of two families who needed it the most. This might be the best Christmas Mary ever had. Except for when she was with Sidney of course. She had given a lot of thought to what she was doing, and in spite of Edgar's persuasive words, she stuck to her guns and wrote the checks.

Edgar was out at two o'clock in the morning delivering two presents that would alter the course of the lives of the two families. It was so beautiful outside at this time of night, with all of the snow. He felt like Santa Claus, only better. This was not only going to be a nice surprise, but it was going to change their lives tremendously. His first delivery was Greg Morgan. He knew Greg was getting close to not being able to get out of bed. He'd never seen anyone so brave and so determined to not show his illness to his family. Getting through this Christmas season will be the toughest thing Greg could ever do, but now, with this present, he would go to his grave knowing he had taken care of his family. His house would be paid for, and the car. He would have no debt and his wife could begin a new life feeling secure and safe. What better gift to give a dying man?

Edgar found tears streaming down his face. He didn't know why he liked Greg so much, but that man really tugged at Edgar. He was proud to be a part of this gift as he had put some of his own money in the envelope. Like Mary, he had saved and been frugal in his life, so he did have a good savings. Now it was coming full circle to give some of it to someone like Greg. He walked slowly up to the house and opened the glass door, placed the envelope under the door knocker, and turned and walked away.

Greg heard something outside and had peeked out the upstairs window. He had laid down with his younger son to get him to sleep, when he thought he heard something at the front door. It was snowing so heavily that it was a little difficult to see, but he thought he saw a figure walking away from the house. *Who could it be?* He strained to see if he could recognize the person but it was just too hazy with the snow, and very dark outside. He carefully went down the steps, trying hard not to lose his balance, and opened the front door. There was another envelope on the door, under the knocker. He picked it up and held it, afraid to open it. Something told him it was going to be different this time.

—   —   —

Edgar was in his car driving to the next location. Even with snow tires it was dangerous to be out driving tonight. Edgar was headed to the house around the corner, where the husband had died and the wife was left to raise the kids alone. He was torn because he sort of wanted to give it to Doug, because he knew his wife was struggling and hanging in there with a man who may have physically abused her. Doug seemed to have changed since he first met him. That was impressive, considering his probable background. He went ahead and left the envelope at the house he and Mary had discussed. The Dickerson house was dark and there were no Christmas lights anywhere to be seen. He was worried that no one was home, but he could hear a dog barking somewhere inside the house. He opened the screen door and put the envelope into the crack of the front door. He turned to walk away and heard a noise from inside the house. He didn't mean to scare this woman, so he hurried away so that she wouldn't be afraid to open the door. He knew she would be surprised and relieved when she opened the envelope. He wished he could tell her about Mary. But he had made an agreement on the front end of this venture and he intended to keep it.

He made one more stop before heading home. He pulled into Doug's driveway and left another envelope on his own. It wouldn't pay off Doug's house, but it would help provide clothing or pay off some bills that might be hanging over their heads. He had brought this envelope with him, not knowing for sure if he would leave it or not. But now he was glad he did. This was going to be some kind of Christmas for his neighborhood. It was getting colder and the snow was continuing to fall heavily. A full blown white Christmas. *Who would have thought this much snow would fall this year? It was not even in the forecast. Made you wonder sometimes.* He pulled into his driveway and sat there a moment before heading into the garage and closing the door behind him. Inside, he cranked up the heat and climbed into his bed, pulling the covers up to his neck. He was freezing but happy.

I better enjoy this short holiday season, because I have a lot of work ahead of me when the New Year hits. He fell fast asleep, not moving one inch until morning.

—   —   —

Mary was up late wrapping presents and piling them under her tree. She had managed to get out and shop before the snow started falling. She looked outside her window and couldn't believe the amount of snow coming down. She turned to look at her tree; it was the prettiest tree she had ever seen. Lacy and Linda had helped her decorate it, and it turned out that Linda had a knack for design. She draped the ribbon and tucked things into the branches. It was fabulous! But what the two girls didn't expect was to wake up with a lot of presents to open. Mary was having a ball and making the most of having company in her large house. It felt like she had a purpose again, with Edgar giving away her money for her, and now this little family living in her house. She almost hated for Linda to leave, but she had a feeling this was going to be short- lived.

The last thing she did, after leaving out cookies and milk for Santa, was to place an envelope on the tree for Linda. Edgar and she had agreed that a new car was what she needed the most. So inside the envelope were the keys to a brand new Nissan Crossover. It was perfect for a mother with a child, and Lacy would soon be having friends over to play. There was room for a stroller and all the toys she would accumulate. Standing back to look at all the lovely bows and paper, Mary yawned. It was late and she needed to go to sleep. Tomorrow was going to be a very busy day for her. She undressed, put on her gown, and sank into her bed with the down comforter pulled up to keep out the cold. She was sound asleep until eight o'clock the next morning.

Early, before Mary and the girls had time to get up, Edgar walked across the lawns to Mary's house and made a huge snowman with a carrot nose and coal for eyes, a big scarf around his neck, a hat, and coal for a smile. He was perfect and Edgar was proud of himself. He hadn't made a snowman since Jane was a little girl, and this one might be the best one yet, because the snow was just the right consistency for making snowmen. He went inside to clean up and waited for Mary. Breakfast would be welcomed this morning, as Edgar was hungry. He had a big present for Mary. He had purchased her a lovely new robe and slippers from Bradford's. He also bought her some new perfume and bath and body crèmes. He had the salesperson at Bradford's wrap it before she mailed it to him. It was in a lovely silver box with wide satin red ribbon. She would be so surprised. And Mary loved surprises.

CHAPTER 18

Linda barely opened her eyes and the smell of Christmas breakfast overtook her. She couldn't help but smile, for this was going to be the best Christmas she'd ever had, just being around two people who really did care about her. Lacy was still asleep, so Linda got up and took a quick shower. She wanted to look halfway decent when she went downstairs. She was still very sore from falling and hitting her head on the park bench. She tried hard not to think about Jesse this morning. Plenty of time for that.

She woke Lacy after she was dressed, slipped her feet into a pair of shoes, and they went downstairs to see the magic that Mary had created for them. Lacy was beside herself, for she was old enough now to really appreciate the Christmas tree all lit up, and the pretty presents. She had a little tricycle under the tree, and a doll and stroller. She was so excited that she was squealing.

Mary was in the kitchen getting breakfast ready, and Edgar was coming in the front door laden with his own presents to put under the tree. They all went to the kitchen table and sat down and enjoyed a lovely Christmas breakfast. Mary had made muffins, eggs, and oatmeal for Lacy, toast, pancakes, an egg quiche for Edgar, and all kinds of fruit juices. Country ham was stacked on their plates and fresh fruit. It was more than anyone could eat at one meal, but they all laughed and had a wonderful visit before presents were opened.

Linda couldn't hold back Lacy any longer, and Mary began handing out presents to the two girls. Linda opened a lovely sweater with gloves and a hat to match. She also got a new winter coat and a new purse. Lacy opened up a box of doll clothes, toys, wooden puzzles, musical instruments, a learning computer, and there were still presents left for her to open. Mary pulled at the bow on the lovely box from Edgar and nearly died when she saw the plush robe and slippers. It was more than she could have expected from Edgar. She knew it was expensive and frowned at Edgar. He only winked at her and handed her another gift to open.

Edgar opened his gifts from Mary and set them aside. He was waiting to see what Linda did when she got the envelope from Mary. There was paper strewn everywhere and bows, and so many toys you could hardly walk. Mary reached over and pulled the envelope off the tree and held it in her hand. Linda looked at Mary and raised her eyebrows.

"Surely you have done enough for us, Aunt Mary. I'm overwhelmed with your kindness and generosity. You and Edgar went out of your way to make sure we had a wonderful Christmas and there are no words for me to say that will tell you how I feel about all of this. What more could I need?" She looked at all the things piled under the tree and smiled. There were tears running down her face. She felt so loved and cared for that it was going to be very difficult to leave.

"Well, there is one more present for you, angel. I want you to know that this is from Edgar and I to you, to help you get started on your new life."

Linda took the envelope and opened it. At first she was confused. *A key. What was it for?* She looked closer and saw it was a car key. "What in the world have you done, Mary? Edgar? Don't tell me this goes to a car! I can't accept this from either of you. You have done enough already. She handed the key back to Mary.

"Oh yes you can! I want you to come with me and look in the garage, Linda. And I don't want to hear a word about it." Mary took her arm and walked her to the garage. Inside was a brand new white Crossover, with a big red bow on it.

"Oh my gosh! I'm speechless! It is beautiful." Linda slowly walked up to the car. She was so shocked that she hardly could speak. "I don't know how to thank you both for what you've done. This will help me so much. I was planning to go back home and get a good job and start my life over. Now I don't have to ride the bus to get there."

Edgar came over and hugged her and told her that she was going to make it after all. Mary hugged her too, with tears coming down her wrinkled cheeks.

"It's going to be okay, angel. One step at a time. Just know you can trust both of us to help you, no matter what you are dealing with. Don't try to handle it all by yourself. Sometimes things are too big to handle alone. Will you remember that?"

"Yes, I'll try. I know my life is complicated right now, but things will get better. I'm going to see to that."

Edgar heard her say that and cringed. He was pretty sure she was going to call Sarah Stryker after the New Year rolled in. There was nothing he could do about it right now, as he had not spoken with Fred yet. And he didn't want Linda to think he was spying on her. So for now, he only smiled and sat down in the living room to watch Lacy play with her toys. He was getting sleepy and nodded off a few times, letting his head fall back on the sofa. It had been a long night, and he was exhausted and so full after eating such a huge breakfast. He had to talk to Mary about cutting back on so much food.....

Outside the snowman was standing tall, guarding the yard. Mary was looking out the window at the snow and noticed the snowman, and called Linda to the window. They both smiled and turned around to look at Edgar. He was sound asleep on the sofa and Lacy had curled up beside him and fallen asleep herself. Too much excitement for one little girl and a mailman.

—   —   —

Greg was still in shock Christmas morning when the kids all came down to see what they had gotten. There were presents everywhere and paper strewn all over the living room. He sat down next to his wife and held her hand. She didn't know about the envelope; he wanted to surprise her. She handed him presents to open; books to read, a new shirt, and new tennis shoes. He handed her some presents, and then handed her the envelope. He prefaced the envelope with the story of how he found it last night in the door. And he told her he saw a figure leaving the house, obscured by the snow that was falling so hard. He didn't know for sure who it was, but he had an inkling. He kept it to himself until he was sure.

Susan opened the envelope and screamed. *What in the world had happened? Who had done this thing?* There was a cashier's check for enough money to pay off their house, their car and then some. There was a typed note saying that the giver wanted them to have this money so that they could be debt free and focus all their energy on Greg and the time he had left with his family. The donor wanted to remain anonymous for many reasons, and wished them a Merry Christmas and Happy New Year. There was no signature on the note. It was strange to Susan that someone would give them such a large sum of money. It had to be someone who knew them in some way. She was relieved but confused and full of mixed emotions about Greg and his illness. She wasn't ready to live without him, and tried to remain positive that something would turn this thing around. The check sort of made her feel that he was dying. *That it was a done deal.* She hugged Greg and gave him the money back.

"I don't want to sound ungrateful, for this will let you have a great peace of mind, and also provide for me and the kids after you are gone. But it is hard right now for me to swallow the fact that you may not finish out the New Year with me." She walked out of the room to clean up her face, because she didn't want the boys to see her crying. They already knew the situation, but she didn't need to remind them of it on Christmas morning.

—   —   —

Mrs. Dickerson opened her door on Christmas morning to see the snow piled up around the yard and front door, and let the dog out. An envelope addressed to her fell to the ground and she bent over to pick it up. She was smiling because she was thinking a nice neighbor had remembered her at Christmas. This was an especially tough Christmas as it was the first one since her husband's death that she had had to share with the kids alone. She got the dog back inside and opened the envelope. It was a cashier's check in the amount of fifty thousand dollars. At first she thought it was a joke. She sat down and looked it over carefully. It seemed legal enough but why would someone give her that amount of money? She looked in the envelope again and saw a small note inside that was typed.

Please accept this money from someone who really cares about your life. I hope it helps you find your way, and not feel so alone. Have a Merry Christmas and a Happy New Year. And never lose hope.

There was no signature on the note. That was it. Nothing more. And no way to find out who it was from. She sat there a few more minutes and then she started crying. She cried harder than she had ever cried since her husband died. *Maybe there was a God after all*, she thought. She had felt scared and alone for this whole year, not knowing how she was going to make it. Now she had the money to keep her safe and take care of her children. *What a relief this will be in the coming years. I will have to manage this money very well, and do my best to find a good job so that I don't use it up on living expenses. It just might be the motivation I need to get myself back into living my life again. It's been on hold for so long that I have forgotten how.*

Her mind raced to figure out who would have done this thing. But there was nothing but white snow and footprints up to her door.

CHAPTER 19

L inda couldn't wait until the holidays were over. She was thrilled about her
new car and would be forever in debt to Mary and Edgar for this new start.
But she wasn't letting Jesse off the hook that easy. Had he been nice to her,
things might have been different. He took the other road and was as ugly as he
could be. It was shocking how he treated her in the park. So she was going to
take action as soon as New Years day was over. She had decided to visit Sarah
when Jesse was at work. She would take Lacy over to her house and let her see
her husband's child. That would play on her heart and she would understand
Linda's situation better. Linda just didn't know if she would get anything out of
Jesse if she did this. It was going to cause the marriage to end, but would she see
any money? It would feel so good to get revenge, but would it taste so great if
she never saw any money out of it? *Probably not, because the joy of revenge wouldn't pay
her rent.* She decided to text Jesse one more time and let him know she was going
to talk to Sarah. If he didn't respond, then she would do it.

The only other choice she could think of was to have Edgar talk to Jesse.
She had been toying around with that idea for a day or two, and it was sounding
better and better. She just hated to involve anyone else in this mess. She knew
Edgar would tell her not to let Sarah know right now. If Edgar agreed to talk to
him, it might calm Jesse down a little; but it could backfire because he wouldn't
want anyone else to know about it. The more people that knew, the bigger
chance that Sarah would eventually find out. She couldn't take that chance. He
would come after her big time if he thought she was talking around town about
him. She knew that for sure.

*So what is the best answer? If I go home with no money, I'll have to move in with my parents
and they already have said they don't want anything to do with my marriage splitting up. They are
disappointed in me and aren't even trying to find out how I am. That isn't a good feeling, but I
have reconciled in my mind that it was too much for them to deal with. I'm so thankful for what
Mary and Edgar have done for me. It is way beyond what I ever expected. I have never met anyone
like Edgar in my entire life, and I am pretty sure I never will again.* Mary had followed suit
and taken her in like her own daughter. There was nothing she had wanted for
during her stay with Mary. She treated Lacy like her granddaughter, and Lacy
adored her from the first meeting. But she did have to go home. She couldn't stay
in Portersville and make a life for herself as long as Jesse was around. He would
make her life miserable, she was certain.

For the next two nights Linda was sleepless, trying to figure out what in the world to do. On the outside, in front of Mary and Edgar, everything was fine. But on the inside she was in turmoil. She was leaning toward telling Sarah again, because there didn't seem to be another answer. Jesse hadn't responded to her text. This didn't surprise her, but it did make it tougher for her to make a decision. She knew if she drove over to Jesse's house, life as she knew it would not exist. *All their lives would change. But would it change for the better for me? Sarah needed to know her husband was a jerk. In fact, she probably already knew that. My guess is that this will be the straw that breaks the camel's back,* she thought. *It may not be the first time Jesse has strayed. So many unknowns. It is time to make a decision.*

— — —

Edgar was ready to place a call in to Fred Perkins. He dialed the Sheriff's office and asked to speak to Fred. He was put on hold and the next voice he heard was Fred Perkins.

"Hello. This is Sheriff Perkins. How can I help you?"

"Sheriff, this is Edgar Graham. I would like to make an appointment to talk to you, if that's possible. Are you available anytime this week? The sooner the better."

"I can find the time, Mr. Graham. What is this about, if I may ask?"

"I would rather talk to you in person about it, if that's okay with you, Sheriff. I assure you it will not be a waste of your time."

"Okay, Mr. Graham. I will see you on Thursday morning at nine o'clock. I look forward to it."

Edgar hung up the phone and wiped his brow. He was a little nervous about getting back into the business, but ready to do a good job for Portersville. It might seem odd to Fred Perkins that he had retired from the FBI and was content to deliver mail. To most people that seemed like an odd thing for him to be doing. But actually it kept Edgar informed about what was going on in the town, in the best way possible. Talking to the people always brings information you don't hear in the paper or on the news. And because he was a mailman, people weren't on the defensive if he asked a lot of questions. It could actually be a plus if he continued delivering the mail, if the sheriff would allow him to go undercover.

He had ulterior motives for wanting to be an undercover cop. He wanted to check out Jesse Stryker thoroughly, to see if he could dig up anything on him. He also wanted to snoop around the department to see where the leaks were, and what was going on behind Fred Perkins' back. He had a nose like a bloodhound, and nothing got past him. Absolutely nothing. It was almost eerie what he could come up with, given enough time with someone. This time he wanted to get close enough to Jesse to figure out about his son and the drug lords. There was a connection there, but he didn't know for sure what extent Jesse was involved.

Edgar was excited about his meeting on Thursday, and thought about it all day while he was delivering his mail. He was also worried about what Linda was planning to do. He had almost called her to meet him somewhere, so that he could let her know he saw her that day in the park; that he saw what Jesse did to her. He knew she was in a dilemma about what to do about getting money from Jesse. That had to be the conversation she had with Jesse in the park. There was no other reason for her to meet with him. If he told her that he had been there in the park watching, would that make her not trust him, or would it relieve her? He didn't know. He had only a little time to make that call, because he knew she was going to act pretty soon. He thought about contacting his friend in the FBI and getting him to help her intercept her cell phone calls and texts, but it might not be necessary. He didn't want to wait too long, for Linda was apt to do something on a whim. She was cornered in a way, and a person feeling cornered cannot make a wise decision.

— — —

Linda was so close to calling Sarah Stryker that she could hardly contain herself. She had a few more days to decide, and then she either had to act, or drive home with no money. She decided to wait until tonight and if Jesse had not responded, she would call in the morning when she knew Jesse had time to get to work. She put it out of her mind for a while and tried to enjoy the day with Mary and Lacy. She watched Disney movies and ate popcorn; she laughed and looked at old photo albums of Mary when she was younger. Inside she was sick and scared. But she allowed no one in. This was her baby in more ways than one.

CHAPTER 20

Edgar did not miss one single nuance that came across Linda's face, or her body language. He knew she was struggling and this was a different struggle. She was deciding whether or not to ruin a marriage or walk home empty handed. He stayed unusually long at Mary's, waiting for the right opportunity to talk to Linda. What he had to say to her would surprise her for sure, but he hoped it would give her a better direction and a clearer picture on things. Mary was yawning and pretty tired, so she excused herself and went to bed earlier than usual. Lacy was sound asleep on the sofa and Linda decided to carry her up to bed. Edgar made his move.

"Hey Linda! Before you go upstairs, let's go onto the sun porch. I have a few things I want to talk to you about, and I would rather not wait until morning if that's okay with you."

"Sure, Edgar. I was going to take Lacy upstairs, but it can wait." She got up and headed to the sun porch and sat down in her favorite chair facing the window. It was cold and dark outside, but the moon was shining bright against the snow. It lit up the whole side yard and everything took on a hazy, distorted shape.

Edgar sat down in the chair next to her and was quiet for a moment. They both were watching nothing outside, just letting their minds wander. "I don't know exactly how to begin, Linda. I have so much to share with you. I'll begin by tellin' you that you are a very brave young woman. And you have one heck of a little girl. I can see you love her and that you are a good mother to her. That is huge nowadays."

Linda was a little nervous about the way Edgar was talking to her. She had never heard him talk this way, and his voice was slow and deliberate. She wasn't sure what he was going to say, but she tried to trust what she knew of him so far. "Thank you, Edgar. I do try to be a good mother and be there for her. She is the joy of my life."

"Listen. I know you don't know anything about me, and what I'm about to share has to remain between you and me." Edgar paused, staring out the window for a moment. "I was worried about you the other day; I could tell somethin' was up. I followed you when you went to the park." He watched her closely for a reaction to this news. "For some reason I was worried about your safety. I saw Jesse and you talkin' in the park, and put two and two together. I know now he is the father of your child. Am I right?"

"Yes, Edgar." Linda was tearing up. She didn't know what to think. He followed her? Why would Edgar follow her? Her heart was pounding in her chest...

"I wanted to make sure you were not gettin' in over your head. I don't know Jesse, but I think there is more to this story than meets the eye. I think you're tryin' to decide whether or not to push the money situation with him, or go to his wife. That would be any woman's intentions right now. I understand totally why you are doin' this, okay?"

Linda shook her head, but she was still in the dark about what Edgar was up to.

"I want you to totally trust me, like you did the night I saw you standing out in the cold with no place to go. Okay?" Edgar paused and put his hand on her arm. "I want you to allow me to step in here and provide the money for Lacy, and let it go with Jesse. That's a dead end street right now. I know you want him to care and to pay for this child's welfare. But he is angry and doesn't want you to mess up his life. I can feel it. He could have really hurt you out there in the park, and thank God I was there in the trees, watching. I wouldn't have let him do anything more to you, I assure you. I didn't step in when you fell, because I wanted to see what he was up to. I was ready to protect you, but didn't want to ruin anything you were doing either."

"It doesn't seem fair, Edgar, to let him off so easily. He needs to face this responsibility because he might do it again sometime to another young girl. It has changed my life forever. Who is going to want me now? I have been married, and my husband left me because I had a baby that wasn't his. Who is going to want me now?" She bowed her head and started crying, but her hands were in a fist. She was very angry at Jesse.

"I know you're hurtin' inside and very angry at him. I don't blame you one bit. But please, let's just let it go for now. He will pay the price at some point because his wife is not stupid. He'll slip up and get caught if he's runnin' around on her regularly. I just don't want your whole life to be focused on makin' him pay. You have a lot of life to live and I want you to have a happy, clean life. Start over. And make it right this time."

"I already owe you big time, Edgar. There is no way I can keep taking from you and Mary, after all you have done. I appreciate your offer, but I don't see how I can do it."

Edgar was quiet for a moment, thinking. "I can't say any more than I have already said. You are going to have to trust me on this one. I can set you up with a bank account and I will put money in it on a regular basis. You won't have to ever wonder if the money is goin' to be there. If I should die, there will be enough to take care of Lacy until she graduates from college. I know Mary is going to want to help on this one, so don't be surprised about that. She and I are doin' some pretty cool things together, and you're a part of that venture."

Linda was quiet. She didn't know what to say. She was stunned, but at the same time, not all that surprised that Edgar was capable of doing such a thing as this.

"I know you need to think about all of this. I want you to leave Jesse alone, Linda. He is a bad seed, and you don't need to mess around with him. We know he has a bad temper and could take it all out on you. Sleep on it, and we can talk in the mornin', okay?"

"I'll think about it, Edgar. I'm so overwhelmed by the whole thing that I don't know what to say. I do want a good life, and this would help me so much. I'm just not sure I can let go of wanting Jesse to pay." She stood up, shook his hand, and headed up the stairs.

Edgar let himself out, locked the door, and headed home. It was dark and cold outside and Edgar was worn out. But his mind was racing ahead to a talk with Fred Perkins. He laid in bed and lined up what he wanted to say to the sheriff, and dozed off to sleep around two thirty. He woke up with the worst cold he had had in years. And he still had to get dressed and deliver mail. He decided for the first time since he began delivering mail to use his car. It was just too cold and he was too sick to walk.

—   —   —

Linda laid in bed tossing around what Edgar had shared with her over and over in her mind. She might allow Edgar and Mary to help her with Lacy. It was very tempting because that meant she could get out of town sooner and start her life over. But one day she would make Jesse pay. There was no reason why he should be allowed to escape having to take responsibility for what he did. If she gave herself time, she was sure she could come up with something. An answer to all of this. Jesse was intimidating. And he was very determined to protect his marriage. But it was too late now for him to expect her to keep quiet forever. He would regret the day he met her for the rest of his life.

She yawned and fell into a restless sleep.

—   —   —

In a dark room across town, Jesse woke from a sound sleep dripping wet with sweat. He sat up in bed wondering what woke him up. And why was he sweating so much? He got up and went into the bathroom and wiped his face with a cold rag and leaned over and looked into the mirror for a moment. There he saw a stranger looking back at him. He may have gone too far this time. He may have made a mistake that he could not cover. He turned and walked back to bed with his shoulders sagging. He sat down, looked over at his wife sleeping quietly next to him, and lay back on his pillow. *That stupid girl. I couldn't make a deal with her and have her around the rest of my life. I need to think of something that will take care of it once and for all. She has a lot of nerve showing up here, in my hometown. Calling my house. Texting me. She's out of control. I have to find a way to deal with her.*

He shut his eyes, but sleep would not come easy. He dreamed of walking along a path covered in moss and it was cold and damp. He came up on a bench and noticed a young girl sitting there. She looked up at him with the saddest eyes he had ever seen in his life. He tried to speak to her but no words would come out of his mouth. He tried to move his arms to reach out to her but they would not move from his side. She got up and looked at him one more time and turned and walked away. More than anything he wanted to run after her and say something. But for the life of him, he could not move. He watched her walk away and tears fell from his eyes. He noticed that her feet were in a strong light as she moved farther away from him, but when he looked down, he was standing in utter darkness, alone.

CHAPTER 21

Sheriff Perkins was a man who believed in justice and the good of mankind. He tried hard to keep his department up to a certain standard, but this year it seemed to have gone awry. He was afraid that Jesse Stryker might be part of that, but was hoping he was wrong. He answered a phone call, made a few of his own, and then checked his watch. Edgar Graham would be here any minute and he was very curious about what this guy wanted. He had done some checking around town and found out he was a local mailman, with nothing else of substance going on in his life. He didn't run a background check on him, but would do it after he heard what Edgar had to say. He got busy filing some folders that had been stacked on his desk when he was interrupted by a knock on his door. He looked over the filing cabinet and stared right into the face of Edgar Graham.

He found something out about Edgar in the first five minutes of the conversation. He looked right through you with black eyes, and seemed to already know what you were going to say before you could get the words out of your mouth. It was very disconcerting at first, but Edgar also had a way of putting you at ease, so Fred relaxed and listened.

"Fred, it may seem a bit odd to you that a mailman would want a meeting with you. However, when you hear my background you won't be in the least bit surprised by what I'm askin' of you. I've lived in Portersville for some years now and have established a group of friends and acquaintances over the years. I've been a good citizen and tried to help people when I can, and direct them to someone else if I can't. I pay my taxes like the rest of the people here, and vote for who I think should be in office. I've reached a plateau that I thought I was over, and it has taken me back a little. So I've come here this mornin' to share information about my background and see if you are interested in my offer."

Fred was looking intently at Edgar, amazed at the ease with which he spoke. For a mailman, he was very forthright and knew exactly what he wanted. "I'm all ears, Edgar. You have certainly piqued my curiosity, so let's have it. What do you have in mind?"

"I spent fifteen years being an FBI agent for the government. I know that seems odd, but let me finish." Edgar got up and paced the floor. He was getting excited. "I retired because I got tired of havin' my life threatened and bein' in the line of fire all the time. I decided Portersville looked like a nice, peaceful place to live, so I settled here and applied for a mailman's job. Odd as that may be, it was a perfect way for me to get to know the people in the town and also keep up with what was goin' on. I hear things that the newspapers never print. I know what goes on behind a good many closed doors, and keep it all to myself. I have reached a point where I'm no longer satisfied with just bein' a mailman, and wanted to approach you about going undercover for your department."

Fred was completely blown away by this and sat back in his chair, rubbing his chin and thinking. There were beads of sweat coming up on his brow and he wasn't quite sure why. Definitely, Edgar was very intelligent and would be an asset to the force. He just wasn't expecting this at all, and it made him uncomfortable to be caught so off guard.

"Go ahead, Edgar. Don't stop now. Let me know what you're thinking about."

"Okay Sheriff. Well, I've noticed a lot of drug activity in Portersville. I've heard a lot of things that you might not have heard, as I deliver on my mail route. People tend to think that a mailman does not pay much attention to anything while he's on his route. They say all kinds of things in whispers, thinkin' I'm not payin' any attention. So I would like to remain a mailman, and also go undercover. I know I could make a huge dent in the drug traffic if you would allow me in. Does this appeal to you in the slightest, Sheriff?"

Fred pushed his chair back and stood up to look out of the window. Portersville was a great place to live, but it did seem that corruption was creeping in. He could use some help from someone like Edgar, especially if he was willing to go undercover. It was exciting to think he used to be an FBI agent, and now he would be working for him. He stood up straight and turned to look at Edgar. "I would be delighted to have you on the force, Edgar. Let's do some background work on you and have you fill out some paperwork. You and I can meet again on Monday morning or whenever it is good for you, to nail down exactly how you want to work this out. I'm very interested in what you have to say, and can tell by this conversation that you have a lot of experience that is needed on this force. I might add that you may not be received very kindly by some of the men. Maybe even Sergeant Jesse Stryker. I suppose you are used to that kind of behavior in your line of work, so just wanted to give you a heads up."

"Sheriff, it won't bother me in the least how the other men see me at first. I will prove my reputation to them, and that takes time. I would just as soon remain in the background as that's where I do my best work. I would ask that you don't make a big deal about me joinin' the force, and don't share with the men right off the bat that I was an FBI agent. It will cause them to feel defensive towards me, and that isn't what we need here. I want to silently blend in; that's my style in a lot of areas of my work. I know I can be an asset to the Portersville Sheriff's Department, and I'm thrilled that you are willing to give me a chance."

"Well, I'll do some checking on my own, Edgar. But it looks like we may be a good match, you and I." Fred stood up and shook Edgar's hand. " I'll see you on Monday; please call the front desk to let me know when you'll be in."

—   —   —

Edgar whistled all the way to his car. This went so much better than he had hoped. Maybe he was hitting Fred at a perfect time, with all the things that were going down in the town. Drugs were everywhere and it was time that something was done about it. Now he had something to look forward to in his work. He had to keep quiet about it, for that was the point of going undercover. He could tell his daughter though, and he couldn't wait to do that later on tonight. He knew she would be thrilled; she never did quite get the mail route thing. He smiled, knowing this was going to be a very interesting year for him. Now he could sink his teeth into something and do some good at the same time. He wanted to tell Mary so bad, and might at some point do just that. Right now he needed to keep everything under wraps. He didn't need his previous life to get out in the open; it was going to come in very handy in tracking down a lot of drug lords. As soon as the sheriff gave him the okay, he knew exactly where he was going to start.

Fred didn't waste any time checking out Edgar Graham. It didn't take him long to find the records of his FBI tenure and all the accolades he received during his 15 years. Fred was shocked that this caliber of an individual would even be remotely interested in working for a small town Sheriff's department. But he wasn't going to question Edgar's motives. A guy with this kind of record you simply welcomed into your family. He basically would give Edgar full freedom to do what he needed to do, because he knew the press was always pushing the latest drug-related murders, and it was time some of these thugs were stopped in their tracks. He couldn't wait for their meeting on Monday to see what Edgar had in mind. Now he was almost getting excited about the New Year that was already under way. Maybe at last his department would shape up. He didn't forget Edgar's warning; to keep his FBI record under his hat for the time being. Edgar Graham just might turn out to be the saving grace of Portersville.

CHAPTER 22

Dinner was served at Mary's house at six thirty. Linda and Lacy were front and center at the table, as they knew by the aroma coming from the kitchen, that this was going to be a fabulous meal. Edgar had made a bad habit of eating dinner with Mary and Linda, and it was so cold he was looking forward to a hot meal and good company. When he came in the door, Lacy jumped down from the table and ran into his arms. He was getting attached to this little girl he found outside a storefront, on a cold winter night.

The table had so much food on it, that there was hardly room for their plates. Mary had outdone herself. She had cooked all afternoon and served up a huge roast, potatoes, fresh string beans, acorn squash, bread pudding, fresh yeast rolls, a fruit salad, and pie for dessert. They ate in silence for a while and then the conversation turned to Linda and Lacy heading home. Mary could hardly talk about it, for her house would be empty when they left. She had gotten very attached to Lacy and tried to convince Linda to stay longer. Even for good. Linda would hear nothing of it and said she had to go. It was not a place she felt she could live for the rest of her life, and her friends were in Illinois.

Edgar recounted their first meeting, and how he felt when he looked over and saw the two of them standing out in the cold with nowhere to go. His heart went into a knot thinking about how they looked when he approached them. "I'm amazed at how you trusted me, Linda. Just thinkin' back on it, you really were very open with me from the beginning."

"Well, I knew I was in trouble, Edgar. I had no money and Lacy was freezing. We couldn't stand there all night just hoping someone would walk up and give us some money."

"I know. I just never realized that it would turn out like it did. Mary, you have been a lovely host to these two girls, and have gone over and beyond what you had to do to make them feel at home here." Edgar put his hand on Mary's hand, and they looked at each other and winked.

"Linda, I know you are resisting our help any further, but we have already set up a separate account for you in Illinois where you will have money each month deposited out of our accounts. This will help you start a new life and not feel so dependant on a man. Take your time in finding your way, okay? Don't rush into anything. I can only imagine what it would be like to raise a child alone, as I did have Sidney with me until he got older."

Linda teared up and looked down at her plate. "I still can't believe that this has happened to me. I would've never dreamed I would be staying with such a lovely generous woman, and that you both would go out of your way to set my feet on solid ground. I don't take this lightly; I hope you both know that. I didn't want to accept the money, but right now I have no choice. So I thank you from the bottom of my heart for helping me offer a future to Lacy. I'll keep you both posted on how she is doing and send photos of her to you as she grows. I'm sure we will come back to see you some day."

—   —   —

Mary cleared the table with a lump in her throat. This had been a very special evening and everything could not have gone any better. She only hoped that Linda would work through the issues that brought her here in the first place, and not let them hang her up. She had a lot of life to live, and a lovely little girl to share things with. She knew that Edgar had knowledge of some things he had not shared with her yet. She would wait until Linda was gone to ask. She was old but her mind was sharp as a tack; she knew that Edgar had not been a mailman all his life, but she hadn't figured out yet what his past entailed. *Give me time, Edgar. I will have you all figured out,* she thought.

Edgar asked Linda when she would be leaving, and the answer surprised him. "I was thinking about leaving in the morning, Edgar. I know that's quick, but if I stay around here any longer, you both will talk me into staying here permanently, and I don't think that's the best thing. You know what I am talking about, right Edgar?"

"I can understand your situation perfectly. It's a wise move you made to accept this money, so that you can let go of Jesse and not worry anymore about his meeting his obligations to Lacy. That was and is a dead end street that you don't need to go down. After the other day in the park, I'm convinced that Jesse could have hurt you big time if he had wanted to. He has that in him, Linda, so you are leavin' at just the right time." He stepped over and hugged her and smiled into her blue eyes. "I'm so glad we met and that we were able to help you for a time. Stay in touch with us and know you will always be welcome here. I know I can speak for Mary on that."

"I can feel that, Edgar, and it makes me sad to leave you. You've made me feel safe, almost like a father does with a child. I trust you totally and know you want what is best for me. I know I can call you if I get into a mess and that feels so good to know. Hopefully that way of living is over and from now on I plan to make sound decisions about my life and Lacy's."

"I like the sound of that, Linda! Let me know if you need anything. There is money in an envelope for you so that you have money for gas and food on your way home."

Edgar walked back into the kitchen to say good night and to let Mary know that the girls were leaving tomorrow. "I know it's going to be hard on you Mary, but I can see why she wants to go on home. There is nothing here for her now."

"I am sad. My house will be so empty! Yet, I do want her to get started living her life. I think we have done all we can, Edgar. I just hate to see them go." She dabbed her eyes with her apron and walked out to the living room where Linda and Lacy were sitting.

"I love you both and will miss you terribly. I will be up early and fix you a good breakfast so that you will not leave on an empty stomach. Is there anything you need, Linda? I do have a large suitcase that I no longer need. I'll bring it into your room so that you can pack. We did do quite a bit of shopping and you both got so much at Christmas! Let me know if you need anything else."

— — — — — —

Edgar left the three women and walked across the lawns to his house. The snow was slowly disappearing and the brown dead grass was peeping through. He was anxious to call his daughter and shoot past her what he was planning to do in Portersville. She would not be all that happy, but would understand his reasons.

"Hey! How is my girl doing?" Edgar loved hearing her voice.

"Hey Dad. How are you?

"Just got back from eatin' dinner at Mary's house. We said goodbye to Linda and Lacy as they'll be leaving tomorrow for Illinois. It is sad to see them go in one way, but good in another. She did agree to accept our offer, by the way."

"I know that was a big relief to you and Mary both. Jesse sounds like a loose cannon and she does not need someone like that in her daughter's life, anyway. So what is your next move, Dad? I know you are up to something. Am I right?"

Edgar laughed. "Yes, I am, Miss know-it-all. Just because you're an attorney does not mean you can foresee the future." They both laughed.

"I've approached the local sheriff to see if I can go undercover for a while. I'm getting' restless, like you said I would, and need somethin' to do that's more challenging. I see so much around town that the sheriff may not see; that's the cool thing about my job. So I'll keep the mail route and do the police work after I'm done with the route. I can even go out at night if I want to, and see what is happenin' on the streets."

"Dad, I'm glad you're doing this. I know you get bored delivering mail; I didn't know how you were ever going to adjust to that in the first place. However, there'll be some risk in this position and I thought we were done with all the risk taking."

Edgar sighed. He knew that was coming. "I know, baby. I know. It's just that when you see some things goin' down, and know how to expose them, it's hard not to want to get involved. I realize my age, and all the reasons why I shouldn't do this. But the good thing is that I can quit anytime I want to."

"Have you ironed out the technicalities yet? Does this sheriff realize you want to do things your way? Does he have any idea who he is hiring?" She smiled to herself, and shook her head.

"I'll take it slow, I promise. It's a small town, and they do things differently here. I'll respect that. However, my being around may light some fires under some rookie cops that sit on their butts all day in their cars, doin' absolutely nothing. I'm sure I'll find some dirt or dead wood in the department as well."

"Oh, there's no doubt. Well, have a ball, Dad. Only remember you have a daughter around, will you? I'm not ready to be fatherless yet. I love you too much."

"That goes without sayin', Jane. I love you too. I'll keep you posted on things and also let you know what agreement I have with Fred. I know you'll get a kick out of what we come up with."

—   —   —

Edgar hung up and smiled. He had a feeling life was going to get much more interesting.

CHAPTER 23

Linda got up early and showered, packing her bag quickly so she would be ready to go after breakfast. She was actually excited about going back to Illinois now that things were settled here. She had stayed up late last night thinking about the whole situation, and made a decision that Edgar would not like.

Lacy was waking up, so she pulled her up and brushed her hair, loved on her, whispered that they were going home today, and changed her into her clothes. She was a little fussy, and Linda picked her up to head downstairs for breakfast. Mary was in the kitchen getting their plates ready, and turned when she saw Linda and Lacy coming in the door.

"Hey girls. You sleep well? I sure hope so. I know you have a long drive ahead of you, Linda."

"Yes, we slept pretty sound. There was a lot on my mind, but I did finally conk out! Lacy slept like a log. She loves that bed up there."

"I have your breakfast ready. Here. Sit down and eat all you can, for this is your last home cooked meal for a while. I took the liberty of making you a few sandwiches to take on the road with you. Hope that was okay."

"Oh my heavens! Mary you're something else. You think of everything. We're hungry and this looks so tasty. We are nearly packed and ready to go; it'll be hard to leave this house, but we have such good memories to take with us, Mary."

Breakfast was eaten in silence, with Mary and Linda lost in their own thoughts. The dishes were cleared and Linda ran upstairs to get her suitcase and all the toys for Lacy. Mary sat down on the sofa in the living room to talk to Lacy one more time. And then it was time to say goodbye.

"Mary, I have grown to love you in these few months, and hate to leave. But you know I need to get on with my life. Please know I'll remember this the rest of my life. You and Edgar are the best! Take care of yourself, and when I get settled, I promise to send you my address and phone number. Maybe you will break down and get a computer so that we can email!"

"I'll miss you both, terribly. Now go, before I try to talk you out of it! Be very careful on the road." Mary hugged them both and hurried them out the door. She was about to lose it and did not want them to see her cry.

— — —

On her way out of town, Linda dialed the Stryker residence. A woman's voice was on the other end of the line. Linda had planned exactly what she wanted to say, but when she heard Sarah's voice, the words were stuck in her throat.

"Hello? Is someone there?"

"Hello?"

Sarah was about to hang up and she heard someone sobbing. "Hello? Are you ok?"

Linda got control of her voice again and answered in a quiet slow voice. "You'll never know who I am, Sarah. I'm just a young woman on the other end of the phone. But I wanted to tell you that my life has been ruined because of your husband. I had to call and talk to you before I left town. He is nothing but a liar. A worthless liar. I trusted him, Sarah. I believed him. And all the words he said were empty. Meaningless. I hate him now." She was about to hang up but Sarah screamed into the phone.

"Don't hang up! Please! Don't hang up!"

Linda sat there holding the phone, not sure what to do. "I'm here, okay? I'm still here."

"You don't have to tell me who you are. I don't need to know that. What do you mean he ruined your life? What did he do?"

"He got me pregnant on a one night stand, and now that my daughter is here, he wants nothing to do with supporting her. He wined and dined me, told me lies about how much he wanted to be with me. All lies. Then he hurt me physically when I tried to talk to him about it. All I wanted was some money to help raise my child. He would not even listen. I don't want anything from you, Sarah. I just had to call and tell you the truth."

Sarah stood there holding the phone to her ear. There was a dial tone on the other end. She started shaking as tears were streaming down her face. *What had Jesse done?*

— — —

Jesse was sitting at his desk smiling to himself. So Linda had gotten the message that he was not going to put up with her pressure. He hadn't heard from her except once since he saw her in the park. A short text saying she wanted to talk about the money. He turned his chair around and looked at the picture of his wife and kids on his desk. *Sarah would never have to know this even happened. Maybe Linda has left town and it is over.*

He picked up his keys and walked out of the office. He was headed for an early lunch, because he had a meeting around noon with Fred Perkins.

In the quiet of his empty office, the phone rang about ten times. The caller left a message that was brief but to the point. And this message would alter Jesse's life forever. And he never saw it coming.

CHAPTER 24

Edgar was early for his appointment with the sheriff. This was going to be the most important meeting he'd had in a long time, and he didn't want to be late. He had in mind what he wanted to say to Fred Perkins, and he also realized that the salary of an undercover agent in Portersville was not going to be very big. Thankfully, he didn't need the money as badly as he needed the job.

Edgar walked around the building, killing time until his appointment. He peeked in and out of rooms, and got himself familiar with the location of everything. He had worked so long as an FBI Agent that it wouldn't take him long to familiarize himself with the routine here at the Sheriff's Department. In fact, that might be his strong suit; summing up a situation and fitting in so well that he was almost forgotten. Until he produced results that were extraordinary. Then the other men would pay attention to Edgar Graham.

— — —

Sheriff Perkins was waiting in his office when Edgar came to the door and knocked. Without either one knowing it, they both were equally excited about this endeavor, and equally apprehensive about drawing up a deal they both would be happy with. Edgar shook his hand and sat down. He respected Fred immediately and felt like they would communicate very well with each other. He was not as sure about Jesse Stryker.

"Good morning Edgar. Please make yourself comfortable. Would you like some coffee or water?"

"No I'm fine, Sheriff. Looking forward to our coming to an agreement on my working here with you."

"Well, that makes two of us, Edgar. I couldn't wait to come in to work this morning, as this is the first time someone of your caliber has ever applied for a job here in Portersville. To tell you the truth, I'm a bit nervous. So let's get started. What are you thinking about, Edgar. Tell me what you want."

"Well Sheriff, what I want is simple. But it's a lot to ask on our second meeting with each other. So stop me if you think I am askin' the impossible, will you?"

"I have a feeling that I won't find what you want hard to swallow, Edgar. Please feel free to speak your mind."

"As I said the other day, I want to be an undercover agent for your department. I especially want to work on weeding out the drug dealers, but will work in some other areas too. Fred, I have worked in the most bizarre environments you can imagine, goin' undercover around the worst of society. I fit in wherever I have to, to get the job done. What I want from you is complete freedom to do this. I can find moles hiding in the weeds. And I know how to pull them out. I assure you, I go by the book on everything, but at the same time will do what I have to do to get the job done."

"I see, Edgar. So what you are telling me is that you will work for the department but you want total freedom while on the job to act in whatever way you have to as long as it is in compliance with the rules and regulations, to get the job done. Is that correct?"

"That's correct. I don't want someone standin' over my shoulder all the time, tellin' me what I can and can't do. I know this isn't the FBI, but I do know the rules. Unless Portersville is different than the rest of the world, I know exactly what I can do and what I can't do. I also don't want some over eager cop blowin' my cover or showin' up at the wrong time."

"Believe me, Edgar. I can identify with that. I've been undercover myself and that has happened to me before. It actually took the desire out of me because too many times the bad guy goes free and you can't get him back to save your life. I will keep the other guys under control and let them know their limitations. I want to introduce you to Captain John Davis and Lieutenant Lee Smith. Both of those men are sharp and at your disposal. I also want you to meet the two undercover guys I have on the force."

"What I would love is to meet your whole deputy force so that I can size up all the men here. I would like to hand pick the men I work with. I know this sounds cocky of me, Fred. Please don't take it that way, okay? I just know who I want to cover my back, and if it's not the right guy, then it won't work. Know what I mean?"

"I get it Edgar. I also want to talk about salary. We don't have a lot of money in the department but I can offer you a part time salary of about twenty five thousand dollars. I know that isn't much, Edgar. I'm working on getting us more money, but we are the last in line next to teachers in getting a raise."

Edgar laughed. He wanted to put Fred at ease concerning the money. "Hey Fred. I'm not takin' this job because I need it to make a living. I made my living years ago. I want to do this to have somethin' purposeful to do. I've found that deliverin' mail isn't enough challenge for me at this point in my life. So this is a perfect fit for me, as long as we can work together for a common purpose."

Fred got up and took Edgar into another office and introduced him to John Davis and Lee Smith. They were two great men and Fred had nothing but the highest respect for them both.

"Edgar, these two men help me run this department and keep a hand on all the men here. They run it by the book and can be trusted explicitly."

Edgar looked both men in the eye and knew immediately that they could be trusted. What he didn't know was if they would accept how he did things. *I guess we'll find out,* he thought.

—   —   —

They walked out of the office and stood in the hallway. "All the men are not here today for you to meet. I'm going to have a special meeting with all the deputies and the undercover cops so that you can meet them all at the same time. Do what you need to do to get to know them and let me know what you think."

"I know this is highly unusual, Fred, for me to pick the men I want to work with, but I do appreciate your respectin' my background. I promise you I'll do my best to produce results. That's the bottom line; to bring in the people who are corruptin' the town. I just want you to be prepared for what I find."

"I will call you after I set the time for this meeting. In the meantime, let me know what I can do for you. Otherwise, I'll be in touch with you shortly. Thank you, Edgar for wanting to be a part of this team of men. I hope it works out like you want it to. I'll do my part to make it happen."

Edgar walked away with a good feeling about his decision to work with the sheriff. He felt pretty good about Davis and Smith. What he was worried about was choosing two men he felt confident about to go undercover with him.

—   —   —

Jesse Stryker walked back into his office and saw a light blinking on his telephone. Someone had left a message. He pressed the button, and the words he heard were the most dreadful words of his life.

Edgar was passing by Jesse's office when he pressed the button. The words of Sarah Stryker floated out into the hallway….. and Edgar could not get home fast enough.

CHAPTER 25

Mary was home cleaning, stripping beds, washing sheets; turning her house upside down to keep herself busy so that she wouldn't cry. Her favorite guests were gone and she was thankful for such a wonderful opportunity to help someone. Yet it left her life very empty for a time. She would just have to adjust again; she knew it was possible to live alone and be happy. She had done it when Sidney died, and she could do it now. But gosh it had been nice to have someone in the house. It brought new life to the old house and it was invigorating. She had not cooked like that for years and it was nice to know she still had the touch.

She didn't hear Edgar come in, as she was in the back of the house. He walked into the kitchen expecting to find her and found instead a fresh pot of coffee and sweet rolls. He sat down at the table and helped himself, waiting for her to come down the hall. When she came in to the kitchen, it did not surprise her one bit that Edgar Graham was sitting at her table.

"Good mornin' beautiful." Edgar grinned with a full mouth of sweet roll. He had just eaten a quick lunch but could not resist homemade sweet rolls.

"Well, what do I owe this honor at this time of day? I thought you would be out on your route by now."

"I should be. But I have somethin' to talk to you about. Sit down, Mary. You'll find this interesting."

Mary pulled out a chair and sat down, piling her dust rags on the table and sipping the last bit of her morning coffee. "Okay, I'm all ears. This must be important for you to hold off delivering your mail."

"It is important. I found out a lot while Linda was stayin' with you. I don't know if you figured out that Lacy didn't belong to Linda's husband, but she shared with me earlier that someone here in Portersville was the father. That was why her husband left her, Mary. Lacy didn't belong to him."

"I was thinking that might be the case; just putting together her standing in the cold in front of the grocery store and not having any money. No mother would put her child in that situation unless there was a real problem at home. So go on, Edgar. What else do you know that you haven't told me?" Mary raised an eyebrow and smiled at Edgar with that disarming smile she pulled out on occasion.

"That is why I'm here this mornin'. The father is Jesse Stryker. I know that is a shock to you in a way, but hear me out. He ran into Linda in a restaurant where she was waitin' tables in Illinois. He was supposedly there for business. He sweet talked her and they slept together and Lacy is a result of that one night together." Edgar paused to let Mary digest this news.

"Now, when she arrived here she texted him to see if he would help her out. He didn't meet her text with friendly words. He was at the very beginning obstinate and cruel to her. She panicked because she had no place to go. Then I showed up and took her to the hotel and later to you. You know the rest of the story. However, I followed her one day to the park where she met Jesse, to discuss his givin' her child support so that she could raise Lacy and know she had college money set aside as well as money for clothes and other needs. Jesse would have none of it; he wanted to give her a small sum of money and run her out of town with threats. He actually pushed her down and she hit her head on the park bench. Then he stood her up, shakin' her and hit her in the stomach pretty hard. This man is holdin' a lot of anger and frustration. He is a loose cannon, Mary."

"Oh my gosh Edgar! What in the hell was he thinking? Excuse my French. This child could be his daughter for heavens sake. I imagine this wasn't the first time he ran around on his wife. So what happened next?"

"Well, you and I talked and decided to give her some money for Lacy, and set up a bank account for the child so that Linda would not have to worry about whether the money was available or not. It took a lot to get her to agree to take this deal from us, but along with that I made her promise not to contact Sarah Stryker or keep pleadin' with Jesse. It was my opinion that if she continued pesterin' Jesse, he might do something a lot worse than hittin' her in the stomach. She made that agreement and left town. Apparently on her way out of town she must have phoned Sarah Stryker, because as I left the police department today I walked by Jesse's office and heard him listenin' to Sarah's phone message. Their marriage is over. She didn't sound too happy."

"I see," Mary said. She sat there a moment and thought about the predicament Linda was in. "I can almost understand her wanting Sarah to know. If I were Sarah, I would want to know. However, what did Linda gain in telling her now? I guess just revenge. She didn't want Jesse to get off scot free after her life had been so damaged. So what are you going to do, Edgar, if anything?"

Edgar sipped his coffee for a moment before answering. He didn't want to share with Mary about his going undercover. It could put her in danger. "I went to the police department to chat with the sheriff; I thought it would not hurt for me to get to know the guy in case anything came up. I have no way to contact Linda until she lets us know where she is. I'm worried that Jesse might try to find her and kill her, or beat her up at the very least. I'm sure he is capable of all of the above. I didn't let on to the sheriff about any of this; just a friendly visit. But I wanted to get you up to date on things in case you should hear from Linda. I don't know if she'll contact you or me first, after she's settled in her apartment. One of us needs to know how to get in touch with her and her address."

"I agree totally, Edgar. I'm so glad you came in and shared all of this with me; I'm a little hurt that you didn't tell me this before. Was there a good reason for that?"

"Mary, I was asked by Linda not to tell anyone. It was very difficult not to tell you this, but I had to keep my promise to her so that she would continue to trust us. Can you see that?"

"Of course I see it, Edgar. It's a lot to take in; however, it would've been more of a shock if you had told me in the first place. And I wouldn't have been able to keep my mouth shut. I forgive you Edgar, because I would have worried my self sick if I had known. What a mess this all has been, and I don't know how in the world Linda has dealt with it all. I promise I'll let you know if I hear from her, and you do the same. I pray that Jesse doesn't do anything to Linda or her child. He will have you to deal with if he harms her anymore." She paused and wiped her eyes, worried about Linda even more now. "I'm going to fix chicken tonight and rice if you are interested. You have a key so come whenever you like."

Edgar stood up, hugged Mary and reassured her that everything was going to be okay, and walked out the door. He felt bad not telling Mary about his new job, but it wasn't the right time. She would understand some day. But not for now. He really had to lay low so that no one figured out what the local mailman was up to.

—   —   —

Linda had pulled into a motel after driving in the snow most of the day. She was close to home but just couldn't take it anymore. Lacy was restless and getting fussy, so she just decided to pull off the road and start fresh in the morning. They had checked in and ate at the small restaurant across the street. Both of them were tired and went to sleep soon after eating supper. In the night, Linda woke up and her phone was vibrating. She had a message. She opened the phone and it was from Jesse. She smiled at first and then was scared to play it. She pressed the button and the message played on speaker phone.

Listen you little punk kid. You are messing with the wrong person. If you have messed up my marriage, I will come after you. I can find you no matter where you go. That is what I do for a living, remember? You need to call Sarah back and tell her it was all a lie. If you don't patch this up, I will find you and you will not live to raise that child you say is mine. And yes, for the record, that is a threat.

— — —

Linda leaned back on the headboard and tears streamed down her face. She was afraid all over again. Blown away at the callousness of Jesse. Now what was she supposed to do? She closed her eyes and she saw the face of Edgar Graham. She opened her eyes and dialed his phone number, not remembering it was the middle of the night.

Edgar was dreaming an absolute nightmare when the phone rang by his bed. He looked at the caller ID and couldn't pick up the phone fast enough. "Hello, Linda? You okay?"

"Edgar! Edgar! I'm in trouble. I'm so scared. I did what you told me not to do. I phoned his wife on my way out of town. I think I have awakened a dragon! Jesse isn't going to back away from this without fighting me. Maybe killing me. You should have heard his message...... oh Edgar! I'm so afraid!"

There was silence on the other end of the phone. Edgar was thinking. *Awakened a dragon? Well old Jesse was about to meet the dragon slayer of Portersville, dressed in a mailman's clothes.*

"Stay calm, Linda. And don't call his wife anymore. I want you to trust me now more than you ever have trusted me. Okay? I'm goin' to take care of this, and all I want you to do is watch your back a little. Find an apartment where a lot of people are around, and get focused on livin' your life. I'll keep you posted, angel. Let me know as soon as you can what your new address is and your phone number. Get an unlisted number. And it might not be a bad idea to have a roommate, an old friend who might even put the lease in her name. See what you can come up with, and I'll talk to you sometime tomorrow to see if you are okay."

Linda hung up the phone and laid her head down on the pillow. She may have just made the biggest mistake of her life by calling Sarah Stryker. She made up her mind to do what Edgar told her to do, for that was her only lifeline at the moment. And she had learned to trust him with her life. Literally.

CHAPTER 26

Sitting in his garage where it was freezing cold, Doug checked all of his supplies. He dialed Mary's number to see if she was ready for him to do the work on her sun porch.

"Hello Mrs. Williams. This is Doug Peterson. I hope I've waited long enough after the New Year and holidays to call you 'bout the work you needed me to do."

"Well hello Doug! Yes, you have timed it perfectly. My guests have gone home and the house is empty. Please come by and we can go over what needs to be done. I'll be here all day."

"I'll be there 'round three o'clock, if that's okay with you, Mrs. Williams."

"That will be fine, Doug. Just knock on the door, as I'll be in the kitchen doing some paperwork."

— — —

Doug was nervous as he stood at Mary's door. He needed the work so badly but couldn't help but feel guilty for hurting her and taking her money. He hoped the guilt was not written across his forehead as Mary opened the door.

"Hello, Doug. It is nice to meet you. Please do come in so I can show you the sunroom."

"Thanks, Mrs. Williams. I'm anxious to git' started on this work. It's been a long winter and things are slim right now." Doug was feeling too familiar with the surroundings and that added to his guilty feelings. She walked him into the sun porch and he sat his tool box down.

"I see the boards that need replacin', Mrs. Williams. And you mentioned paintin' it too, is that correct?"

"Yes Doug. I am going to leave you here to measure the boards and could you work up an estimate for me? It really isn't a big room, and the sun comes in here in the afternoon. I'm not sure why the boards have rotted, but let me know if you think there is a leak somewhere."

Mary walked out of the room and left Doug to his work. He sounded vaguely familiar to her but she could not place him. She knew she had never met him, but there was something about his voice that was ringing a bell.

Doug came out after about fifteen minutes and walked into the kitchen where Mary was sitting. "Well, I've done the measurin' I needed to do. Do you want me to match the paint that's there already? I can take a small piece of board to match the color, if you aren't changin' it to another color."

"I may be boring, but I am keeping that color. I like it so well and it is such a bright room that it does not take a lot of color in the room to make the room warm. Were you able to estimate the cost of this Doug?"

Doug swallowed. This was the toughest part of his job; working up a fair price. "I think I can do it for 'bout four hundred dollars, Mrs. Williams. Does that seem fair?"

"That is way below what I expected, Doug. Be sure you cover yourself, now."

"I will. Thank you for lettin' me do the work. I'll come back tomorrow at nine o'clock to start if that's okay with you."

"Perfect. I will be ready for you, Doug. Have a good evening."

— — —

Doug ran down the steps and jumped into his truck. It was tough, but now the ice was broken. He felt some better about working around Mary, but was hoping the guilt would ease up. She was such a nice lady and he hated that he had acted so mean to her just for a few dollars. It made him think about the mindset of a thief. *They are not really payin' attention to the person they are robbing. Their mind is solely on the money.*

— — —

Mary finished paying her bills and fixed a pot of coffee. Doug's voice was beginning to bother her, and she wanted to just sit in the quiet of the house and think about why it sounded familiar. The house was very quiet with just the ticking of the clock. Mary got up and walked into her living room and stood there thinking. *When could I have ever met Doug?* She moved toward the kitchen again and something felt familiar. She stopped dead in her tracks and stared at the kitchen table, this time seeing her purse dumped out and the robber going through her wallet. The robber's voice seemed more gravelly than Doug's but the words sounded the same. *The accent. Am I wrong? Could it possibly be that Doug robbed me and now wants to come into my home to do more work? Will he rob me again?*

Mary rang Edgar's cell phone and he picked up on the second ring. "Hello, Mary. You okay? Anything wrong?"

" Edgar. I've just thought of something. Doug was just here and gave me an estimate on the sun room. I kept thinking that I remembered his voice for some reason. I've sat here in this quiet house thinking and thinking and now it comes to me that he might be the person who robbed me. I can't swear on it, Edgar. I wouldn't want to accuse him wrongly. But something is pulling at me about his voice. What do you think?"

"I don't know Mary. I thought all along it might be Doug, but he doesn't seem hesitant to come back to your home. Let's watch him closely and if you feel the slightest bit uncomfortable around him, give me a call. I'll keep my eyes and ears open. I'm only a call away, Mary"

"I'll lock up my house Edgar. So if you try to open the door, the dead bolt will be on. Just ring me so I know you are coming over."

"Okay, Mary. Just relax. It's a long shot that it could be Doug. But we can sure keep our eyes open. I will check in on you later."

— — —

Edgar sat there in his car with a feeling in his stomach that usually meant something was wrong. He didn't want to accuse Doug if it wasn't true. But he hadn't trusted him the first time they met on the street. The creases in Edgar's brow were getting deeper and deeper. He loved Mary now, and didn't want anything to happen to her. He almost felt responsible for her. *Time will tell*, he thought. *Time will tell.*

Chapter 27

Edgar had spent some time mapping out the streets in certain areas of Portersville. He knew most of them like the back of his hand. It was hard to believe that drugs were lurking in the houses on his mail route. But Edgar had been around too long to think otherwise. He had a plan and had chosen two men to work with him from the sheriff's office. They were not the ones already assigned to undercover; those boys were not right for Edgar. The two he chose were men who were quiet, observant and had no egos. When they all got together, the three men fit like a glove.

Edgar had a tent in the back of his car, and he changed clothes to fit into his new surroundings. He was growing his hair longer and hadn't shaved in three weeks, preparing for this job. The excitement was building and he was really looking forward to his first attempt to fit in with a certain crowd. Tonight he was going to put up a tent underneath the bridge on Front Street. There were a lot of homeless people there and it was a great place to get the feel for things. He bundled up, wore plenty of layers, and packed some food that looked appropriate for a homeless person. He drove over to the bridge and parked his car in a lot that was a short distance from the bridge. He told the two men to come later in the night and do the same thing he was doing.

Setting his tent up, he heard men talking about him, and some of them were drinking and sarcastic. "Hey dude, what's up with the tent?"

"Just trying to stay warm, man." Edgar kept busy fixing his space and went inside his tent and got his bag out that held some clothing, soap, toothbrush and toothpaste. He didn't bring much, because none of them had much. He had messed up his hair and had dirt on his face and under his nails. He was used to fitting in like this, so he was very comfortable in his own space. A few men walked over to introduce themselves. They were living in boxes that were getting torn and were a little wet. It was getting late and Edgar yawned and acted like he was tired. Someone had built a small fire and a few of the men were huddled around it laughing and drinking something. Edgar snuggled down in his tent and zipped himself in. He dozed off easily and woke himself up about four o'clock. He quietly got out of his tent and noticed that the other two men were set up down the way from him. There were two men standing under the bridge talking and exchanging something. Edgar saddled up to them with his hands in his pockets. He had a limp and coughed, sounding like he was pretty sick. The two men looked up at him and then went back to what they were doing. They didn't see him as a threat at all.

Edgar could see that one of the men was holding a bag of white powder and the other man was digging in his pocket for money. The taller man was yelling at him and pushing him a little. Edgar could feel the tension and squatted down near them, warming himself by the small fire. He kept coughing so they would not think he was listening. He pulled out a bottle and took a swig and put it back in his pocket. Then the other two undercover cops came near him and squatted down. They offered Edgar a weed and he took it and sucked in the pungent smoke. The two men were watching and walked over to Edgar and his buddies. They squatted down with them and asked if they wanted to buy some white powder. Edgar shook his head no, but his buddies said yes.

"Hey dude. How much you want?"

"Whatever you have, dude. Just a small amount this time, okay?"

"Sure. We have what ya' need. You got any crisp?'

"I got as much as you need, buddy. Just get me the white powder."

The two men walked away laughing. It had begun. The trade was coming down soon. Then Edgar could find out where the source was. It would take some time. You could buy this stuff anywhere; schools, restaurants, on the streets. But getting to the source was something else. Edgar winked at the two men and they all got back into their tents. Edgar's name was Streetdog. His two cop friends were Shorty and Bluejack. They slept sound because they had to get up in a few hours and work their day jobs. The other men under the bridge stayed up late and slept during the day.

Edgar phoned Fred after he got home that morning and reported what had taken place.

"We have a ways to go, Fred. But we'll get it done. I'm confident we can snag the dealer and bust this ring that has been goin' on for years underneath that bridge. You know it takes time, Fred. And there are fingers that spread into the schools and businesses all over Portersville. We'll try to get the source. You have my word."

"I am amazed at you Edgar. You're so calm doing this. I guess it's become second nature with you with your background. Whatever you need, let me know."

—   —   —

Changing back to his normal clothes, Edgar was going to deliver the mail early today. He knew he might go back out on the street tonight and didn't want to be late getting back to his tent. He also wanted to visit a bar that was down on Fourth Street to see what was happening there. He had heard that it was a hot spot for drugs and wanted to check it out. He told the other two cops not to show up tonight because they couldn't always show up as a group.

Before he started his route, he popped his head in to see how Mary was doing. He was a little worried about their conversation yesterday about Doug. "Hey woman. You up?"

He loved to ask her that, and see her get mad.

"I was up before you ever thought about getting up, you simple man."

"Whoa! Hey Mary, that was a pretty good comeback! I just wanted to see how you are this mornin'. Hope you aren't too worried about Doug!"

"I decided in the middle of the night that I was not going to worry. If it was Doug, and he is stupid enough to come back into my house and try something again, then I will be ready for him. You forget I do have a pistol in my bedside table. I'm going to keep it in my kitchen in a drawer from now on. What do you think of that, Mr. Edgar?"

"I think that's a great idea! Just be sure he doesn't find it and use it on you."

"I already thought of that. I'm a good shot. I trained on that gun when I purchased it after Sidney died. A woman alone all the time is easy prey."

— — —

Edgar left and hurried to begin his day. He felt alive for the first time in a long time. What he didn't see was one of the men who lived underneath the bridge, standing on the street corner near his first mail delivery. The man started walking towards Edgar and stopped just before he was right up on him. "Do ya' know Jesse Stryker? I'm lookin' for him. He owes me some dough."

Edgar was caught off guard but didn't make any facial expression to show it. "No, I don't know Jesse Stryker. I'm sorry. What did he do to you?"

"He owes me a lot of green stuff, man. I was hoping you knew who he was. You deliver mail, right?"

"Yeah, but I don't deliver his mail. I know I would recognize that name, and he isn't on my route. What does he owe you money for?" Edgar knew it had to be drugs, and the guy was not going to admit it.

"Nothing, man. I'll git it done my way." He turned and walked away, laughing. His laugh made the hair on Edgar's arm stand up. He phoned his buddies and told them to get on the street and watch for this guy walking around town.

He described him down to his shoes and socks and told them to keep an eye on Jesse. This didn't really surprise him at all about Jesse, because of his son's death.

"We will take care of it, Edgar. Immediately."

What did bother Edgar was the fact that this man was in a good neighborhood walking out in the open, obviously comfortable here. Way too comfortable.

CHAPTER 28

Jesse Stryker lived on Monroe Street at the end of the block. Edgar could see his house from where he was parked, four houses down, in the pitch dark. He had some luck digging up information on Jesse. He had done his homework. Someone ratted on old Jesse, and it couldn't have come at a more opportune time. Once the guy started talking he didn't shut up. Guess he had been stung by Jesse pretty bad. The sergeant was the source for half the drugs coming into Portersville. Edgar hadn't seen it coming, but once he heard about it, things started adding up. Several men in the department opened up and talked, when normally they wouldn't rat on a fellow cop. There was a warehouse outside of town where Jesse stored kilos of cocaine, and he had a team of people on the street to sell it to the kids, to the homeless, to anyone who would buy it. Edgar was surprised at how smooth the operation was going, considering how hot headed Jesse was.

Inside the house, Sarah and Jesse were arguing over what he had done with Linda. It was not going well, and Jesse was getting more and more enraged. Just when he was about to haul off and hit his wife, the doorbell rang and Jesse jumped. He scrambled towards the front door and opened it, finding himself looking straight in the face of Edgar Graham.

Edgar could see the tension in Jesse's face. He was ready for it. Edgar also noticed that Jesse still had his uniform on and his side arm.

"Jesse, could you step outside? I would like to talk to you for a moment."

"I'm a little busy here, Edgar. Can't we talk tomorrow at the department?"

"No, Jesse, this is way too important. I think you need to calm down anyway. Looks like you're pretty worked up in there."

"That is none of your business, Edgar. Now why don't you go back home and be a good mailman and leave me and my wife alone." Jesse started to slam the door in Edgar's face, but Edgar was too quick. He shoved his foot between the two doors and it caught Jesse off guard. Jesse instinctively grabbed his gun and pulled it out. "I said you need to go, Edgar. I'm not in the mood to talk to you tonight. What in the world do we need to talk about that would bring you all the way over to my house, anyhow?"

Edgar stepped back on the porch and smiled quietly. "Well, for one, we could talk about your little meeting in the park the other day. Now do you think we need to talk?"

Jesse lifted his gun and aimed it straight at Edgar. Sarah was screaming at him to put the gun down. But Jesse was already way past being pulled back. His life was going by him at the speed of light, and it was ruined. All because of a stupid kid he got pregnant. He had no idea that Edgar had found out about the drugs. He shoved Sarah away from him and she fell against the piano. Edgar remained planted on the porch, calm and cool.

"Put the gun down, Jesse. You don't want to do this. I think if we talk you might change your mind about some things. I have been doin' some checkin' on you; you're familiar with a man called Bennie Jay? He is known on the streets as Poco. He seems to know you real well, Jesse."

"I don't know what in the hell you're talkin' about, Edgar. Hey! You all of a sudden decide you want to be a cop and you're tryin' to tell me what to do? Who do you think you are, Edgar? You're nothin' but a punk mailman who got bored with his life! Now get off my case, damn it!" Jesse tried to close the door again but this time Edgar pushed it open. Jesse felt his temper go past a red zone and pulled the trigger on his gun. Edgar fell flat on his back. He lay motionless and Jesse ran out the door. He panicked. His mind had literally stopped working. He was feeling like a caged animal and as he ran towards his car, someone came around the corner of the house and shot out his front tires. Jesse was confused. Who was shooting at his car? He thought Edgar was down. He heard a voice calling his name and he turned around and Edgar was standing up with a gun aimed at him.

"Jesse, put down your gun. The game is over. You are under arrest for selling an illegal substance. We found a man walking the streets tonight wanting to know where you were. He talked, Jesse. He told us a lot about you. So come on down to the station without a fight and we'll talk to you about it." Edgar walked slowly over to Jesse and took his gun away. "There's another matter we need to discuss too, Jesse. Linda. Need I go any further with that?"

Jesse kicked at the ground feeling rage come up in his gut. He put his hands behind his back glaring at Edgar. He was even more shocked when Sheriff Perkins walked around the corner of the house to help Edgar with the cuffs. *How in the world did Edgar find out about his business so quickly? Poco had talked; but what did they promise him to get him to open up. Poco had been around for a long time. He was street wise. Who was this Edgar Graham anyway? He acted like a cop the way he handled a gun. He certainly did not look like a mailman now.*

Edgar grabbed his arms and Sheriff Perkins put the cuffs on Jesse. They turned him around and read him his rights. Jesse looked at Fred and winced. He was curious about how much they knew. Guess he would find out soon enough.

He decided to keep his mouth shut and not give them anymore information than necessary. He was also thinking of the name of a good lawyer.

— — —

Sarah came out of the house shaking her head. *What in the world was Jesse into?* She walked over to Edgar and asked him some questions. "We were arguing about the girl he got pregnant. I had no idea about any drugs he was selling. I've never known Jesse to do any drugs. Are you saying he was doing drugs? I'm so confused."

"No Ma'am. We aren't saying that at all. Jesse ran a pretty complicated drug ring and I just happened to run into his main man on the street the other night who was drinkin' and willing to talk to me. A lot of this was discovered by sheer accident but as soon as I heard it, everything began to make sense to me. I'm sorry, Sarah, to come bustin' into your home like this, but somethin' had to give here. Are you goin' to be okay?"

Sarah felt weak and sick to her stomach. Her life would never be the same now. There was no going back. She lifted her head and looked Edgar right in the eyes. "I'm sure it will take some time, Edgar, but actually it's a little freeing to know the truth. He's been abusive to me for a long time and has had several affairs. This affair with Linda was the last straw. So if I'm honest, Edgar, I'm thrilled you came by tonight. It just made things easier for me in the long run."

Edgar was taken back by her strength. Obviously she had been thinking about leaving Jesse for a long time. This little raucous tonight just opened a door for her that she was having trouble putting the key into. "Here's my card, Sarah. Call me night or day if you think of anything I might want to know about, or if you feel threatened in any way. If I were you, I might take a trip somewhere; go see some family. Because of the people who were involved with Jesse, I cannot promise you are safe right now. Do you understand that?"

"Yes, I do, Edgar. I don't want to think I'm in danger, but if you say so, I'll leave for a while and visit my sister in Ohio." Sarah looked around the yard and pulled her coat up around her. It suddenly didn't feel like home anymore. Her house no longer belonged to her, because of what had taken place tonight. Her mind was racing, but she thanked Edgar and went back inside the house. She could not even stand to look at Jesse as they pushed him into the backseat of the squad car.

Jesse could see Sarah walking back into their house with her head down. Something grabbed him for a moment and then anger took over again. *Stupid woman. She never did get it about what life was all about. He had to make a living, didn't he? And how was he to do that on the salary a Sergeant pulls?* He shook his head. *She certainly did not mind spending the money,* he thought, laughing to himself. As they pulled out of the driveway, Jesse saw a bicycle leaning against a tree next door, and his children's faces flashed before him. That was about the only thing that could get to Jesse at this one moment in his life. His kids. They would never know how he got started in this mess, and they would never believe anything he ever said to them again. Pretty huge price to pay for money. He leaned back in the squad car and listened to the police radio blaring in the front seat. This would be his last time that he would ride in a squad car for the rest of his life. Unless it was taking him to prison.

—   —   —

Edgar drove home in his own car, listening to an old song on the radio. But he didn't hear the music this time; his mind was racing. He hadn't been on the job a week and already had found his way in with the street people. It really wasn't that difficult. But you had to blend in. You had to be believable. He felt bad for Sarah, but in a way, it was the best thing that could have happened to her.

As soon as he got home he undressed and took off the bullet proof vest. *Those things came in handy when the hit came down. Jesse really thought he had put me down,* Edgar thought to himself, shaking his head. The power of the bullet knocked the wind out of him for a few seconds and it was hard to stand back up right away. He knew better than to go to a man's home like that, being that aggressive, and not have a vest on. *Fred was blown away by the information I fed him,* thought Edgar, as he pulled off his boots and socks. He stood in the hot shower and closed his eyes. What a night. Word would get around really quick that this bust had taken place. The sheriff still had to take possession of the warehouse and would probably already have men over there tonight guarding it. *This news would spread like wildfire under the bridge and all over town. Interesting.* He told his other buddies to go back to the bridge tonight and listen. He would have to show up too, so as not to cause any suspicion by suddenly disappearing. But not tonight.

Edgar picked up the phone and called Jane. She was the only person he could call and talk about his new line of work in Portersville. She was home doing some paperwork when the phone rang.

"Hey beautiful! How's my girl?"

"Hey Dad! I'm tired tonight. What's up?"

"Well, a week on the job and we turned up some of the biggest news in town. I arrested the sergeant in the sheriff's department tonight. Can you believe it, Jane? He was running one of the biggest drug rings here. He had so much cocaine stored in a warehouse right out of town, that you would not believe it. He hid it behind appliance boxes. The name on the building was an appliance dealer so no one questioned it."

"Dad, was it dangerous bringing him in? I know you, Dad. Was there any shooting involved?"

"There is almost always shooting involved where there are drugs, my dear. I had on my vest, you know. Hey, how long have I been doin this stuff, baby? You know I'm not goin' to walk up on someone suspected of dealing drugs without my pistol, don't you?"

"Well, I want to be able to talk to you for years to come. I want you around for my children to know. I thought this was all behind you, but you just can't give it up, can you Dad?"

Sweat beaded up on his brow as Edgar tried to think of a good answer to that question. His daughter always had the upper hand, and he hadn't figured out how she did it. "I know, baby girl. I know. But you can't expect me to sit here and be a mailman the rest of my life. I have to have somethin' else going on. If you can think of a career for me, then let me know. Until then, I'm fallin' back on what I already know and love."

Jane sat back in her chair and grinned. She couldn't help but smile because she knew she had put his back against the wall, and she loved doing it. However, she also knew nothing she said would stop her father from having his hand in the pool of mankind. He just had to keep his fingers wet, and nothing anyone said would stop him. She just didn't want him to drown in it.

—   —   —

Jesse sat in his cell, stripped, finger-printed, and numbered. He felt sick inside but the anger had not totally subsided. *I would love to get my hands on Edgar Graham about now. Not to mention Linda! If she hadn't come into town, none of this would have happened. What I can't figure out was how in the world Edgar found all this out so fast. Who was this guy, anyway? Where in the world did he learn the skills it would take to dig this up in such a short time?* He smiled for a moment, but it was a sick smile. He would never trust a mailman again. And the word would spread on the street, if he had anything to do with it. Edgar Graham just might find a bullet on his daily route delivering mail.

Jesse's badge lay on the desk with his other belongings, waiting to be bagged and put in a locker. He had worn that badge for about fifteen years, and now it was over. It meant nothing to Jesse anymore. He did feel a slight twinge when they took the badge off, but really it was more about a loss of power than it was a sadness about his job being over. The amount of money he had made in drugs made him forget who he really was, and the promise he made to uphold the law and keep Portersville safe. It was a joke to Jesse, and some of the other men in the department. They used the badge to help them achieve what they wanted. Personal gain.

— — —

Sarah booked a flight to Ohio to see her sister. She would leave on the early morning flight and arrive there before eleven. She decided to just tell the kids that she was visiting her sister for now. Better to wait until she got settled and then spend time telling them the whole story. They would want to see her, but she was going to try to keep things as normal as possible in this huge transition in her life and theirs. She knew Stan would feel sorry for his father in a way, but after he heard about the whole thing, he would understand her situation.

She breathed a sigh of relief and locked up the house, climbed the stairs to her bedroom, and never heard the man breathing silently, standing in the corner of her room, in the dark.

CHAPTER 29

The phone was ringing in the Stryker house, but no one answered. The answering machine kicked on and a voice came on. "Mom? Are you there? Mom? I got your message about your plane flight to Ohio. What is going on Mom? Are you okay? ...Mom?"

Nothing but silence. Silence, because Sarah Stryker was gone. The front door stood open, there was a television on in her bedroom, and all of her clothes and belongings were still in their proper places. Nothing in the house was touched or damaged. It was just empty. No trace of forced entry, no trace of an intruder. Just an empty house that looked like someone had run out and left everything...

Jesse was sitting up in the jail cell, sore from sleeping on a hard bed. He knew he was facing arraignment and bail. Only there was no one to put up the bail for him. So he imagined he would be sitting in jail until the trial. He was going to have a court appointed attorney for the arraignment and a court date would be set.

He lay back down on the bed and covered his face with his arms. *What a mess I've created. Everything was going great until I slept with Linda and got her pregnant. What I want to know, and will find out somehow, is how Edgar Graham got involved in my life. Where in the world did this guy come from?* It nearly drove Jesse crazy thinking about it all. He needed to find a way to contact someone on the outside to get some answers. He hoped, stupidly, that maybe one of his goons would come and see him in jail. He knew the word would be out by now that he had been arrested. He also knew it might be plastered all over the morning paper, and maybe anyone who knew him or was involved in this mess would stay hidden until it blew over.

He started the process of going over every single aspect of his business to think about whether it was safe from discovery or not. *The warehouse was exposed already and would be emptied out immediately. No point in wasting any thought on that. His money was overseas in about six different offshore banks, so it could not be found or touched. It was not taxable and no one knew it was there except him.* Sitting in jail dealing with what he may have to face, he realized that this might not have been such a great idea, to not have anyone know about the money. In fact it was pretty naïve on his part; what was he thinking? If something happened to him, that money would just sit there and rot. He should have told his wife. He wondered if she would break down and come to see him? He was hoping against hope that she would. He needed someone to be able to post bail, and she might be his only hope.

Suddenly a guard came in and said he had a visitor. Jesse stood up and walked to the bars and looked out at the doorway. He just knew it was Sarah; he was shocked to see Poco standing there. The guard left them alone but stood at the other end of the hallway so that he could still see them both. There were cameras everywhere so it was not like he could get out or anything.

"Dude! What's up wid' you? Thought you owned it, didn't you, dude? I told you, man, if you scrapped me, then I would lay you down."

"I didn't scrap you, Poco. I was goin' to pay. I just needed more time. You sure did screw things up for us, dude. Look what you did by rattin' on me to Edgar Graham. What were you thinking? Obviously you weren't."

Poco walked up close to the bars and looked Jesse square in the face. "When I said sum words to this so called Edgar Graham dude, he wuz' a bum on the street. He said he been scrapped by you and asked if I'd had any trouble gittin' my dough from you. So we had a rap and got some words said. That was it. How'd I know I was talkin' to a damn undercover cop?"

Jesse rolled his eyes and walked back to his cot and sat down. He put his head in his hands and rocked back and forth. *All of this crap has happened because of Edgar Graham. Somehow I am going to bring that guy down. Big time.*

"Okay Poco. You spilled the beans on me. So what now? How do I get outa' here?" Jesse whispered because the guard was staring at them like they were two girls in bikinis.

"I don' know, dude. You got problems fo' sure. Whut I wan' to know is, where's my dough? The crisps? You owe me and if'n you don' pay up, I'll take you down the alley myself."

"You'll get your money, big dude. But don't threaten me, Poco. I've done you right all this time. Just wait and give me a chance to get outa' here..."

Yeah, right dude. There ain't a 'torney for miles 'round who wants yur case. You goin' to be stuck with a court mouse who culdn't find the cheese if it was sittin' under his nose."

Poco stepped back and motioned to the guard. He took one more look at Jesse and shook his head. Jesse sighed and rubbed his face. *I have to find a way to get some of my money to Poco. How can I do that locked up in a cell? And where is my wife?*

— — —

Two hours passed before Jesse saw anyone again. He was getting hungry and thirsty when the guard came in with a hamburger and fries and a coke. Jesse asked if he could make a call and the guard shook his head. *Alone is not the* word that would describe how he felt right now, in this cold empty cell. He was just about to feel sorry for himself when a court appointed attorney showed up to get his story. In shorthand form. This was the mouse that Poco was talking about. Jesse had never seen anyone write down so much information on such a tiny pad in his entire life.

"So basically man, you are guilty but don't want to go to jail. It's my understanding that you would have to give up a lot of information that the court would see as helpful in containing this drug movement in Portersville, in order to have a lesser punishment or walk free on this one."

"I don't know that kind of information, man. I have a small drug business and don't play with the big boys around here. If I did, I would already be dead. They wouldn't tolerate my being caught like this."

The attorney got up and walked to the door of the cell and motioned to the guard. "I'll do the best I can, but you best get ready to spend some of your life behind uglier bars than these."

— — —

Meredith was worried now. She had placed a call to her mother and there was no answer. She called the airlines and checked all flights to Ohio; her mother was on none of those flights. She phoned her Aunt Sue and she hadn't heard another word from her since the original phone call saying she was coming for a visit. *Now it was time to call the police,* she thought. She reached for the phone and dialed the sheriff's department and waited for the someone to pick up.

"Hello? Is this the sheriff's office? I need your help! This might be an emergency but I can't get my mother to answer the phone at her house, and she isn't on the flight she booked to Ohio either. Can someone go over to her house and see if she is okay?"

"Hold on, ma'am. Who is this, first? And secondly, who is your mother?"

"This is Meredith Stryker. My mother is Sarah Stryker. My parents live at 1455 Monroe Street. Please hurry, I think something is wrong."

"I would say something's wrong, Miss. Your father is sitting in our jail under drug arrest."

There was dead silence on the other end of the phone. "What? What are you saying? My father is in jail because of drugs? Are you crazy? He never did drugs in his life. What do you mean drug arrest?"

"I can't tell you anymore than I have, Meredith. You may want to hop a plane and come to see your father. He probably could use a family visitor about now."

"I need you to check on my mother, sir. I'm worried that something has happened to her. Would you have a patrol car go by her house and make sure she is alright?"

"Will do, ma'am. What is your phone number, so I can call you back? If we find your mother is okay, we will have her call you. Otherwise, you will hear from one of us here at the station. Is that clear?"

"Yes, thank you. Hey! Is there anyway I could speak to my father? Please? Please? I just want to talk to him for a moment. Please let me talk to him!"

"I'll give you five minutes with your father. Hold on please."

Meredith's mind was going ninety miles an hour. *What in the world was going on? My father in jail? And where is my mother?* She felt sick and was about to lose it, but she wanted desperately to speak to her dad. The voice she heard on the other end of the phone did not remotely resemble her father's voice.

"Hello? Meredith? It's Dad! I'm sorry you had to call and find me in this position. I don't want you to worry, Meredith. I'll be fine. It's all a big mistake and I'll get to the bottom of it shortly."

"Dad! I'm worried sick about you! And where is mother? She's not answering her phone, and she isn't on the flight that she booked. Where do you think she is, Dad?"

Jesse stood up. *What is going on?* "I don't know, sweetheart. I'll try to find out the answer from here. You need to calm down and not get all worked up, baby. I'll try to find out about your mother and let you know. I don't know how many calls I get, but someone will call you back shortly and let you know if your mother is at home."

"Dad. This is crazy! You never did drugs did you Dad?"

"Of course not, Meredith! It's all a big mistake. Just take it easy, stay put, and wait for me or someone here to call you back."

—   —   —

Jesse put the phone back in the cradle and looked up at Stuart, the deputy working the desk tonight. "Stuart, you get a damn car to my house pronto. Something smells here and I don't like it one bit. If something has happened to my wife, heads are going to roll. Call that Edgar dude and let him know. Since he knows so damn much, pull his butt out of bed and get him on this."

Stuart looked at Jesse in disbelief. *Still giving orders from the cell.* It just blew his mind to watch him. "Jesse, you are in no position to be giving me orders, you hear? Now get back in your cell. I've already phoned this one in and someone will be at your house in minutes."

— — —

It seemed like hours before Meredith got a call back. She was sitting by the phone, talking on her cell phone to Stan. They both were shocked and wondering what was going on. Their family had been like the all- American family; nothing in the closet. Not perfect, but pretty damn close. Now all hell had broken loose. Meredith was shaking and crying and Stan was trying to reassure her that things were not what they seemed. The phone rang and Meredith picked it up.

"Hello? This is Meredith. What did you find out about my mother?"

There was a pause on the other end of the line, and then bad news. "Well, Ms. Stryker, we just got back from your mother's house and it's empty. She isn't there. But strangely, the front door was open, the television was on, and nothing was disturbed. Almost like she had just run out of the house. We have police there now checking out the house. Do you know where she might have gone? Any friend she might have run to?"

"I have no idea. She didn't have that many friends in town. Her sister was her best friend, and she lives in Ohio. We know she isn't there now."

"If you think of anything let us know immediately. She may try to contact you, so if you hear from her, please call us back. I have your number if she shows up here."

"Thank you so much. I'm so worried! Please find her, will you? Ask Dad if he knows where she could be?"

"We'll handle it on our end. Just let us know if you hear anything. My advice to you is to stay put because she will need to be able to reach you if she's in trouble."

Meredith hung up the phone and relayed the information to Stan. He decided to come to her house and wait it out with her. He was in the next county but it was only an hour's drive away. She hung up the phone and just sat there, stunned. Her world had just been ripped apart. *Where in the world is Mom?*

CHAPTER 30

===========

Edgar got a call on his cell phone late in the night. He jumped out of bed, grabbed it and heard the voice of Fred Perkins on the other end.

"Sorry Edgar. Hate waking you up like this, but we got a problem here. Sarah Stryker is missing."

"I'll be right in, Fred." *This is not a good sign*, he thought.

"Hey Edgar. Go on over to the Stryker house. We have detectives there now, but I need you on the case. Please find this woman. It doesn't smell good, Edgar."

"I'll do my best, Fred. I have men on the street already and I'll notify them to help me find out what is going on. Words will be flowing on the street like water tonight."

The two other undercover cops were already under the bridge listening to what was being said. Word was that Poco had made some phone calls to the head man, and he had sent a man over to the Stryker house to pick up Sarah. It appeared that Jesse owed this king pin some money and was late paying. Now that the drug bust had happened, the king pin wanted his dough. He doesn't wait to be paid, and Jesse was aware of that fact. Edgar had a quick chat over the cell with one of his men.

"Hey dude. Anything you find out to help me find Sarah would be appreciated. I know you're cold. Bundle up best you can. The longer we go without finding her, the less likely she'll be alive."

"Ditto. Will check it out. Get back 'atcha quick. Gone."

Edgar hung up and rubbed his eyes. These guys were ridiculous. He pulled on plenty of clothes and jumped into his car, and drove like a maniac to the Stryker house. He had a gun tucked into his pants and one in the pocket of his coat. *You just never knew with these guys on the street. White powder men. Snowmen. You watch your back with a snowman.*

As soon as he pulled into the driveway his cell rang. "Yo, Edgar. I got one second here. People everywhere. I may have somethin'. Will get right back to you with a name. Gone."

He checked his watch. It was three in the morning. *What a time to be up tryin' to break a case. Oh well, I did it for years. Suck it up, man,* he said to himself. He didn't hear the other men complaining and they were sleeping out in it tonight. He went over to the house and walked up the steps. There were way too many people in the house. He hoped they hadn't touched anything.

"Hey Edgar. Fred is in the bedroom and wants to see you."

"On my way there now." He walked into the bedroom and Fred was leaning over the bed. He had found one small piece of tape that had fallen on the floor near the bed. Packing tape. He also found mud near the window by the bottom of the curtain. Edgar cleared the room except for Fred and stood at the doorway. In five seconds he sized up the situation.

"Fred, this is the deal. She was gettin' ready for bed, laid down, and someone was hidin' behind the curtain. They walked out, grabbed her, pinned her down and taped her mouth. My guess is this is about money. About someone gettin' paid. I'm waitin' on a phone call now from one of my men to tell me what's goin' down in the streets."

Fred nodded and they walked back into the living room.

"There's no point in you guys all being here. I want two men here and the rest can go back to work. Keep your eyes open and your radios on. I have all your cell numbers so I can reach you no matter where you are. Report anything you see to Edgar."

— — —

The arraignment took place the next morning. Jesse was a dead man walking. Since he had shot a deputy, there was no way the judge would allow him bail. So he was going to sit in jail until the court date, and try to figure out how to communicate with someone on the outside so that he could get money to that idiot Ranko. The jail was pretty quiet and the odds of someone else coming to see him were pretty slim. Or that was what Jesse was thinking when Edgar Graham walked in.

"Good mornin' Jesse. I hear you've had your arraignment and the court date is set for two months from now. Let's get to the point, Jesse. Who do you report to? Who is the big dog on the block?"

"And what do you think you're going to do with that information, Edgar? Call him up?" Jesse smirked. *This guy really could get under your skin.*

"Hey dude. If you are so damn smart, what are you doin' behind bars? And why in the world would you shoot me at your door? I had not pulled my gun out, and didn't plan to use a gun on you. Just wanted to talk, that's all. You flipped out, Jesse. Lost your temper. And now look at you? You may be in for life, do you realize that? We are talkin' the rest of your life."

"So answer my question, Sherlock. What are you going to do with the name of my source?"

"I would find him and pay him off. That's what he wants. Do you realize that your wife is missing? Did anyone bother to tell you that little tidbit of info?"

Jesse nearly fell off his cot. "Meredith phoned last night and told me she was not home They were supposed to let me know last night and I fell asleep waiting on someone to get their butt back here."

"Well I just came from your house, and someone was in your wife's bedroom late that night. She never made it to sleep. They hoisted her right out of the bed and left barely a trace on their way out of the house. The television was still on."

Jesse was sitting there with both legs moving and his eyes were jerking back and forth. *I did not intend for my wife to ever be involved in this mess. Now look what happened. It was all because of this punk in front of him, puttin' his nose where it didn't belong.*

"You better find my wife, Edgar. Her blood is on your hands. You should never have come to my house that night. None of this would have happened. I will blame you if she dies." Jesse stood up and glared at Edgar.

"Don't bother tryin' to hit me, Jesse. You wouldn't last five seconds with me. Stop being such a hot head and let me in on this dude's name. I need to get busy finding your wife, and anything you know that could help me, you need to tell me now. Otherwise, I will try to get it from another source." Edgar pushed Jesse down on the bed. "And by the way, just to jog your memory a little, this whole damn thing is your fault, not mine. You didn't love your wife, dude. You cheated on her. How many times, Jesse? And to top it off, you, a detective for years, sellin' drugs in your own hometown. How stupid is that? In fact, I'm amazed at your naivety. You would have been found out sooner or later; right here under the nose of the law you claim to work for. It was really not that difficult to find you out. When you don't pay someone in the drug world, they come to you. I had a man walk straight up to me, askin' me if I knew you. Think about it, Jesse. You need to talk to me so I can save your wife. Now where do I get some money, and who do I need to pay off?"

Jesse knew he was right. He hated to admit it, but if he wanted to find his wife, he better cough up a few names. "The main man is Ranko. He's a mean dude, Edgar. He doesn't live here, but he has his own plane. If you let word out on the street that you want to talk to him, believe me, he will show up. I do owe him money. Exactly one million dollars. Just where are you going to come up with that kind of money, Edgar?"

Edgar whistled. "One mill? Are you nuts? You owe someone money who would slit your throat for a dog bone? You aren't as smart as I thought, Jesse. How did you run this hairy business of yours making decisions like this?"

"I've done pretty damn well for myself, Edgar. If you hadn't joined up forces with the department, I would still be making money."

"Well, if you have so much money, fork over some of it to pay this guy off. I need to know where some of your money is and how to get a hold of it. Start talkin', Jesse. The guard isn't out in the hallway; he trusts me explicitly. So if you don't want me to tear you apart for shootin' me, then start talkin'."

Somehow Jesse knew Edgar was being serious here. He bowed his head and wanted to disappear. "I have one account here in town under the name of Michael Jones Barringer. It's at the main branch of State Trust Bank. If you have a pen, I can give you my account number. Or if I can make the phone call, I can transfer that sum of money into your account. Then you can write a check and cash it."

Edgar shook his head. It was amazing how Jesse still tried to take control of the situation. "That is exactly what you're goin' to do right now. I want one million in my bank account today. Here is my cell phone. Now call and let's get this transfer done."

— — —

Sarah Stryker was taped down to a chair in a cold warehouse. She was shivering, hungry, thirsty and had wet herself about three times since she had gotten there. The men were totally ignoring any requests that she had, and she could feel herself getting dehydrated. They would not allow her to go to the bathroom, or give her any food. Finally, when the others were outside, one of the men came over with a cup of water and allowed her to drink out of it. She drank and drank, cursing inside, because she knew she would eventually have to go to the bathroom again. She had no idea where she was, or what they were going to do with her. She tried to listen to what they were saying, and basically figured out that they wanted money from Jesse, and were waiting for some type of contact from him or one of his buddies. She started shaking again and crying. No one noticed. Her only hope was that her daughter would realize she was gone and that something was wrong. She could not count on Jesse to save her. She closed her eyes and felt so alone. But the one face that kept popping up in her mind did not belong to her husband. It was the face of Edgar Graham.

CHAPTER 31

The money came through the accounts in a split second, no questions asked. Edgar took one last look at Jesse and spoke in a cold tone. "You better hope we find whoever has your wife and that this amount of money is enough for him to release her. Usually these bad boys need interest on the money you didn't pay. See if you can stay out of trouble, Jesse. I may need your brain."

Jesse looked at Edgar and sat back down in the cold cell. Things were not turning out like he had envisioned. He had to find a way to contact someone on the outside. The worst thing he could do was sit here and do nothing.

— — —

Edgar's boys were on the street talking to everyone they could find that even looked remotely like they did drugs. Word was definitely going down on the streets that Jesse had gotten bagged. Apparently everyone knew who he was and they weren't too happy about the arrest. He was a big source for drugs for a lot of areas around town, and out of state. The lines were going to jam up now.

Edgar was in constant contact with Sheriff Perkins, and as soon as he had a name they were going to put it in their computers and give it to the guys who read the lines on peoples' lives. They would find out everything there was to be found on this guy, if they could just get his name. Time was ticking by at the speed of light, but information was coming in slow motion. It was about to get on Edgar's nerves when his cell went off. He grabbed it and got in a corner of the deli to hear better.

"Dude. We found the snowman. He's not local, but will be here tonight, flying his own bird. He's dangerous. He carries tools with him. We'll keep you posted. Gone."

Edgar did not say a word, but read between the lines of what his guy was saying. It was not going to be an easy deal. He made a trip home to pick up his 357 Magnum and made sure he was wired so that they would never find it. It was a new type of mic that was wireless and so small it was the size of a human hair. It was so sensitive that it picked up the sound of a raindrop falling on the ground. He put on his bulletproof vest and leg covers, put the money in a pocket on the inside of his vest, dressed like a homeless man and headed out the door. He had plenty of time, but wanted to check in with the sheriff to verify that their communication was impeccable.

— — —

Sarah was losing hope one minute at a time. She did not allow herself to cry when anyone was around, but her hope was being swallowed up by her immediate needs. She was so hungry now that she could hardly stand it, but her thirst consumed her. It was like torture watching them come and go with cokes and all kinds of drinks, not offering her anything. She was tired, she was dehydrated, and she had not gotten out of the chair now for twenty four hours. She could see a clock on the wall in the far room, and she tried hard to keep up with night and day. There were no windows in the room so she didn't know if is was dark or light outside. Very confusing. She didn't know how long she could last like this, but she willed herself to be strong for her children.

If she ever got out of here, she was going after Jesse with all that she had. He would never set sight on her again, or the children, if she had her way. She could hear the men talking and tried hard to hear what they were talking about. She would hear Jesse's name mentioned every once in a while, and a lot of cussing. They weren't too happy with her husband. It sounded like he owed the main guy a million dollars. This was beyond her thinking. She couldn't grasp her husband owing a drug lord that kind of money. Or even being involved in drugs, for that matter. They were talking about a ransom note, but she didn't know for sure if they had talked to anyone or not.

— — —

Suddenly, for no apparent reason, something changed in the room. Ranko, who seemed like the head of this drug ring, phoned and was heading into Portersville from Chicago. She could only hear bits and pieces, but suspected that somehow the police or someone had gotten in touch with Ranko. The men were scurrying around and no one even looked at her anymore. They seemed to have one thing on their minds. Money. She asked one more time for water, and one of the men came over and threw coke in her face. She opened her mouth and felt some of it land on her tongue, but not enough to help her parched throat. Another guy came up and let her drink water out of a bottle, but it tasted like something else was in it. They all laughed as she drank nearly the whole bottle. In five minutes she had passed out. Dead to the world. They cut the tape off her arms and untied her hands and feet, and moved her to a cot that was in a room off the main area. It was cold and dark in the room. She did not hear it, but the door closed and locked, and she was alone. She was out for a very long time, but as she came to, it was very disconcerting to not be able to see. She thought at first that they had blinded her. She stared for a few minutes in one spot and suddenly saw a thin light at the bottom of the door. Her eyes adjusted to the darkness and she finally realized that she was in a small dark room. She tried to get up but felt very dizzy. She waited for what seemed like hours and tried to move again. This time she made it up and walked along the wall to the door. It was locked. She slid down to the floor and cried. *What are they going to do with me? Is anyone looking for me? Can I get out of this alive?*

She had no answers. No voices talking. Nothing but silence.

— — —

Edgar was on the street, mingling with the street people, and it was getting colder outside. Some of the men had started fires in old metal garbage cans, warming their hands as they talked in low voices. There was an apprehension in the air, and the talk of the night was Jesse Stryker. They couldn't believe he had gotten nailed. Some of the men laughed and said he was so cocky and sure of himself, hitting on the people who had no money and making deals with them, knowing they did not have the wherewithal to pay. He was constantly setting people up to benefit himself. This time just might be payback time for Mr. Jesse.

Edgar just listened and nodded. He chose to keep his voice very low and talk very little. This wasn't the time to get to know any of the men standing around him, and he moved from fire to fire, just trying to get a feel for what was going on. He was really waiting on the call from his men… to hear if Ranko had landed. He wasn't nervous at all; in fact, the stress of the situation actually acted like a tranquilizer to Edgar. He worked best when the odds were against him, and that made him a perfect FBI agent. He had the skills to bring things down that just had no way of working out. The impossible was possible anytime Edgar Graham was involved.

Even though he was busy and waiting for that call, he was also praying against hope that Sarah Stryker was still alive. She didn't deserve to die over what her husband had done, and it would infuriate him if that happened. *Jesse deserved the death penalty if she dies,* Edgar thought with a smirk on his face. He had just about had enough of his mouth and his cockiness. He thought he knew everything and ended up knowing nothing.

Time ticked by. No call. Nothing to do but wait.

CHAPTER 32

M ary was getting a little worried about Edgar. He had not come by for his usual breakfast in the last two days. She didn't mother him and would choke before she called to track him down. But she had gotten spoiled to his popping in at all times of the night or day, and now there was no sight of him anywhere. She wondered what he was up to...

Doug was almost finished with his work on the sun porch. He had done a stellar job and she was very pleased. He was quiet, on time, and very neat in his work. This impressed Mary and almost made her not think about his voice. She had offered him lunch everyday and they sat and chatted about his family and how hard it was to make a living. She was growing to really like Doug and wanted to share it with Edgar. The thought crossed her mind that she just might give him a call tonight.

— — —

Doug was winding up his work and ready to call it a day. It was nearly seven and Shelley would be wondering what was taking him so long. He was tired but enjoyed his work in Mary's house. It was quiet and she left him alone to do his magic to her room. It was a great room; a lot of windows that allowed the sun to come in during the afternoon hours. He was hoping she would come up with more to do, but she had not mentioned it during lunch. His bills were biting him in the butt and he did not answer his phone anymore if it said 'Caller unknown'. He hated living this way, paying one bill and not the other, but until his business picked up, he was doing the best he could to stay afloat. He thought about asking Mary for advice, but was too ashamed to ask. He was setting aside money in an envelope, and when his work was done, he would decide how to leave the money for her to find. He was going to pay her back for what he stole from her. It was the right thing to do. *I can't live with myself anymore for hurting this sweet old lady, who is now giving me a job to do that would help me stay afloat. How ironic is that?*

He walked out into the living room and saw Mary through the doorway, standing at the kitchen sink. He yelled her name so that he would not scare her, and she turned around and smiled.

"Hey Doug. Are you through for the day?"

"Well, Mrs. Williams. I am actually finished with the job. I need you to come look at what I done and let me know if it's alright. I want to please you, Mrs. Williams, so if you need somethin' else done, you'll call me to do it." He smiled at her and waved her back to the sun porch.

She walked behind Doug and checked out the room. She was so impressed with what he had done; it blended right into what was already there so well that you could not see where his work began and where it stopped. That was a sign of a good repairman.

"Doug, you have amazed me at how well you did this room. You are very skilled! Thank you so much." She reached out and shook his hand. Then she walked back into the kitchen to get an envelope she had sitting on the counter.

"Here Doug, this is your payment for doing the room. I told you I would pay you well, and I meant it. It was very important to me for this to be done right. This house is old like me and I want to keep it up as long as I can."

"Thank you, Mrs. Williams, for the work. If you ever need anything else, please let me know. I'll put you as a priority if you need me."

Doug walked back to his truck and climbed in. The door creaked and groaned when he shut it. The passenger window would not go down, the heater barely worked, and the radio was completely gone. *What a piece of junk.* But at least it got him to and from his work. Right now he could not be too picky. He was broke. He laughed at himself and drove home. When he pulled up in the driveway he could see Shelley looking out the picture window. She was so pretty. He loved her with all his heart.

He gathered his tools up and picked up the envelope. He had almost forgotten to look inside to see what Mary had paid him. He had asked for four hundred dollars for the job. He imagined she might give him another hundred since she knew he was broke. He opened up the envelope and nearly fell out of the truck. *What in the world was she doing? There's $1,000.00 in the envelope. I can't take this from her. That is way too much for the job.* He nearly started the truck and drove back over to Mary's to give her the money back, but he caught a glimpse of a note in the envelope underneath the money. He pulled it out and read her slanted handwriting.

Doug- this may seem like too much money for your work, but it meant so much to me to have it done right. You were so neat in your work and you stayed late every single night. I want to show my appreciation to you so I'm giving you more than you asked for. Please let this

help you get through the winter, and perhaps keep you from trying to find other ways of making money. Your family needs you home.

Warmly,

Mary Williams

Doug sat there feeling a chill run up his spine. *Did she recognize me? Does she know I stole from her?* He felt sick suddenly and leaned out of the truck and threw up his lunch. He wiped his mouth and laid his head on the steering wheel. *Maybe I am wrong. But what else did she mean about "finding other ways of making money"? Maybe nothing. Maybe I am over-reacting.*

He got out of the truck and walked into the house. His girls ran up to him and held on to his legs, screaming for him to pick them up. He looked at his wife who was walking through the kitchen door, smiling at him. Doug took one look at her face and started crying. The kids let go of his legs and he walked over to Shelley and put his arms around her neck. He tried to control himself, but he was overtaken with guilt and with the astounding gift Mary had given him. He was going to pay her back now, for sure. And he couldn't bring himself to share with Shelley what he'd done months ago. He did show her the envelope, and she cried too. It meant they had food for the winter, and could pay some of their bills. Shelley was shocked to see Doug so emotional; she was used to his anger, not the tears. But she shrugged it off because the money meant less struggle for a month or two.

—   —   —

Mary sat at her table and put her head in her hands. She knew it was Doug who robbed her for she had finally placed his voice, but it was not the same Doug who repaired her sun porch. It was a broken, scared Doug who didn't know which way to turn. She hoped the extra money would ease the tension of making it through this rough winter. Maybe she would find more work for him to do, but at the very least, she had helped him over a hump. It had shaken her at first when he called across the room to her and something about the tone of his voice rang a bell. But she didn't think too much about it because she had seen a good side of Doug. He did rob her and push her down. But she knew at the time that he wasn't wanting to kill her. All he got from her was the money in her purse. He could have taken a lot of jewelry and other valuable things she had in the house, but he didn't. He wasn't a professional thief by any stretch of the imagination. Edgar might say she was being foolish, but she was going to give Doug a second chance to prove himself. And in fact, he did prove to be a great repairman. She decided to keep this revelation to herself, not because she didn't want Doug to know, but because she didn't want the scolding of Edgar Graham.

— — —

Doug lay in bed thinking of what Mary had done, at how unworthy he was to receive it. And how much he wanted to give back to her what he took.

CHAPTER 33

"The snowman is on the ground, dude. Stay tight. Waiting for the road map. Will get right back to ya. Gone."

Edgar closed his phone and waited. *Ranko is sure taking his sweet time getting here. I don't know how much longer Sarah Stryker can hang on.* He looked at his watch. It had been three days now, and he still had no idea where she was. He knew without a doubt that Ranko's men had her, but knowing where was a shot in the dark. There were warehouses all over the city. No point in moving too far without talking to Ranko first. He hoped this deal went down, because it was his only bird in the hand. He didn't have another option at the moment. That was not to say he couldn't come up with one. But the second option usually meant someone was going down. It would not be Edgar Graham.

Edgar's men were in another area of town talking and waiting. News had it that Ranko had landed and would be looking for Edgar. He would put the word out on the street that he was looking for Streetdog, and it would find its way back to Edgar. It was not the fastest way to hook up, but this was how it was done on the street. There was nothing Edgar could do to speed up this part of the deal, so he sat down on the curb around some other men, and listened. They had come to accept that Edgar was the quiet one. He learned so much from them, and they got nothing from him. That was how he wanted it. Most people want to talk about themselves anyway. If you sit with them long enough, they'll tell you things they've never spoken out loud before. It's human nature to want to talk about all that we know. So Edgar just sat there quietly and took mental notes on what was important, and let the rest go over his head.

— — —

Four hours later, Edgar got a call on his cell. He looked at his watch and it was midnight of the third day and he was finally getting the call he had waited for. "Streetdog, snowman in the field. 4th and Anderson Street in twenty. Loaded. Got company. Gone."

Edgar slammed his phone shut and got up and walked slowly out of the area. Then he took off running and got into his car and rode to 4th and Anderson Street. He actually beat Ranko and his men there by about five minutes, so he had time to check out the scene. There were no people around at the moment and the street was not as well lit. He understood the importance of darkness.

He decided to stand in the shadows where he was not clearly seen, to give him a slight edge. It would not last long, and he had to be ready to fire if he had to. He was well protected everywhere but his head, and unfortunately that was easy access.

He checked his watch again and he had about two minutes left before they showed up. Sure enough a black Mercedes with blacked out windows pulled to the curb and stopped. Five men got out of the car, all dressed in black. Ranko had to be the tall thin guy coming out last. The other men were his goonies, all had guns and all were mean as yard dogs.

"Streetdog. You bein' a shadow man? Come out and talk where I can see you, dude. You better be a lone tree or you will be a dead tree, get it man? I'm here for one reason. Jesse Stryker owes me big time and I hear you got the crisps. So let's get this thing goin' down so I can get outa' here. I got things to do."

Edgar stayed where he was and remained calm. "I got what you want, Ranko. No problem there. But you need to call your dogs off, or I'm stayin' right here in the shadows." Edgar had strung an invisible wire across the street right in front of him. It would be a deterrent in case anything went wrong. He also had most of the sheriff's department hidden in the trees and surrounding area. His two undercover cops were behind Ranko's men. They blended into their surroundings so well they couldn't be seen even by Edgar. Edgar was ready to make a move and touched his nose to let the others know what he was doing.

The four men stepped back and lowered their weapons. They looked like they were relaxed and calm but it was just a game. They would kill Edgar in a New York minute if Ranko raised his arm. "Show me the money, Streetdog. We ain't got time to play this game. Just show me the envelope. I called my men back, now I want this thing to move."

Edgar reached slowly into his vest and pulled out the money. "I want the location of Sarah Stryker before you get a dime. And I want reassurance that she is alive. No bullshit Ranko. This is the deal here; I get Sarah Stryker and you get the money you're owed. Are we walking on the same street or not?"

Ranko laughed and shook his head. "You act like you callin' the shots, dog. You don't know who you talkin' to. I can take you out in five seconds, man." He turned to one of the men standing behind him and said something too low for Edgar to hear. The man lifted his cell phone and made a phone call. He put the call on speaker phone and asked someone to put Sarah on the phone.

Her voice was so weak that Edgar could hardly hear her. "Hello? Please help me. Please help me! Hurry! Edgar? Is that you? Please Edgar... they hur..."

The call was cut off and Ranko smiled. His white teeth with gold on the bottom edges glowed in the dim light. "You heard the woman! Let's go! You give me the money and you can have her back."

"Nope." Edgar did not budge. He was more than prepared to take Ranko down to his knees. "I ain't doing nothin' 'til you tell me exactly where she is. Stop the stall job, Ranko. Where is she? Do you want your money or not?"

"Hell, I want the money. The dame aint worth nothin'. She's at the warehouse on the outside of town on Industrial Avenue." He told the goon to place the call again and tell the men to let the woman out.

"I want her alive, and I don't want a damn shootout when I get there. Do you here, Ranko?"

"I ain't deaf dude. Send your men over there to git' her now, and give me that money so I kin' get outa' here."

Edgar made a call on his cell and signaled four men to go to the warehouse. In actuality, there would be about six men going. He hoped that would be enough. He had pulled the detectives and any man that could shoot a gun. Hopefully he had picked the right ones to get the job done. He waited and waited, wanting to hear Sarah's voice saying she was okay.

—   —   —

The six men pulled up to the warehouse, squealing their tires. The lights were flashing on the patrol cars and the men had their guns out. They were prepared to shoot to kill. The door opened quickly and two huge men walked Sarah Stryker out the door. They had machine guns aimed at the police officers. Two were out in front and the other four policemen were behind the two cars with guns aimed at the heads of the two goons. The tension was so tight it would not take much to spring a leak.

Sarah saw the cops and started screaming. The men threw her down and let out some shots. That was all it took. The four men behind the cars let out a string of bullets and the two men went down like flies before they got their second round off. The detective in the group called Edgar back . "We got the prize, Streetdog. Two down."

Edgar pulled out the money and moved forward a few steps. Ranko's goons were trying to contact the warehouse but no one was answering their phone. Ranko was getting upset but wanted the money. He was torn between wanting to shoot Edgar down or take the money and get the hell out of town. He chose the second option and walked forward with the four goons right behind him.

Edgar didn't move up to the invisible wire but came near it. He handed the money to Ranko and turned his back on purpose and walked away.

"Hey dude. Don't back pedal on me yet. I need to count the dough."

Edgar kept on walking.

"I said hold it, Streetdog. I need to count the money."

"I counted it this mornin'. It's all there, Ranko. If I make a deal, I make a deal."

—   —   —

Edgar turned around just before he got to his car and touched his nose. He pulled his gun and shot Ranko in the leg and one of the goons ran toward Edgar and tripped on the wire. The other goons raised their guns to fire. All the men in the trees began to fire and bullets were flying everywhere. The Sheriff came around the backside of the Mercedes and put a gun to the head of one of the goons. "Don't move or we'll blow your head off." Eight men came running and two of them were on Ranko in seconds. It all happened within ten seconds of Edgar firing. Edgar took care of Ranko, handcuffed him and made him lie flat on the pavement. Two of Ranko's men were wounded and Ranko was bleeding pretty badly from his leg.

Fred walked towards Edgar and shook his hand. "Nice job Streetdog. Nice job. We got the money back and we got Sarah. I didn't think for one minute that you couldn't pull this off, Edgar. But I was nervous. Yeah I was nervous." He grinned as sweat poured off his brow.

Edgar laughed and leaned up against the Mercedes. What a job this was! He congratulated the two undercover cops and they talked for a moment about how it all went down. The ambulance came and police cars were everywhere. The goons were cuffed and put into a car, and the ambulance left for the hospital.

Fred was surprised that this all went down without one officer being hurt. Edgar was about the bravest man he'd ever met, and he was the first to admit he couldn't have pulled this off without him. Edgar suddenly felt tired, and said good night to the men. He was ready to go home. Sarah would be taken to the hospital and he would check her out in the morning. What he needed now was a good night's sleep. He thanked the undercover guys again and walked away.

Word got back to the Department that Sarah was alive and safe. One of the guards walked back to the jail cell Jesse was in and clanked on the bars. "Hey Jesse! Thought you might want to know they found your wife. She's safe and has been taken to the hospital." He turned and walked down the hall and closed the door.

Jesse stood up and walked to the cell door. He grabbed hold of the bars and sank down to the floor, sobbing uncontrollably. He had no idea what Sarah had been through, but he was thankful she was alive. He did love her, but it went away somewhere in between having the kids and losing his son. Why, he did not know.

He had nothing but time to think, and he had made a mental list of what he had done right and wrong in his life. The left side of the paper was a little too heavy. He smiled for a moment, but it didn't last long. He did love making that money. For a little while he had been top dog in a very dangerous world. He had not counted on it affecting his wife and children like this. He sure had not counted on spending his life in prison with the thugs that he sold drugs to. *How ironic would that be? He had never used drugs in his entire life.*

— — —

Edgar pulled into his driveway and cut his car lights off before flashing them towards Mary's house. He didn't want her to know he'd been out so late. He could sure go for a good breakfast tomorrow. And that was just what he thought about when he lay down to sleep. That and his dead wife. This was the time he missed her the most. She would have been waiting up for him, and they would have had a glass of wine and talked about the day. He had been alone now for about as long as he'd lived in Portersville. Maybe it was time to find a new wife. Too bad Mary was too old. He smiled.

CHAPTER 34

Sunday mornings were the one time that Mary allowed herself to sleep in. Her bed felt warm and cozy and she could hear the wind blowing around the back corner of the house. The only thing that would make it better would be to look over on her nightstand and see a nice hot cup of coffee. But that would mean Sidney was still around. And he had been gone so long she had forgotten how the wrinkles on his face looked, or how his mustache felt against her mouth when he kissed her. She didn't think she would ever forget those things, but somehow they had slipped too far back into her mind. *There must be a deep pool of water somewhere in the brain that holds all the memories we cannot remember,* she thought. *For it feels like I am swimming in slow motion anytime I try to recall anything about Sidney.*

She finally decided to get out of bed and put on her robe and head downstairs for breakfast. *Who knows? Edgar Graham might just show up!* With that thought encouraging her, she made a fabulous casserole of eggs, sausage, cheese and peppers and popped it into the oven. She cut up some fruit, made cheese muffins, and fixed some crispy thin bacon. The house had a wonderful smell wandering through the rooms, and she hoped that it would find its way to Edgar's nose so that he would get hungry for one of her breakfasts.

She sat down to eat her breakfast and someone knocked on her front door. Then she heard the key and knew who it was; Edgar was coming for breakfast! She smiled and walked to the hallway and greeted him as he was taking off his boots. Edgar smiled back and gave Mary a warm hug. It felt almost like coming home when he saw her. And the aroma coming from the kitchen was enough to heal all his aches and pains.

"How in the world are you, Mary? It feels like I haven't seen you in weeks."

"Tell me about it, Edgar. I have missed you, but hey, my sun porch is fixed, and Doug did a fabulous job!"

Edgar looked at her in surprise. "He finished it already? Man, he must've been workin' late every night!"

"That's exactly what he did, Edgar. He was here early and worked 'til seven every night. I was so proud of him. He seemed to really enjoy his work and I've never seen such a neat carpenter."

"I'll look after I eat. This is the best meal I've had since the last time I saw you, Mary. Any news from Linda?"

"No. I haven't heard a word. I'm a little worried, Edgar. I don't know why she hasn't called us. I would think by now that she would have found a place to stay; somewhere safe for the child."

"She doesn't know yet that Jesse Stryker has been arrested. You and I haven't even had a chance to talk about it. I have a lot to tell you, Mary. I'll wait until after we finish our breakfast before I begin. It's going to take a while."

They sat in silence, both of them lost in thought, eating until they were so full they could hardly move. Edgar needed this big breakfast. He had gone all day yesterday without eating and he was getting a little light headed. He pushed away from the table and patted his stomach. "I can't eat another bite, Mary. Thank you so much."

They both got up and went into the sun room and Edgar checked out Doug's work.

"You're right, he's done a bang up job on this porch. You really can't tell where his work begins and ends. It matches perfectly. I'm proud of old Doug."

She smiled and patted the chair opposite her, for him to sit down. "I have waited too long for this time with you, so sit yourself down and start talking. I'm all ears, Edgar."

He always loved their conversations because Mary was a good listener. She was so interested in what was going on, even at her age, that it made him want to confide in her.

"You have to promise that what I share with you goes no place. It is critical to our safety and perhaps the safety of others, do you understand?"

"Of course I do! Go ahead. I can't wait another minute to hear what you have to tell me."

"I haven't spoken much to you about what I did in my past to earn a living, Mary. In fact no one knows in Portersville except the sheriff. I kept it quiet because I had retired and wanted a peaceful life here in Portersville, without complications."

Mary nodded, with a very serious look on her face.

"I spent years of my life as an FBI agent. I know it comes as a shock to you, but I made good money and enjoyed the heck out of it, even though my life was on the line for years. I lived two lives really; on the outside I was social and was married, had a daughter, and lived like everyone else. But the life I had that no one knew about was harrowing to say the least. When you work for the FBI you don't own your time, your life, or anything else about yourself. You're on call twenty-four hours a day and you don't always know where you're goin' or what you're goin' to be doin'. I trained before that as a Navy Seal, so my background went well with any undercover operations I might be called on to do."

Mary was sitting forward on her seat with an expression of disbelief. She thought he was just a nice mailman, only to find out he had partaken in covert operations. It was a lot to take in for an old woman, and she found herself shaking a little.

"I loved my job; don't get me wrong, Mary. But my life was on the line and my family's lives were on the line. My position had to be kept hidden from my family because at any time they might be questioned about my whereabouts, and it was best they just didn't know. It was government policy that even my family didn't know what my missions were about. A tough way to live your life in one way, but I seem to work best under pressure and enjoyed the years I spent as an agent."

Edgar got up and walked to the window to look out. He stood there with his hands in his pockets, feeling relaxed and glad he could share this with her. He would trust Mary with his life. "I came here after my wife died so that I could relax, have a more normal life, and help as many people as I could on my small salary as a mailman. It is amazing how much money I have saved over the years doing this job, and how many people I have helped. But you know, Mary, I'm bored. I found myself wanting more to do. So I called Fred Perkins and asked if I could become an undercover agent for the department. He has been fabulous about it, and I handled my first operation this week. Jesse Stryker was part of that operation."

"Oh my goodness, Edgar. Don't tell me Jesse was involved with a murder or anything! That would be more than I could handle, thinking about Linda and that baby being out in the park with him alone."

"It was not a murder he was involved in. It was the largest drug operation in this part of the country, and our Jesse was the source for all the cocaine in a three state area. A lot has happened that I won't be able to share with you just yet, but Jesse is in jail and may go to prison for life for what he has done. His poor wife, Sarah, was captured and nearly died tryin' to escape. We got her out last night and the men who captured her were shot down. It was quite a night, I'll tell you that! I'm just glad it's over and we're safe. Jesse has no idea that he nearly killed his own wife tryin' to be a big shot in the drug world."

Mary was speechless. She didn't know what in the world to say. She had no idea that all this was going on outside her door and suddenly felt pretty naïve. "Edgar, I can honestly say that at one time it occurred to me that you might have been a policeman in your former life, but it never ever occurred to me that you might have been an FBI agent. What a background you've had, and to think you are wasting it all being a mailman. I don't mean that like it sounds, but it is a waste don't you think?"

"Not really, Mary. I've paid my dues to society and I don't feel guilty at all takin' a break from it all. I've just decided that for a few years I might want to get back involved and get the streets cleaned up around here. No one was expectin' an FBI agent to show up last night and take down the king pin that had turned the streets of Portersville into a friggin' drug nightmare. It was a perfect set up that just happened and it went off smooth as silk. That was what I was paid to do before and now I'm doin' it because I'm bored and I want to help out around here. I do like this town, Mary. It's a neat place to live, but a lot is goin' on underneath all the niceties that no one knows about. It happens in all towns and cities across America. We're no different than any other town. I'll do what I can, and then I'll retire again from that occupation. You can only take so much of it and then you're fried."

She understood. She needed Edgar around too much to suggest that he stay in such a risky occupation just because he had the skills. She was very proud of him, but also worried about his well being. "I get it, Edgar. All of this is just so new to me and it's hard to take it all in. I'm honored that you felt like you could trust me with this information. I promise you I will not say a word to anyone."

"That goes without sayin', Mary. I know you very well."

"Well," she smiled and stood up. "It is absolutely amazing what goes on in this little town when the lights go out at night. I had no idea. You know I have a gun, Edgar; should I keep it loaded?"

He laughed. "Well Mary, an unloaded gun is no defense at all. It may even get you killed. Load that thing and learn how to shoot it. Don't ever hesitate to pull that trigger if you are caught in a bad situation here at the house."

"I already know how to shoot it, Edgar. But I will put bullets in it tonight. Do you want some of those muffins to take home with you?"

"That sounds like a winner, Mary. You never know when I might be called out into the night again, and those muffins would taste great out on the street on a cold night."

— — —

Edgar walked the two lawns home and set the muffins down on his counter. He no more than sat down to take a short nap on a full stomach when his cell phone rang.

"Edgar, bad news. Jesse Stryker was found dead in his cell this morning. He hung himself in his cell sometime last night after the guard closed up the place. You might want to come over here and check things out, you think?"

Edgar shook his head in disbelief. The nap would have to wait. He grabbed his jacket and walked out the door, grabbing the muffins just in case. This could be an all- nighter again. He needed to check in on Sarah at the hospital anyway. His car took off and all Mary saw as she looked out the window was a trail of smoke. She said a silent prayer that he would be safe. She was depending on Edgar more and more as she was turning eighty five her next birthday in July. She would never tell Edgar her age, but she was getting older and had felt her age lately. Her mind was not like it used to be and she was more unstable on her feet. She had not been to the doctor in twenty years, not counting the time spent in the hospital after Doug had robbed her. Maybe it was time to let the old doctor see how things were inside.

She walked back to her bedroom and lay down on her beautiful bed. She closed her eyes and slept like a child. When she awoke Edgar was still not back home, but she did have a message on her recorder from Linda, with a number to call. She sat down at the kitchen table, dialed the number, and waited for an answer.

— — —

As alone as he had ever been in his life, Jesse had made a tormented decision to end his life. He was filled with shame, and could not stand the thought of seeing his children again, after all that had happened. He knew Sarah was okay and that gave him some sense of peace. Edgar would take care of her, he could be sure of that one thing. The guard had checked in on him once and then turned out the lights. There was no sound in the jail but the nightly news being watched at the front desk by the clerk. Jesse found a way to hang himself from the ceiling of his cell with a sheet on his bed. It was the hardest thing he had ever done, but he had come to that place where there did not seem to be a reason to live anymore. In the morning, someone discovered him hanging there. There was no sound at all as his feet were swinging slowly back and forth.

CHAPTER 35

Jesse's death was both a shock and a relief to Sheriff Perkins, as he waited for Edgar to arrive at the jail. He hadn't gotten along with Jesse from day one, and had to deal with his temper constantly. The other men didn't respect him, and he was up for review soon. Fred was dreading having to put Jesse in prison for the rest of his life; that place would have killed him sure enough. Maybe this was the best answer for everyone who knew Jesse. His wife, included.

"Good morning Fred. I was just going to take a lazy Sunday morning nap and you just had to grab me right out of my bed." He smiled and grabbed Fred's hand and shook it firmly. "We made it through a rough week, Sheriff. I guess it's not over just yet."

"My thoughts, exactly, Edgar. I'm very thankful for what you've done and how smoothly you pulled it all off, man. It was amazing! I still have to pinch myself that it's over with. The town feels better already, even though I realize the drugs are still going to find a way to move around town."

"Yeah, they'll always be around. But we made a huge dent, man. That's for sure. So let me see the jail cell. Who found him, Fred? Is his body gone yet?"

"No. We just found him when I called. So the coroner is on his way and I wanted you to see him before they got here. If you don't mind, Edgar."

Fred led Edgar back to the jail cell where Jesse's body was lying. He was turned a little on his side, the sheet wadded up beside him. He had hung himself on the highest part of the bars. "I don't know how he did it, but he knew what he was doing. It's sad, Edgar. But maybe he's better off dead than in prison."

"They would've eaten him alive in there, Sheriff. You and I know that for sure. All those dudes who used to buy drugs from him are in there. He wouldn't have lasted long, and he knew that. I hate to see him lyin' here but he chose this life, Fred. No one else is to blame but him. He probably could not face his family after his drug connection was revealed. His children would have never forgiven him, especially after what happened to Sarah."

Edgar checked out the cell and looked closely for any signs of entry. There were none. No one had come in or out of the cell since the guard had closed down the jail for the night. "Where is the guard that was on duty last night?"

"He is off today. But we've already placed a call in to him to have him come in for questioning. Maybe he saw something, but I doubt it. I'll let you know what we find out from him, or if you like, you can sit in on the questioning."

"Frankly, I know you know what you are doing, Fred. I'm goin' to sit this one out. If you have any snags, just call me back in. I want to run up and see Sarah Stryker now, and then head on home. You have my cell number, and I'll come back in if you need me to. Thanks for the good work last night, and I'll talk to you soon."

— — —

Edgar headed back out to his car. Instead of going home to take his nap, he headed directly to the hospital to see Sarah. She had to be absolutely worn out from this nightmare, so he wouldn't stay long. He just wanted her to know he cared, and also tell her about Jesse before she saw it on the news in the hospital. That would be a very cruel way to be told your husband was dead. He had a funny feeling she wouldn't even be upset, and he wouldn't blame her one bit. He could only imagine the kind of life she'd had with Jesse, so maybe this would give her a chance to start a new life. He wondered if the children knew. He would have to ask the sheriff if anyone had called to notify them.

He pulled up in the parking lot of the hospital and got out. He was heading into the building when his cell rang. He looked at the number and saw that it was Mary, so he took the call.

"Hey lady. You okay?"

"Oh yes, Edgar. Don't worry about me. I just wanted to let you know I got a phone call from Linda. She has found a place to live; an apartment on the south side of town not all that far from her parents. She has called them and they seem to be willing to mend the relationship so at least she'll have them to fall back on now. I didn't mention anything about Jesse to her, because I knew you would want to be the one to tell her. Is that right, Edgar?"

"Perfect Mary. I'll contact her tonight. Leave her number on my answering machine at the house and when I get home I'll call her. I hate telling her over the phone because it is a bit much for anyone to handle. I think she just might be relieved to know he's not a threat to her anymore."

"I agree. Well I won't keep you, dear. Take care and talk to you soon. The kitchen is always open." She smiled and hung up the phone, glad that she had caught him before he went into the hospital.

— — —

Edgar was tired when he got off the elevator and it was only around two o'clock in the afternoon. What a week it had been. He found Sarah's room and knocked on the door. A weak voice answered the knock.

"Come in, please."

Edgar walked in and took one look at Sarah and regretted he had come. He knew she would be exhausted, but she looked very fragile laying there. Her face ashen and her lips dry.

"Edgar! Oh Edgar! How nice of you to come." She could hardly sit up so Edgar walked to the side of the bed and sat down.

"I know you're weak, Sarah. You're in a good place and they'll get you back to your normal self real soon."

"They've been wonderful to me, Edgar. However, this morning the press came through the door and I liked to have died trying to get them out of this room! Finally the nurses came in and shooed them out. I guess I have that to look forward to when I get home." She tried a weak smile, but it slid off her face like ice cream melting in the sun.

Edgar dreaded telling her the news and felt like she might even be too weak to handle it. He decided to talk to her for a moment before he brought up Jesse. "Have you talked to your kids yet, Sarah? I know they are worried about you."

"Yes, Meredith has called about five times already. She wants to come here and take care of me, but I told her I wouldn't have it. She is finishing up her Masters and needs to tend to her own life. If I needed her I would call her. She fought me on it, but finally relented. I think it's best for the kids to go about their lives as normal as possible. I'm not going to make a major deal out of it to them. They don't know much about my abduction and I don't plan to tell them the torture I went through. They are just kids, Edgar. You know?"

"Yes, I do, Sarah. You're a brave woman." He put his hand on her arm and stared into her eyes. For a moment they locked eyes and then Sarah turned away.

— — —

Edgar got up and walked to the window to look out, trying to decide how to bring it all up. *Boy Jesse had made a mess of things this time for sure.* He cleared his throat and walked by to her bedside. "Sarah, I want to talk to you about the other night. When the officers came and rescued you, and those two men got shot, something else was goin' down on the other side of town." He paused and looked at her to see if she was taking this all in. "Jesse was into drugs big time, Sarah. He wasn't using them himself, but he had a warehouse full of cocaine and he sold it to dealers who then took it out on the street. The man over Jesse, that he bought the drugs from, was a very dangerous man, Sarah. We located him after a lot of hard work on the street and had a shoot out right in the middle of a street on the other side of town. I delivered the money that Jesse owed to this man, and just as he took the money, I shot him in the leg and guns started goin' off. My men came out of the trees and the rest is history. We caught the main king pin who sold all the drugs to Jesse. He'll go to prison for life, and the goons who were with him will follow him there."

Sarah laid there shocked and speechless. She had no idea that Jesse was involved in something this dangerous. "So what happens to Jesse now? Will he go to prison for life, Edgar?"

He knew that question was coming and he knew the answer. He just wasn't prepared to tell her that her husband was already dead. He cleared his throat again and started to try to explain to her what had happened to Jesse today. "Sarah, Jesse would have gone to jail for life for shooting an officer. He tried to kill me at your house. Luckily I had on a bullet proof vest, and was okay. But he still would go to prison regardless of whether I was injured or not. After what took place on the street last night, Jesse was overwhelmed with what he'd done. His life was ruined, his marriage was ruined. He had shamed his children. What else did he have left? He allowed me to transfer the million he owed the king pin and I think he knew it was all over for him then. If the drug world got wind of what had just happened on the street, they would come after Jesse or have him killed in prison. He took his own life sometime in the night, Sarah. He hanged himself in the jail, and was found this morning by the new guard on duty. Sheriff Perkins called me this morning and I went in to check Jesse out. There was no sign of foul play; nothing had been disturbed in the cell. I think that Jesse knew his time was up one way or the other."

Sarah wanted to sleep and never wake up. She couldn't believe her husband was dead now. She looked at Edgar and began to cry. He leaned over the bed and held her close; this was the part he hated the most about being a cop. There was just no easy way to let her know.

"Sarah, it might be best that you get Meredith home. The kids will need to come to the funeral and help you out through all of this. It's a lot for you to manage and you would be bringing them home anyway. Why don't you call Meredith, or do you want me to tell the kids? I would do that for you Sarah."

She looked at Edgar and faintly smiled. "I trust you, Edgar. For some reason I trusted you the first time I laid eyes on you. Which happens to be the night I was kidnapped. Just don't go into too much detail with them. They are young and don't need to know it all."

"I agree with you. I'll only say what I have to. Can I get you somethin' to drink, Sarah? I can go get a coke or sprite. It might taste good to you right now."

"I think I just might take you up on that, Edgar."

—   —   —

Edgar was glad to get out of the room for a moment. His heart really hurt for her and he wanted to help her all that he could. He went to get the drink and picked up one for himself. He hadn't had lunch and was getting hungry again. When he came back into the room, Sarah was crying again. He went to her and gave her a sip of her Sprite and set it down on the table beside the bed. He leaned over and hugged her and wiped her tears. "What is the number, Sarah. Let's get this part over with so you can relax."

—   —   —

The conversation with Meredith was tougher than he'd expected. The girl didn't want to accept that her father was dead. She had no idea about the drugs and was shocked. Edgar took it slow and tried to explain how the drug world works, so that she would understand why her father decided to take his own life. He didn't paint Jesse as a bad man, because he knew the kids needed to have good memories to hold on to now that he was gone. She said she would call her brother and get on a flight as quickly as they could book it. He put Sarah on the phone so that Meredith would know that her mother was all right. They talked for a few minutes and Sarah handed the phone back to Edgar. She was very weak and tired. He put the phone down and looked at Sarah. She was laying there with her eyes closed. He knew she wasn't sleeping, but only trying to cope with all of this. Edgar didn't talk to her but sat beside her until she fell asleep. He tiptoed out of the room and closed the door. He would come back in the morning, because Sarah was going to need help coping with all of this. Her body needed to heal as well as her heart. As he walked down the hospital hallway to his car, he thought how lovely a woman she was. He hoped she found love again in her life. And he hoped it for himself as well.

CHAPTER 36

L inda was sitting in a chair reading to Lacy, thinking about her short talk with Mary. She really did miss being at Mary's house; it was starting to feel like home. She was so unsettled because of the anger she felt towards Jesse, that she couldn't really relax and take in what was there. Mary had been so kind to her and loving to Lacy; it really was wonderful how Edgar and Mary had taken her in. She was just about to take Lacy into her room and lay down with her to get her to sleep when her phone rang.

"Hello?"

"Hey girl! How in the world are you doin'? Mary said you've gotten settled into an apartment. That sounds wonderful."

"Hey Edgar! It is so good to hear your voice!. It wasn't too hard to find something to rent, Edgar. I had no luck in finding a roommate though, but maybe I'll be okay here alone. I have a phone here at the apartment but it's in my father's name." She paused for a moment; it was so good to hear his voice again. "I was wondering what if anything is going on with Jesse and his wife?"

Edgar was ready for that question. "Well, Linda, quite a lot has happened since you pulled out of town! Apparently you must've made your long awaited phone call to Sarah Stryker, and she and Jesse had a bad argument. In the meantime, I had gotten some information coming down the pike about old Jesse, and made a visit to his house just to talk to him, and ask a few questions."

"For heavens sake, Edgar. What in the world did you find out? Was he surprised that you showed up on his doorstep?"

"Oh, I forgot to add that I joined up with the Fred Perkins and am now an employee of the sheriff's department!" He paused and smiled to himself. "Yes, he was surprised. I totally caught him off guard. I tried to talk to him but he lost his temper, which was typical of Jesse. He shot me with a pistol he had in his hand. He was definitely disoriented and tried to run; thankfully I had prepared for the worst and had put on a bullet proof vest so I was unharmed. It did knock me off my feet, however! I got up and went after him and the Sheriff and I arrested him and took him to jail. Turns out he was involved big time in drugs and warehoused kilos of cocaine that was then sold across three states."

Linda was shocked that Jesse was in jail. "Oh my gosh! I had no idea he was involved in anything like that. It's hard to believe, with him being a sergeant and everything. How stupid can he get, Edgar? Good thing I left Portersville, huh?"

She was almost speechless with this news. "Is everything alright now? And what is Sarah going to do?"

"Well, there's more, Linda. The short of it is that I tracked down the king pin of this drug deal and he ended up in jail with four of his goons. Jesse got wind of it all, freaked out, and hung himself in his jail cell. They found him this morning. So I'm calling to tell you that you don't have to ever worry about Jesse Stryker again." Edgar paused to give her time to digest this news. "I know it's a shock to you. All of us here are still tryin' to put things together. But he may be better off dead than spending a lifetime in prison where they would have prob- ably killed him sooner than later. Word gets around, even in prison."

Linda was quiet on the other end of the phone. Jesse was dead. That was hard for her to grasp. She should have had some regret but for some reason she felt sudden relief. "I guess you're right, Edgar. But it's all a bit scary to me. Do you think I'm safe now? I can start my new life and enjoy my daughter without worrying about anything?"

"I sure do, Linda. And we want you to come and see us soon. We're having withdrawals from not seeing you two everyday. Mary is missing Lacy something terrible. So you're family now and are welcome anytime. Do you hear that, girl?"

"I hear you loud and clear. I'll get settled, get a job, and let you know when I can come. It may only be for a short weekend, as I won't be able to take off work. But please let Mary know I miss her too, and will call you both to keep you posted."

When they hung up, Linda sat in shock after hearing the news about Jesse. He was gone. Totally gone out of her life. So many mixed emotions welled up within her, but in the end, she knew it was best for her daughter to never know who her father was. And it was a relief to know she would never have to deal with him ever again.

— — —

Edgar could finally relax and eat supper. It had been one hell of a week and he looked forward to the day when all he did was deliver his mail again. Doing both jobs had been almost too much on him, but he didn't want to give up the mail delivery just yet. He had a feeling it would always provide information for his undercover job, so he wanted to keep it as long as possible. Besides, there was no one around but him when he got home, so what difference did it really make in the big scheme of things?

He fell asleep in his chair with the television blaring. It made no difference to Edgar Graham. He was dreaming about Mason Stryker, buried in James' backyard, underneath the concrete of his shed. He saw Jesse pull the trigger and kill his own son, because of a drug related fiasco. Edgar woke up sweating and sat up ,thinking for a moment, rubbing his face with both hands. *Mason owed Ranko money big time; Ranko must have been pressuring him. But how did Jesse kill his own son? Maybe he knew Ranko was going to take him out; maybe Ranko would have taken them both out. He made James bury his son underneath the place where a shed was to be built. And Jesse even helped James pour the concrete.* The only catch to this nightmare was that Edgar had suspected something and was hiding in the woods when they buried Mason. Edgar had decided right then and there he would never let anyone know he saw it happen. And that decision had no flaw in it until he saw Jesse out in that backyard at night looking for something. How that stupid shoe got left out in the yard was beyond Edgar. Maybe Jesse was making sure there was not another shoe on the ground. It was all so weird and this dream kept repeating itself when Edgar was really tired.

He did end up telling James about his hideout in the woods. And James became the secret keeper along with Edgar. Only James had a loose tongue and drank too much. He was much relieved when James left town. *The little creep stole my money*, thought Edgar, as he tossed and turned. He finally gave it up and went to sleep, wanting to rest and not think about anything.

He fell right back to sleep, only this time there was one single face that crept back into his dream. Sarah Stryker.

CHAPTER 37

Meredith and Stan flew in to the Portersville airport on Monday morning to be with their mother. Sarah was still in the hospital recovering, so they took a cab straight to the hospital as soon as they landed. On the plane they had gone over and over what Edgar had shared with them about their father, but were in total shock about it all. When Meredith walked into her mother's room and saw her pale and lying there so still, she started crying. Stan held her and they both walked over to the bed and sat down by Sarah.

"Mom, what in the world was going on with Dad? Did you know any of this? Are you okay? Do you need anything?"

Sarah patted her daughter and smiled gently. "It's okay baby. I knew nothing about the drugs or the warehouse full of cocaine. Your dad was his own man, and I didn't follow him around. Besides, he was a sergeant and didn't want me to question what he was doing all day. After many years of his being in the Sheriff's Department I got used to him having a few secrets. Not this kind of secret, of course."

"How did this all happen, Mom? How did it get this far? Dad is dead. He hung himself in his jail cell. How did it come to that?" Meredith cried again and Stan got teary eyed. He knew he needed to be strong for his mother and Meredith, but it was tough. He loved his father and would miss him terribly.

"I think your father found a way to make big money, Meredith. He knew I wouldn't approve and just kept it under wraps. I think he got too good at lying and hiding. Edgar came along and the rest is history. I've never met anyone like Edgar Graham in my entire life. He joined the department and suddenly blew everything wide open in the drug world. He basically saved my life, kids. I owe Edgar a lot."

"He does seem like a nice guy, Mom. He was so kind to me when he called to tell me about Dad. I know that was not an easy phone call to make. I nearly died when he told me."

"Stan, how are you taking all of this; you are pretty quiet right now." Sarah put her hand on his arm and pulled him close to her. She hugged him and then he backed off to answer her honestly.

"Mom, it hit me in the gut. I absolutely did not have a clue Dad was involved with a king pin in the drug world, or that he was the distributor of drugs in at least three states. He was so strict on us and didn't use drugs himself. It had to be the money that drew him in. There was nothing else there but the money for Dad." He paused and looked at his mother. "I just don't see how he could have hurt you like he did. Did you argue a lot? Meredith and I talked about this on the way here. I don't recall you guys arguing a lot in your marriage. But I know we are kids. We didn't know what went on behind closed doors."

"We had a great marriage for years. But suddenly he was preoccupied and short tempered. Looking back, he was probably pressured by the drug lords to produce the money for the drugs. It had to be a lot of money. Edgar told me that he owed this king pin one million dollars. That is nothing in the drug world today, but to us it is a huge sum of money. I'm sure Jesse felt a lot of pressure from that, plus the added pressure of not being able to share it with me. We just gradually fell apart. I saw it coming, but didn't know why. I thought he had someone else, to tell you the truth. He had run around on me once before, but only for a short time, that I know about."

"I wondered about that, Mom. Once I heard Dad talking to a woman quietly on the phone. He hung up when he saw me walking into the room. It just didn't feel right, to tell you the truth. But what was I going to say to my own father?"

"I know, angel. That had to make you feel uncomfortable. I hated for our marriage to end like this, but it was bound to happen sooner or later. Now we just have to hold it together and get through his funeral so that we can go on with our lives."

— — —

Sarah looked at her two beautiful children and knew that she had a lot to be thankful for. "I'm happy you both came to be with me. I have been through so much and need you by my side."

"Mom, how did you get hurt? What happened when you were abducted?"

Sarah didn't want to tell them how bad it was, but she did want them to know her life was threatened. "I was taped down to a chair. No water or food for three days. I was very scared that they were going to kill me. I thought Jesse would come looking for me, but didn't realize at the time what was involved. Edgar sent men over to rescue me and there was a lot of gunfire; it was very frightening. I could have easily been shot during the rescue. The men were very skilled and killed the two goons who walked me out of the warehouse. I was very weak at the time and had to be taken by ambulance to the hospital. Edgar came to see me last night and probably will show up today to check in on me. I don't know what I would have done without him. I want you both to meet him before you go back home."

"Sure mom. We'd love to meet Edgar. He saved your life."

— — —

Edgar heard voices as soon as he turned the corner to head for Sarah's room. He peeked in and saw her sitting with her kids, talking. He was about to turn around and head out of the doorway when a nurse came up beside him and opened the door wide open. "Good morning, Mrs. Stryker. My name is Rachael and I'll be taking care of you today. These must be your lovely children?"

Edgar was going to walk out quietly, but Sarah had already caught sight of him. "Edgar! Don't you dare walk out of here without meeting my kids. We were just talking about you."

He walked back into the room with a big grin on his face. "It sure is good to hear your voice so strong this morning. You must be feeling better, Sarah." He walked over to the bedside and shook Stan's hand. "Edgar Graham, Stan. Nice to finally meet you!" Then he kissed Meredith's hand and smiled at her. "Meredith, you are a very brave young woman. I know Sarah is very proud of you and Stan both." He reached over and patted Sarah on the shoulder. "I know you love having your kids here with you. I certainly don't want to interrupt your visit with them. Let me know if you need anything, Sarah, and I'll bring it to you."

Stan interrupted Edgar and stood up to face him. "Edgar, I want to thank you for saving my mom's life. That's awesome and I want to hear more details from you when you get the chance."

Edgar shook Stan's hand again and noticed that he had Jesse's eyes. "I will be more than happy to sit down with you anytime, Stan, to answer any questions you might have about your dad. I'm just thankful your mother is all right. You two watch her closely, and if you need anything at all, here are all my numbers." He handed Stan his business card and walked over to the bed.

"Sarah, I know you're going to be heading home soon. I want you to let me know how you are. I'm not going to butt in while your kids are here. I'm sure they will watch you closely and take good care of you. I'm a phone call away, you hear?"

She smiled and looked at Edgar with gentleness in her eyes. "I won't forget to let you know how I am, Edgar. I owe you my life, for heaven's sake! We are going to have a rough few days here planning the funeral and getting through that. But when it's all over, I want you to have dinner with the kids and me. Just a simple meal at my house. It's a small payback for what you've done for me, but it would mean a lot to all of us if you would come."

"I would love to come to dinner; just let me know when. I'll be at the funeral, so I'll see you then, I'm sure." He gave them all a hug before he left, and let out a deep breath when he closed the door to her room. He wasn't sure why he felt so nervous now around Sarah, but he needed to get a grip.

Chapter 38

Jesse Stryker didn't have the funeral of an honored Sergeant; instead it had the air of shame and dishonor. There were a few people there including all the deputies that had served under him. The whole department was there, but not to honor Jesse. Sarah and her children were seated quietly by the gravesite, and their faces showed the stress of the situation. The press was held back by the guards, in respect of the family, but their cameras were still going off the whole time. Sarah decided that she just didn't care what happened; nothing would make this time okay for her children. They were seeing their father, whom they had loved all their lives, be buried like a man with no name. He had basically lived a good life until the last few years, but what people would remember would be the dark side of his career, not any good he had done. Ironically, he protected the lives of the people of Portersville on one hand, and on the other he corrupted the streets and children, hidden in the darkness. She had lost one son and she always believed it was to drugs even though Jesse denied it adamantly. And now she was burying her husband.

Edgar stood back away from the small crowd, not wanting to attract any attention. Mary was with him and a few of the neighbors came to watch. Everyone was curious about what happened to Jesse; he hung himself in his own jail cell. The town would talk about it for years to come. The weather was appropriate for the mood; windy, cold and gray. That just about described every single thing about this day.

— — —

Normally there were words said at a funeral about the person; good things that were shared by someone who loved the deceased. Not at this funeral. Not one word. Not even a whisper. Just a dead quiet service with no music or uplifting words. It couldn't end soon enough for the family and as the service ended, Sarah took her children and walked back to the car. They didn't even have a limousine. She looked up and saw Edgar standing there, and he took his hat off as she passed by. For a short moment their eyes met, and she smiled a weak smile. Then she turned and walked away with Meredith and Stan. It was the saddest smile Edgar had ever seen in his entire life. But he was all too familiar with the death of a spouse. He knew the empty feelings she was having; only hers were worse in a way. For she had been robbed of not only a husband, but of all the days they had spent together in the past. Like footprints on the sand in a desert being erased by the winds that blow across the flat plains, the memories she had in her heart were simply gone; as if they never were. Not a trace of Jesse in her life at all. And he didn't even look back to tell her he loved her; or goodbye. For he had been looking forward all along, not collecting memories or building a love with her. Years ago his mind had left the invisible bond that had been established in their marriage; and he had gone on to other things.

Edgar watched the car pull away and took Mary's hand to lead her to his car. She was quiet, for she knew Edgar had a lot on his mind today. Unknown to Mary, he was thinking about Sarah. They drove home in silence, and then she asked him if he wanted to stay and have lunch with her. He agreed, knowing it would be good to talk and laugh and get their mind off of this sad event. She had figured he would say yes, so dinner was already cooked and ready for them when they walked into the door. He was surprised of her assumption and told her so.

"I can't believe you knew I was coming here for lunch, Mary Williams. Am I that predictable?"

"I've known you for quite some time now, Edgar Graham. I haven't met a man yet that would turn down a home cooked meal over a TV dinner, no matter what time of day it is!"

They both laughed and he sat down at the table to watch her get things ready. Mary served both plates and they started eating, talking about Jesse, how it all happened and how it ended up.

"It just doesn't seem possible that all of this was happening right under our noses, and we didn't see it. I've lived here forever and I don't miss much. But drug traffic seems to be invisible to me. Do you ever see it going on, Edgar?"

Edgar smiled. "Of course I see it, Mary. But I'm trained to see it. It happens on our own street, I promise you. There are few families who aren't touched by the drug trade now. In my job as mailman I talk to so many people and they share things with me that they wouldn't ordinarily tell anyone. I don't know why, but they seem to think I don't talk to anyone, so their secret is safe. They do it right in front of me."

"Well, this time it went too far. Things got out of control. Were you ever scared? I would have had a heart attack knowing you were out there fighting these thugs on the street. And how in the world did you get Sarah out of the warehouse with those men holding her?"

"It was pretty harrowing, Mary. I'm not going to say I wasn't nervous. But I was never afraid. I lost that ability years ago, and it's a good thing that I did. No one can do their best if they are full of fear. It's immobilizing. So it's better to focus on the task at hand, than to think "What if…." You know?"

"I can see that, yes. You're a very brave man, that's all I can say. I feel safer at night knowing you're two houses away from me." She smiled and paused for a moment. "Now tell me about Sarah Stryker. Is she getting better? Have you seen her lately?"

"I'm staying away right now, because she has her children with her. They need private time together. It's difficult enough for her because of the press always hanging around her doorway, hoping to get a word or two out of her as she goes to and from her car. That's an awful way to live, and it can make you bitter. She's an amazingly calm woman who has had a very tough life. I'm proud of her, and will do anything I can to help her get on with her life."

"I need to run, Mary! This meal was wonderful but the talk was better. I hope you understand more about what has been going on. I did not mean to keep things from you, but now you are up to speed on it all. Thanks again for the meal. You outdid yourself, as usual!"

Mary held back a grin and cleared the table, watching Edgar walking out to his car through the kitchen window. He needed someone in his life. Maybe someday he would allow another woman in. *I've had such a rich life and looking back, it would have been so lonely without a husband to share things with. Edgar goes home to an empty house every single night. I know he has to be lonely. I hope he finds someone soon that he can love. He is too kind a man to live alone.*

——— —— ———

When Edgar got home, for some reason he thought about James Edsom. He had never heard back from him, and wondered how he was doing. *It would be fun to hear from him and feel him squirming, wondering if I had figured out that he stole my money*, he thought. He dialed the number from his house phone, which would not show up on Caller ID. Sure enough, James' brother picked up the phone.

"Hello? Hello?"

"I'm calling for James. Is he in?"

"Yep. Let me git him."

A long silence. "Hello?"

"Well hello James! Good to hear your voice. Edgar here."

James nearly dropped the phone. His knees went weak and he started stuttering around. "Lo' Edgar. I know you're wundering why I never called you back, but truth is that I been workin' hard at findin' a job, and in the meantime workin' odd jobs for some money to help pay rent for my brother. Times is tough, Edgar. Times is tough. But I did think 'bout calling you. Just didn't git around to it."

"That's okay, James. No problem. I was just wonderin' how you were getting' along, that's all. And I did have something interesting to share with you. You read the papers lately, James?"

"No. Can't say I have, Edgar. What's up?"

"Jesse Stryker is dead, James. Got caught distributing drugs in three states and was arrested. His wife was abducted for money, but we got her out safe and sound. Jesse got so scared he hung himself in his jail cell. Pretty interestin' really. I found out a lot during the last two weeks. You missed out on all of this, James, being gone."

Dead quiet on the other end of the line.

"Say, Edgar. Is our secret still a secret? I mean, I ain't told nobody, I'm here to tell ya'. I would swear on my mother's grave that I ain't told a soul."

"Relax James. Now that Jesse is gone, no one will ever need to know. He shot his own son, James. I saw it go down, so you're fine. I don't want you ever to talk about it, though, James. Do you hear?"

"That's cool, Edgar. Loud and clear."

"I called to see when I could expect any payment for the money you stole from me, James. That was actually the point of my call."

There was such a long silence on the end of the phone that Edgar thought maybe James had hung up on him. He could hear him breathing, and was sure that James was freaking out on the other end of the line.

"Did you hear me, James? I need to know when you expect to pay me back. I had that money saved to help people. And you stole it. Now when you goin' to pay me back?"

"Now Edgar, how do you know I took that money? Anyone coulda' stole it. You had it right there in the open for anyone to see who came in your house. It woulda' been easy to steal, I'm here to tell ya'. But I didn't take it, Edgar. I swear on my mother's grave I didn't take it."

Edgar could hardly keep from bursting out laughing, but he pulled it together long enough to finish the conversation. "Well James, if you didn't take the money, why is one of your black gloves sittin' right under my desk? And you dropped your lighter on the way out of the door."

"Wait, Edgar. There was no way…. I couldn't have dropped a glove. My gloves are right here… well one of 'em is. My lighter? No way! How do you know it's my lighter?"

"I have seen it in your hand for the last two years, James. I know your lighter. No one has a lighter like this. Hey, just admit it, man. You took the money to pay off a drug deal. I know you too well. I expect you to be sending me monthly payments as soon as you get a regular job, you got it, James? This is a new year, so turn over a new leaf. Tell the truth for a change and see what that does for your life. You been lyin' all your life, James. How's that workin' for ya? It isn't. It isn't workin' at all."

"Okay, okay, Edgar. You made your point. I took the damn money to pay a goonie who was on my back. I didn't know what else to do. I was embarrassed to ask for the dough and I was scared you'd say no. The other choice I had was to be shot. Know what I mean, Edgar? And I didn't like that choice. So I let you down; my only friend. I want ya to know, Edgar, that I felt like a dog taking that money from you."

Edgar smiled and shook his head. James was a piece of work. He could almost make you feel sorry for him. "Well I'm certainly relieved to hear that, James. Just pay me back, okay? Then we'll call it even. And I promise not to turn you in to the sheriff's department if you stick to your promise. We got a deal?"

James sighed. There goes the idea of a new truck. "Yeah, yeah. We got a deal. Well I better go, Edgar. I got work to do, or I never will get a new truck."

Edgar hung up the phone and had a good laugh. James had not changed a bit. He would never change. He was about as reliable as the weatherman. *I knew he took the damn money. What a jerk. But it will be a cold day in hell before I get it back. At least he knows now that I know. That phone call was almost as good as getting the money back. He was so shocked.*

James hung up the phone and stood their shaking. *How in the heck did Edgar find me out? I can't do anything right. I couldn't sneak up on a deaf mouse.* He grabbed his cap and walked slowly outside, his shoulders sagging under the weight of what he'd done to his friend. He was so angry at himself he could hardly breathe. One day he would get that money back to Edgar. If it was the last thing he ever did.

— — —

Sarah lay in bed, looking back over the day with a great sadness. She was so proud of her children for holding up like they did. They were troopers; there was no doubt about it. It was a damn shame that their lives had to be disrupted like that because of the stupidity of their father. Stan was really shaken over what his father had done. He wouldn't forgive him for allowing those men to take his mother. Sarah was having the same issues and felt a lot of anger and bitterness. Meredith just didn't want to talk about it. She was done thinking anymore about it, and wanted to move forward. Sarah would give her space and then find a way for them to work through all of this. Right now it was too raw. They all were in shock. And all three of them were tired of the attention this case had gotten, and were ready to be left alone to live their lives.

She looked at the clock; nine thirty. She wondered what Edgar was doing tonight. He had saved her life. He was a peculiar man; maybe he was on a date. But she knew somehow that was probably not the case. She would have to find a way to pay him back for what he'd done. He went beyond the call of duty to make sure she survived. She would never forget that as long as she lived. He was a very special man.

—   —   —

If the truth be known, Edgar was laying on his bed wondering what Sarah was doing at this time of night. But the phone didn't ring at either end of the line. However, an invisible bond was forming that was unseen by even the two parties involved.

CHAPTER 39

The cold remained in Portersville, but the snow had slowly melted away like a snowman whose outer edges slowly began to diminish in the warmth of the afternoon sun. Pretty soon there was nothing left but a puddle, and a memory caught on camera for some young child to see. Edgar was walking his mail route and had approached Greg Morgan's house. He noticed a lot of cars in the driveway and thought at first there was a party going on. He opened the mail box and yesterday's mail was still there. That was strange. Edgar took the mail out and walked up to the front door and raised his hand to knock. Someone opened the door just before Edgar's fist hit the wood.

"I'm sorry to bother you, but the mail from yesterday hasn't been taken out of the mailbox. I don't like to see that, in case someone decided to check out Greg's mail in the middle of the night. Stranger things have happened around here."

"Thank you. I'll tell Greg's wife about this. She'll appreciate your bringing her mail to the door." They started to close the door and Edgar stuck his arm between the door and the frame.

"Excuse me, Sir. Is everything okay in there? How is Greg?"

The man looked down and shook his head. "Things don't look too good if you want to know the truth. I just don't think Greg is going to make it through the night. Hospice is here and the family is in the room just sitting there. Waiting."

Edgar had no idea that Greg had gone down that much. "Can I do anything for the family? For Greg? Can I go in and speak to the family?"

The gentleman backed away and made room for Edgar to come in. Edgar wiped his boots off on the prickly coir mat and stepped into the warm house. It felt good after being out in the cold, but the sadness in the house lay like a thick heavy blanket on an otherwise happy morning. Edgar walked carefully to the back bedroom, following the gentleman up to Greg's bedside. His eyes were closed and his cheeks were sunken in. The room smelled of death. Edgar spoke to the family and hugged the children. Dan was visibly shaken as he was so close to his father. Susan was sitting in a corner of the room with a blank look on her face. She had seen her husband dwindle away to nothing in front of her eyes. Refusing to believe he was going to die, this end stage was even more difficult for her to cope. The love of her life was going farther and farther away from her, and she would soon be left with three children to raise on her own. She was in shock, not feeling much of anything. There was a haze in the room that no one could explain, and it floated into every corner; Greg appeared to be bathed in a soft light.

Edgar bent over and said hello to Greg. His eyes didn't open. Edgar whispered that he would see to it that his wife and kids were alright. He promised Greg that they would never go without as long as he had breath in his body. Edgar had put his hand in Greg's and he would swear later that there was a light pressure on his fingers when he made that promise to Greg. He told Greg what a great father he was, and how highly everyone thought of him. It was very easy to say these things to Greg, because they were true. He was exemplary of a great human being on all counts. Too bad his life was going to be cut short; most men would not obtain this level of greatness after living a full life.

Susan got up and went to Edgar and hugged him, thanking him for all he'd done. She whispered that she knew the money had come from him, and Edgar shook his head. No, it wasn't all his doing. But he would pass on the thanks to the person who wished to remain anonymous. He reassured Susan that her family wouldn't have to ever suffer. She was so thankful and teared up, hugging Edgar goodbye.

Edgar bent down one last time to say goodbye to Greg. When he stood up his eyes were wet, and he had no words left to say to the people in living room on his way out of the house. He would have to call Mary and tell her it was almost over, knowing it would make her very sad. She would be so happy that she had paid their house off, now that Susan would be on her own with the kids. Timing was everything. And this time they were spot on.

—　—　—

The funeral for Greg was simple and quiet, not unlike Jesse Stryker's funeral. Only the room was filled with love and not shame. It was a great relief that he was no longer suffering and his wife had a peaceful look on her face, sitting next to her three children in the pew. It was a lovely sunny day, even though the temperature was in the 40's, it felt warmer because of the sun. He was laid to rest on a hill in the cemetery, surrounded by trees. Tall oaks with deep roots, that had seen history fall beneath their great limbs. They would watch over Greg into eternity. And he would have shade against the afternoon sun, and a shelter from the cold winds of winter. Something in a book that Edgar had read made perfect sense when he thought of Greg; *the stillness of a soul is not unlike a body of water that has been stopped. Even though it is not moving, trees can come by the water's edge and drink so they do not whither. So we can drink of a single man's life, though he be still as water, hoping to gain knowledge that we would otherwise not find on our own path.*

CHAPTER 40

It had been twelve months since Edgar joined up with the sheriff's department and went undercover. In that year, Edgar had leveled the drug traffic and brought it almost to a halt. He had made quite a few enemies, but they never connected him to the mailman who walked the streets of Portersville. He made quite a few arrests and put several men behind bars for life. It was hard on him to work both jobs, but he loved it so much that it made up for the sleep he lost, and the pain in his back. He had developed a close relationship with Fred Perkins and huge respect for the man who put his neck on the line to hire him when no one even knew who he was. They seemed to click right off the bat, which was rare in men who work at the level that Edgar worked at. You tended to keep to yourself and withdraw from society, because you had put your life on the line so many times. He had seen too much to trust anyone. So he was better off living alone, having his breakfast with an eighty five year old woman who could put any young cook under the table with her chicken pot pies and apple strudel.

Edgar made his way home, noticing the signs of spring everywhere. Buds were coming out on the trees, and tulips were popping up. The birds were singing, and lawn mowers were being taken out of storage and cleaned up for the coming mowing season. People were outside more and talking to each other after being shut up all winter. Walking up his driveway he suddenly realized that he was tired of coming home to an empty house every night. He was tired of living alone. Maybe he was just missing his daughter. He hadn't seen her in way too long. Or maybe he was just getting old.

Inside, he changed his clothes and started supper, listening to the news on the television. He put his plate on a tray and walked into the living room like he did most nights, so he could relax and watch a few specials on television tonight. He was about to take his first bite when the phone rang.

"Hello, Edgar? This is Sarah. How in the world are you doing? I haven't heard from you in months and wanted to know how you are."

Edgar lost his appetite in five seconds. *Sarah Stryker?*

"Hey Sarah. What a nice surprise! I was just about to eat my egg sandwich and chips when you called. How are you? How are the kids doing?"

"We're doing much better than the last time you and I spoke. The children are enjoying their jobs and finishing up on their masters. I'm proud of them, Edgar. They are amazing resilient young adults who are headed down the right path in life. Both of them are dating and stay so busy that I hardly ever see them." She paused, smiling. "So tell me what you've been doing with yourself these days. Any more drug busts?"

"Oh, we've made a big dent in the drug situation around here, Sarah. It started with your husband, and just kept on goin' from there. I'm very happy about what we've accomplished in such a short amount of time. I feel much better about the school situation and have camped out under the bridge a few times to see if anything new is goin' down. Kind of boring, actually. There just isn't a whole lot goin' on. That isn't to say it won't come back, because I'm sure it will. But we'll be ready for it when it does."

"I expect nothing but the best from you, Edgar. I owe you my life."

"Well, I tell you what, Sarah, you were pretty amazing yourself, managin' to stay alive during your capture. A lot of women would not have been strong enough to handle what you went through."

Sarah grimaced just remembering the terror of it all. No one would ever know how tough it really was. She shook her head, took a deep breath, and got to the point of her phone call to Edgar.

"I was just wondering if you might come for dinner on Friday, Edgar? I know you're busy, but I would love to have a nice relaxing visit with you. What do you say?"

Edgar was speechless. He had allowed Sarah a long time to heal after losing her husband and basically her life. He had stayed away because he didn't want to upset the children and it would give her time to start her life over without having someone else to deal with.

"I would love to come over, Sarah. What time would you like me to be there?"

"You can come anytime, but dinner will be served around seven. Dress casual, Edgar, as we will be sitting outside when the sun is going down. It is so lovely here looking out at the lake in the early evening."

"I'll be there at seven, and thanks so much for calling. Your voice is refreshing after a long day's work. You have no idea how you just brightened my evening."

Sarah hung up the phone and walked over to the picture window. She had allowed herself space to heal and get strong again. Jesse could have ruined her life, but she wouldn't allow it because of the children. It would be wonderful to see Edgar and have good food and conversation with him. It felt strange in a way having a man over for dinner, after being married for so long to Jesse. Yet, Edgar had a way of putting her at ease. He was the most unusual man she had ever met;

mainly because of his background, but also because he seemed to know what you were going to say, before you even got the words out of your mouth. But the one thing he did that Jesse had not done in all the years of their marriage; he made her feel special.

Edgar didn't get one single hour of sleep. He tossed and turned and finally got up and made some coffee. She had certainly turned his night upside down. He dressed and went for a walk, trying to work through his feelings that he had pushed way down inside. He was not sure what he wanted out of life anymore. This way of living had worked since his wife had died. He let no one in, and he was content with that. Then he had to go and meet Sarah Stryker and that just put a wedge in the door he thought was closed permanently.

The morning was beginning and Edgar took a deep breath. He had learned one thing for sure in his life; you could not count on anything in this world remaining the same.

CHAPTER 41

Edgar came to dinner not expecting anything but a meal to happen. He had made up his mind that he wasn't going to allow himself to get too attached to Sarah. It hurt too much when he lost his wife and he had really shut himself down after that, supposedly for good. But when he walked up to the door and knocked, she opened it and that plan went out the window. She couldn't have looked more beautiful; her hair was loose, and she had a smile that took down the wall he had spent the last 10 years building.

"Come in, Edgar! It sure is nice to have the weather a little warmer so we don't have to bundle up so much. I have everything ready, but I want you to come outside with me and see this sunset. I'm so glad you came early, otherwise you would have missed it."

Edgar followed her into the house and out onto the deck. He stood there breathless looking at a sun as large as he had ever seen that had turned blood orange and was sinking slowly into the pool of water in the back of Sarah's house. The color that ricocheted off the clouds near the horizon was unbelievable. It was not like he had never seen a sunset before, but this looked like it was just for them. Right in her back yard. He turned and gave Sarah a big hug and thanked her for having him over.

"I really didn't know how this would go, Sarah. I guess you had your own misgivings about having me over. Or even us being close friends."

"I will agree that it was a decision that didn't come easy. But I feel very comfortable around you, Edgar. Let's go have dinner and enjoy this lovely evening."

— — —

What Edgar didn't know about Sarah was that she had her own life aside from Jesse's career and the raising of the children. She was working in an orphanage on the bad side of town, with babies and children who were abandoned by women who used drugs. It had kind of taken over her life since Jesse was gone, and she was really making headway in getting donations and programs started for the children.

"I'm amazed that you even started working in this orphanage, Sarah. It would rip the heart out of most women to even set foot in there. How do you stay strong for those kids?"

"It was very difficult at first and I came home crying time after time. Then I realized that I might be the only person this group of children had that would go to bat for them and see to it that they were really taken care of. Their education is pertinent because we don't want them to repeat what their mothers did."

Edgar pushed his chair back from the table and stretched. "Well I want to tell you this might be the best meal I've ever eaten. I might add that I don't cook much at home, but I have a wonderful neighbor I want you to meet that cooks like a chef and is the sweetest thing to me. She is goin' to love you, Sarah. And no telling what you guys will cook for me!"

"Edgar, come and sit out on the porch with me. I want to hear all about your life, your past, what you used to do for a living, and what you dream of for your future. We've been talking about me too much. Now it's your turn to open up to me, if that's possible." she stopped and looked directly into his eyes, and those eyes looked straight into Edgar's heart for the first time.

Edgar squirmed a little because he was not used to talking about himself to anyone. This time is was different. For the first time in ages he really wanted her to know who he was and who he had been. "Well, Sarah. I've had a very interesting life, but most of it was lived alone. I haven't shared much of it with anyone since my wife passed away. I really don't have a good starting place except to begin after I lost my wife. Up to that point my life was like everyone else's life. When she died, I became an FBI agent for the U.S. Government and nothing ever was the same again. That job kept me so busy that I had no time to deal with the loss."

———   ———   ———

It was late into the night before Edgar got in his car to drive home. The sun had been replaced by the moon, which seemed to have cast a spell on Edgar. He had come to her house with a determination to stay strong and silent. Instead, he had told her his whole life story, and even some things he had never shared with anyone. *What in the world is wrong with me? Am I getting weak in my old age?* All the way home his stomach was churning and he had this nervous feeling that he hardly recognized. He had held her in his arms for a moment. He had kissed her mouth and watched her lean her head back and laugh. Her laughter was healing wounds he didn't know he had. What a connection he felt with her; always had. But he never dreamed he would ever hold Sarah Stryker in his arms. Edgar rested his head on the steering wheel of his car, parked in front of his house. *It's almost too much…all the complicated events that had to happen to bring us to this place. It's a wonder she lived through this nightmare. Most people couldn't have held up under that kind of stress. Sarah is a strong woman, but when I hold her, she feels so fragile. I don't think I even deserve Sarah; but maybe I didn't deserve my wife dying either.* Edgar rubbed his eyes with hands that were worn and weathered. He would never admit it later, but a tear found its way down the wrinkles on his face and dropped on the leather seat of the car. Suddenly all the years of holding in, all the nights of coming home alone, and all the feelings he had stashed so far away that he forgot they were there, came rushing in. Edgar started to chuckle; then the laughter came and Edgar leaned his head back and laughed in the quiet of the night until the tears came.

He got out of his car and looked up at the sky. There was a freshness in the night that felt so good to his face. He shook his head and started up the steps to the porch with a smile on his face, knowing that over breakfast with Mary in the morning, he would share about his evening with Sarah. He already knew what Mary would say.

Epilogue

Edgar and Sarah were married on the fifteenth day of May in her backyard, with the sun setting in that great pool of water. They lived a quiet life, sharing their love for helping others, and turning Portersville upside down. When Mary Williams died, she left Edgar half of her estate. The other half went to her children that she hardly ever saw. Edgar and Sarah used part of the money to rebuild the orphanage and house more children. They not only helped children who were victims of drug abuse but opened the doors to any child who was homeless. It soon became a model orphanage and administrators from all over the United States came to see how this orphanage was structured.

Edgar continued with his undercover work for the next 8 years, and was shot in the line of duty while exposing the largest drug ring in a five state area. His unique ability to read people and understand the complicated drug world led him right to the heart of the problem every time. He never lost one of his men while working the streets of Portersville and developed a lasting friendship with Fred Perkins until the day he died.

Fred spoke at his funeral, which by the way, was attended by every single person who lived in Portersville that could get there. The newspapers and radio and television covered the entire funeral and burial. It almost looked like the President had died.

During the funeral, people stood up to share how Edgar had changed their lives. It was then discovered that all the money that people had found in their doorway, in an unmarked envelope, was from Edgar Graham.

Edgar Graham had changed a town in his lifetime, one envelope at a time, walking a mail route in gray clothes, gray rubber boots, and a gray hat. He went unnoticed for years until one day, he died, and the town found out they had a saint living among them.

No one was aware that Edgar Graham carried his secret about Jesse's son to his grave. At the far end of the room, wearing ragged clothes and a dirty hat, sat James Edsom. He was crying and smiling at the same time. Edgar was his hero. Slowly, with heads turning, James walked up to the casket with something in his hand. He leaned over and laid an envelope in the casket, under Edgar's hands that were folded. He turned and walked slowly out of the church, got in his truck and drove home.

When James arrived home from the funeral, he was tired from the long drive back to his brother's house. He walked into his bedroom and sat down on the bed. There lying on his pillow was the lighter he had dropped on the floor at Edgar's house when he stole the money. James picked up the lighter, and smiled. Even in his death, ole Edgar could find a way to have the last word...

Edgar Graham was a good man, but he was not perfect. But then, neither are we.

—   —   —

Nancy Veldman resides in Destin, Florida with her husband. She is an author, watercolor artist, and pianist and has released nine cds of her music. Currently she is working on her sixth spiritual book, her tenth cd, and a third novel is in the wings. Nancy has a non-profit ministry that has ministered to hundreds of cancer patents and abuse victims and her music is being played in many hospitals and cancer centers across the United States. She has been proprietor of a gift shop called Magnolia House, in Grand Boulevard near Sandestin Resort for seventeen years. In everything that Nancy achieves, her main goal is to affect the most people in her lifetime for the good. Nancy and her husband have two sons, two daughters, and ten grandchildren. You can read more about Nancy at magnoliahouse.com where her music and books are available. Her two novels, The Box of Words, and Edgar Graham, are also available on Amazon.com and on Kindle.

Other books by Nancy Veldman

Coming Home
The Journey
Withered Leaves
Dream Catcher
The Fisherman
The Box of Words, a novel

6257332R0

Made in the USA
Charleston, SC
03 October 2010